# THE PRINCE'S HEART

## BEN CHALFIN

T0349432

RISING ACTION

Text copyright © 2024 by Ben Chalfin

Cover Illustration © Cover Ever After
Distributed by Simon & Schuster

ISBN: 978-1-998076-92-5
Ebook: 978-1-998076-93-2

FIC027190 FICTION / Romance / LGBTQ+ / Gay
FIC027030 FICTION / Romance / Fantasy
FIC027450 FICTION / Romance / Royalty

#ThePrincesHeart

Follow Rising Action on our socials!
Twitter: @RAPubCollective
Instagram: @risingactionpublishingco
Tiktok: @risingactionpublishingco

*For Mommom Annette, Pop Al, and Pop Bob*
*I miss you every day*

# THE PRINCE'S HEART

# CHAPTER ONE

Everything in the grand ballroom sparkles and glitters with reflected light. Glowbulbs hanging from ornate chandeliers illuminate a large dance floor surrounded by tables covered in immaculate white linen. From my vantage point near the entrance, I can see there are quite a few people here, which is annoying but to be expected for a ball as fancy as this one. The air is thick with conversations, the cacophony combining with a lively tune played by virtuoso musicians. On the dance floor, people wearing brightly colored outfits dance in time with the music, spinning and twirling like flower petals caught in the wind. Other attendees stand off to the sides, chatting with their friends, or they sit at tables, eating dinner.

All in all, it's quite a beautiful scene, and yet it's a struggle to keep myself from turning around and bolting like a startled deer. I look over at my brother, Samis, who's standing a few feet away from me, looking as resplendent as ever in his red-and-gold formal outfit. "Are you sure this is a good idea?"

"Of course it is, Darien," he says, rolling his eyes. He runs his hands through his short, russet-brown hair, looking every inch the perfect prince that he is. "Say what you will about Lady Gerreso, but she knows how to throw a ball. Plus, she has the best chef in the city." He grins and gives me an exaggerated wink. "And I promised to introduce you to someone, remember? What kind of brother would I be if I let you down now?"

It doesn't surprise me that the quality of the food was part of the allure for Samis—perhaps the greatest mystery in our family is how he can eat twice as much as any of us and still be as skinny as a stick. "I'm sure the food is good," I concede. "But I'm still not sure about this."

"Really? I'm *shocked*." His voice is infuriatingly calm. "Although, perhaps I should be, because as I recall, *you* were the one who asked *me* for help."

"That's not how I remember it," I mutter. Then, louder: "What if your friend isn't here?" *More importantly, what if he is here?*

Apparently oblivious to my discomfort, Samis shrugs. "I'm sure he's around here somewhere. And if not, you can still find some way to enjoy yourself, right? It's just a party, Darien. What's the worst that can happen?"

Despite my nerves, I only have to think about it for a moment. Samis and I may not always agree with each other, but I can admit when he's right. Usually. Plus, I suppose I *did* ask him for advice. "Alright, I'll try. But no guarantees."

His cerulean eyes light up, and he gives me his most charming, princely smile. "Excellent! Now, come on. Let's go find my friend. I think you and he will get along *quite* well if you know what I mean."

I glare at him, already regretting my decision to go along with this. But Samis starts to walk toward the morass of attendees, striding purposefully, his shoulders back and his chin held high. After one more moment's hesitation, I sigh and follow him.

We don't get very far before I hear a familiar voice somewhere to my right, "Excuse me, but what are you doing here?" The surprise is so thick it's almost palpable. "And what in the world are you *wearing*?"

I stop and turn to see a woman about a foot shorter than me wearing a well-cut white-and-gold dress. Her entire look is impeccable, from the intricately woven braid in her light-brown hair down to her shoes, which appear to be covered in pearls. I've known Ivy Tirellon for more than twenty years. She's always been far more fashionable than me, and she never lets me forget it. To be fair, her talents aren't limited to fashion—the Tirellons have a reputation for producing swordmasters going back to the days of the old Empire, and Ivy's no different, as she's repeatedly proven during our training sessions.

"It's good to see you, Ivy," I say, as Samis joins us. "And what's wrong with my clothes?" I add. "I thought we agreed that purple looks good on me."

She fingers the lapel of my jacket. "Not this shade. It makes you look like a grape." She says it with an expression that's half-joking and half-serious, and I can't help but laugh. "It's good to see you, too, Darien. I suppose you look ... acceptable."

"Thanks for that." I roll my eyes at her. "You look good, too. I have to ask, how many knives did you bring with you tonight?"

She grins at me. "Not that many. It's just a ball." Knowing her, this could mean anywhere from one to twenty; she's ingenious at finding ways to hide them in her clothes, so I really can't spot any, even though

I'm only a few feet away from her. She smiles. "'Always be prepared' and all that, you know?"

I shudder as I recall our lessons with the palace weapons tutor, Earon. He was always full of pithy sayings like that. I still remember a good amount of them even though I gave up trying to learn how to fight with a sword—or any weapon, really—some years ago. Ivy, on the other hand, still trains with him three times a week. "If you say so."

She nods as if to say, "*I do say so*," and turns to my brother, bowing slightly to him. "Your Royal Highness, forgive me, but I must ask: how did you manage to drag *him* to a ball as fancy as this?"

"It wasn't easy," Samis says with a grimace that better be fake. "Believe me, it took quite a bit of cajoling."

"I believe it, Your Royal Highness." She gives us an expectant look. "Is your sister here, too?"

I shake my head. "No, Emma's back at the palace. Apparently, she got up before dawn to work on one of her projects, and she said she wanted to get some rest tonight." I don't need to tell Ivy that the last part was almost certainly a lie; we both know that Emma will be working on her mysterious project all night instead of resting. Sometimes I don't understand how she can function as well as she does with so little sleep. "She did ask me to give you her regards, though."

"That's too bad. But in any event, I'm glad you're here, if only to make me look better by comparison." She winks at me. "Want to explore the library with me? Lady Gerreso's wife just got back to Cedelia recently, and I heard she brought a copy of the first edition of *The Travels of Menha Termon* with her from Raktos."

That definitely makes me perk up. I thought all of them were destroyed! I mean, I did promise Samis that I'd meet his friend, but surely that can wait a bit? And if I don't meet his friend tonight, there's always the next ball, right?

With my mind made up, I'm about to accept Ivy's gracious offer when Samis clears his throat. "Sorry, Ivy," he says, "but I promised to introduce Darien to a friend. The two of you can read all about Maria Tarkon's travels later. It's not like this book is going to get up and walk away, you know." He gives me a loaded look. "But my *friend*, on the other hand, just might."

Ivy gives me a knowing look. "Ah. In that case, I'll leave you to it. Until we meet again, Your Royal Highnesses." With that, she bows slightly and leaves, soon lost in the crowd.

Our momentary detour evidently complete, Samis resumes walking toward the mass of people around the dance floor. After a brief, regretful glance at the exit, I trail behind, feeling like a prisoner being led to his execution.

"So, are you going to tell me about this friend of yours?" I ask, trying to sound like I'm not panicking. "You haven't told me what he looks like. Or even what his name is, for that matter."

"You'll find out soon enough." He turns to face me, briefly giving me a wide grin, before facing forward again. "Trust me, you'll like him. I'm sure of it."

*Not this again.* "You've said that before. Several times, in fact."

This time, he doesn't even bother to turn around. "And I was right, wasn't I? Just because you didn't end up courting any of the other men I've introduced you to, doesn't mean you didn't *like* them."

I have no response to that, so I remain silent. He's not wrong, I suppose—he's a pretty good judge of character, and, by this point, he seems to know what I'm looking for. With one not-so-minor exception, that is. Not so minor to me, at least.

Deep down, though, I appreciate that Samis is willing to take charge and make these introductions on my behalf. After he got married and our parents shifted all their focus to finding an acceptable match for me, Samis could have easily left me to fend for myself. Instead, he's been encouraging me to stop spending all my time in the library and actually meet people. Maybe he views this not as a chore, as I would, but as more of a challenge and he's always loved challenges.

Deftly dodging servants carrying trays of food and drinks, Samis makes his way through the crowd, greeting people with a nod or a few words as he passes. I follow quietly in his wake, my mind racing. *What if this one is just like all the others? How many more times do I have to go through this?* Samis grabs two glasses of wine from a passing servant and hands one to me. I drink mine quickly, as though the answers to my questions are written on the bottom of the glass, but none are waiting for me once the wine is gone.

After a minute or so of wandering, Samis stops meandering and makes a beeline in one direction, and my anxiety ratchets up even more. *This is it*, I think, trying and failing to boost my confidence. *Here goes nothing*.

I take a deep breath just as Samis stops before a good-looking man, about my height, with short, blond hair framing a heart-shaped face, eyes the color of a cloudless sky, and full lips. He smiles when he sees Samis, and my heart skips a beat.

"Samis, my friend!" he exclaims. "How have you been?"

"I've been just fine, Petris," Samis says, smiling widely as the two of them shake hands. "Enjoying married life. Not that you'd know anything about *that*, of course."

They both chuckle while I stand there trying not to fidget.

Apparently, it's not quite awkward enough for Samis yet. "Speaking of which," he says, "please allow me to introduce my brother, Darien." He frowns ever so slightly. "Well, *technically* I suppose he's Prince Darien Garros to you, but he won't mind if you just call him Darien. I told you about him a few weeks ago, remember?"

"Of course I remember." Petris turns to me. "Pleased to meet you, Darien," he says with a bow. "I've heard quite a bit about you."

"It's nice to meet you too, Petris," I say. He holds out his hand and I take it, his grip warm and firm. "Samis has only told you good things about me, I hope?"

His grin widens as he releases my hand, making my heart skip a few more beats. *I'm going to need a healer by the end of the night if this keeps up.*

Petris is about to respond when Samis jumps in, a smug look on his face; I'm willing to forgive him for it, just this once, and I bet he knows. "If you'll excuse me, I'm going to find Kenessa," he says. "Have fun together. But don't get into *too* much trouble." With that admonition, my brother turns to go find his wife, and most likely something to eat.

With Samis gone, I'm worried about my grape-like outfit, hoping that it—or, more importantly, my complete lack of social skills—doesn't put Petris off. "How do you and Samis know each other?" I ask, my voice an octave too high.

In contrast to how I'm feeling, Petris looks relaxed: his head is slightly tilted, and his blue eyes hold my gaze. "My family breeds racehorses, and Samis purchased one of our best a few years back. Evidently, the filly we sold him won a few races, and he kept coming back to try out some other horses. Over time, we became friends. I have to say, Samis is one of the best riders I've ever seen. It took quite a few tries before I managed to win a race against him."

"At least you managed to beat him. I don't think I ever have."

Petris laughs again; this time, it's much deeper, a full, throaty sound that makes me blush. "Knowing your brother, I can believe it." His eyes flick down before he looks back up, a hint of a roguish grin on his beautiful face. "I'm certain that you're quite skilled in *other* ways, though."

I feel a flush that has nothing to do with the wine I drank, along with a slow smile. Maybe I don't regret coming here after all.

I spend the next few hours with Petris, enjoying myself far more than I thought I would. At first, I feel a bit bad for monopolizing his time, but he doesn't seem to mind, and I'm certainly not complaining. Something about his easy manner calms my nerves, and after talking to him for a while, I almost forget I'm surrounded by other people.

After we've been chatting for a half hour or so, Petris somehow convinces me to join him on the dance floor, which is quite a feat. By the time we make our way to the center of the room, Samis and Kenessa are already there. I barely notice when Samis gives me a conspiratorial wink as we pass by each other, my attention almost completely on the attractive man a few inches away from me. I try my best to not trip over my own two feet, and to my great relief, I mostly succeed. At some point, I even start to *enjoy* it. *Maybe Samis was right about him.*

After we've danced for what feels like both hours and a few seconds, the music stops and the musicians leave their seats, presumably to get some food and take a well-deserved break. For perhaps the first time in my life, I'm upset to see them go, impatient for them to finish eating and come back so I can keep dancing with Petris. It's a strange feeling.

From the look on Petris's face, he's feeling something similar; just seeing his expression and knowing he was enjoying dancing with *me*, of all people, makes my heart race even more.

"Well, that's a shame," he says. "Would you like to go outside while we wait for them to come back? I think I could use some fresh air."

I nod, realizing how flushed I am. "That sounds like a wonderful idea."

He grins and leads me wordlessly to a side door and out into a small courtyard. The cool spring air, a contrast from the stuffiness of the ball, hits me like a sheet of ice, but it does nothing to dull the fire burning in my chest. Despite the cold, there's a good number of people outside, enough that the air still buzzes with the hum of conversation. Paths lead away from three sides of the square at odd intervals, with plants crowding in around them. Light pouring from the ballroom windows, augmented by the full moon and glowbulbs hung from strings running between the larger plants, gives the garden a soft golden radiance.

Taking me by the hand, Petris guides me across the courtyard and down one of the gravel paths, stopping at a marble bench surrounded by empty flowerbeds. We sit quietly for a few moments, breathing in the fresh air, before he turns to me, his handsome face shining in the moonlight. "Thank you for spending time with me tonight, Darien," he says. "I really do appreciate it."

I can't help but raise my eyebrows at that. "I should be the one thanking you. I'm having a wonderful time. I can't remember the last time I danced that much at a ball."

"Really? I would have thought dancing is part of the job description for a prince."

"Perhaps it is. But that doesn't mean I enjoy it."

He takes my hand, his warm, soft skin pressing against mine. "Maybe you just needed to find the right partner." His eyes look bigger than they did before, and it takes me a second to realize it's because our faces have drawn closer together, our foreheads almost touching. I close my own eyes in anticipation, ready to find out whether his lips are as soft as his touch.

Before our lips can touch, though, I feel him pull back, just a bit, and I open my eyes again. "Forgive me if I'm offending you," he says, his quiet voice ringing in my ears, "but I have to admit, I was surprised when Samis suggested that you and I meet."

"Oh? Why is that?"

He shrugs. "I just meant that, from the way he described you, it seemed like you and I don't really have similar personalities. Don't get me wrong—he didn't badmouth you or anything like that. But I got the feeling you weren't really, you know, my type."

A wave of fear that's colder than the night air washes over me. *Is he telling me he doesn't like me*? Somehow, the prospect seems much worse than it would have just a few hours ago. "I don't doubt what he told you is true," I say, trying to keep my voice steady. "But you still agreed to spend time with me and to come out here, so it can't have been *that* bad, right?"

The sweet smile he gives me lessens my fear somewhat. "Of course it wasn't *bad*," he says. "I don't mind that you're shy. Not everyone can be a social butterfly like Samis." He squeezes my hand. "Besides, it's not like it matters whether you're my type."

Just like that, any relief I felt has gone, replaced by a sinking feeling that I'm all too familiar with. "I'm glad it doesn't bother you," I say, my heart in my throat. "But why doesn't it matter whether I'm your type?"

He looks at me, his face bathed in reflected moonlight. "Isn't it obvious? You're a *prince*, Darien." He says the word 'prince' like it's made of gold, and my heart immediately plummets from my throat down to my feet. "I don't care what your personality is like. Not that I don't like you—you seem nice enough, even if we're not perfectly matched. Maybe if you were someone else, it would be a problem. But you're part of the *royal family*. I'm more than willing to ignore some personality differences if it means I get to court someone like you."

He squeezes my hand again, but the spell has already been broken. *Not me, just someone* like *me*. "I'm sorry, but I don't think this is going to work out," I hear myself say as though from a distance. "I should go."

His face falls so quickly that it might be funny if I wasn't so upset. "Wait, Darien, what's wr—"

Before he can finish the sentence, I stand up so fast I feel lightheaded. My vision blurs from unshed tears. "I'm sorry," I repeat, knowing he won't understand, that he *can't* understand. He calls my name as I walk away, but I ignore him, not even bothering to look back, until his voice fades away in the distance.

# CHAPTER TWO

"What happened with you and Petris? You two seemed to be having a good time together last night. From what I saw, at least."

I look up from the paper I'm holding, my eyes bleary and my mind still half-asleep. Samis stands before my desk, looking as resplendent as ever. Even though I've known him my entire life, I still don't understand how he can be so chipper, so animated, this early in the morning. Even his hair, a few shades lighter than mine and a bit longer, is perfectly coiffed, like he slept with his head floating several inches above his pillow.

"Could you keep it down a bit?" I ask him. "Some of us aren't fully awake yet."

He tilts his head slightly and raises his eyebrows. "You're kidding, right? It's eight o'clock already. Besides, I asked Joram, and he said you got up an hour ago."

I suppose I can't expect my steward to lie to the crown prince, but it would be nice if he would bend the truth once in a while. "There's a difference between getting up and *being awake*, you know."

"If you say so, Prince Sleepyhead." He snatches the paper from my hand and looks at it as though he's never seen anything like it before. "Although, I suppose if I had to read reports like this all morning, I might have trouble staying awake too. What's this one about? Don't tell me Father is making you review the maintenance on the city's sewers again?"

"Be careful with that!" I take the paper back, handling it much more carefully than he had. "And for your information, it's not a report."

"Really?" His eyebrows lift even higher. "And here I thought you'd finally seen the light and decided to get started on your daily work before noon for once."

I roll my eyes and avoid looking at the growing pile of papers on my desk. Occasionally, people are surprised to find out I actually have responsibilities other than lounging around and riding horses and attending balls or whatever it is they think princes do. As with most things in my life, it's Samis's fault—being the raging go-getter that he is, he asked our father to give him some duties as soon as he came of age, and of course that meant I had to do the same when I came of age three years later. Sometimes, I wish I hadn't been quite so insistent back then, but it's too late now. At least our personalities are different enough that we're not fighting over who gets the more enjoyable duties. Generally, the things he enjoys are ones that I would hate, and vice versa. So, while he's off attending meetings of Soeria's Council of State or hosting delegations from foreign countries, I get to stay where it's quiet and review petitions sent to Father or read reports from various government underlings.

"If it's not a report, what is it?" Samis asks, eyeing the paper askance.

"You've heard of the Battle of Cavain, right?"

His blank stare is all the response I need.

"Seriously? Our great-great-grandmother led the victorious army. It's basically the reason Soeria exists in the first place." The fact that there's not even a tiny spark of recognition in his eyes makes me want to groan. "It was toward the end of the War of Dissolution. Our great-great-grandmother Etena led the Soerian army against the Idrian Empire—or what was left of it by then, anyway—and the Empress. After she won, she declared Soeria's independence and became queen. You *really* haven't heard of it?"

"Doesn't ring a bell," Samis says cheerfully. "You know I never paid attention during history lessons."

It is a deep, deep struggle not to roll my eyes again.

"What does that paper have to do with it, anyway?" he asks. He reaches out a hand, but I slap it away.

"It's a first-hand account from a Soerian pikebearer," I explain. "Well, one page of it, at least. There aren't many primary sources from that time—which makes sense, given how many records got destroyed during the war. Or maybe people had better things to do other than write down their memories, I don't know. In any case, it's relatively rare to find something like this without doing some digging. Of course, they wrote it twenty years or so after the battle, so it's not perfect, but it's still better than nothing. It's..." I trail off as I notice Samis's eyebrows have reached their maximum height. "You *did* ask, you know."

"I already regret it," he says, patting my shoulder. "I noticed you completely avoided answering my other question, by the way."

Oh right, I forgot he asked me about Petris. "It went ... okay." I try not to cringe. "Can we maybe talk about this later? It's not like you're going to die if you don't find out right now."

14

"Nonsense," he says. Another thing I'll never be able to understand about him is how he can put so much authority into a single word; it might bother me if I wasn't used to it by now. "Come eat breakfast with me and Kenessa. I want to hear everything."

I don't really want to, but I know it would be futile to resist, so I sigh instead of arguing with him. "Alright, fine. Let me get these papers put away first. I'll meet you there in a few minutes." *Hopefully there will be some food left by then.*

He does as I ask and goes away, his victory secure. A few minutes later, once I've carefully put the page I was reading back where it belongs, I follow him, leaving my chambers and making my way to the rooms Samis and Kenessa share.

Rich paintings and ornate vases line the halls of the Royal Palace, and, as always, I take a moment to admire them while I walk by. The palace isn't large—not for a traditional palace, at least—but it is old, an elegant building made of marble and granite that dates back to the golden days of the Idrian Empire. My ancestors have accumulated quite a bit of art over the years; I've lived here my entire life, and I doubt I've seen even half of the assorted portraits and sculptures.

Since I'm on the third floor, when I look out the windows, I can see the city that surrounds us. Cedelia, the capital of the Kingdom of Soeria, has been ruled by my family for generations—since the aforementioned Battle of Cavain— as monarchs, and before that as viceregents for the Emperor or Empress. Mother once told me that when she first came here from Zeteyon—our neighbor to the east and another former viceregency of the Idrian Empire—she instantly fell in love with Cedelia. "Of course," she said, "I was still a wide-eyed young princess back then, and I wasn't exactly happy at the prospect of an arranged marriage with your father. But it certainly worked out well, didn't it?"

Looking out at the city, I can see why she was drawn to it. Smoke from morning cookfires drifts from chimneys set in red-tiled roofs, and people are going about their daily shopping in the market square that faces the palace. Whoever rebuilt the city after the War of Dissolution designed the buildings close to the palace in such an ornate fashion that they're almost works of art themselves, with gold-topped towers that glimmer and shine in the morning sunlight and intricately carved, wooden window grilles. Seeing them is a nice palate cleanser before I get interrogated by Samis about my exploits—or lack thereof—at the ball last night.

Samis and Kenessa greet me as I enter their dining room; Kenessa looks just as dapper and awake as her husband. Emma, our sister, is with them, which is another surprise—usually she's far too busy to join us for meals. *Maybe she decided to actually take a break for once.* She looks up when I walk in and waves, not showing any signs of fatigue, even though she was probably up earlier than Samis was. I help myself to some sausage, fruit, and toast before I join them at the table.

Unfortunately, I don't get a chance to eat just yet, because Samis wastes no time in getting down to business. "Now that you're here, tell me what happened with Petris," he says. "I saw the two of you dancing, but what happened after that?"

Before I can respond, Emma jumps in, giving me an incredulous stare. "Wait, who's Petris? And more importantly, you were *dancing*? You must really like him if you let him drag you onto the dance floor."

"I did like him. I mean, I *do* like him. We had a good time last night. He seems like a perfectly nice person." I take a deep breath. "But I don't think I'm going to see him again."

The three of them share a look that I've seen several times before, and I suppress a sigh.

"Why not?" Emma asks slowly, her eyebrows raised. "Didn't you just say you had a good time with him?"

"Yes, but ..." *How can I explain this in a way that makes sense to them?* "He said I'm not really his type, which I didn't mind. But then he told me that it doesn't matter whether our personalities are compatible because I'm a prince."

A few seconds of awkward silence pass. "And that was a problem because?" Samis finally prompts.

"Don't you get it?" I shift in my seat and cross my arms, trying not to wither under everyone's collective attention. "He acted like my title was the only thing about me that's important. I mean, he pretty much said he would be willing to court *anyone,* if they were a prince."

"But you *are* a prince." Samis sounds like he's telling me the sky is blue. "It's not exactly a secret, you know. If you like him and he likes you, what's the problem?"

I suppose I shouldn't be surprised they don't understand. This is hardly the first time I've had this conversation with them. "You're not getting it. The problem isn't that he, or anyone, knows I'm a prince. The problem is that's the *only* thing he knows about me. The only thing he seemed to care about, anyway." I pause, trying to figure out how to put my feelings into words. "Look, I don't want to court someone who just sees me as their chance to become part of the royal family. I want someone who actually likes *me* as a person and not just my position. Is that really asking for too much?"

"Darien, I'm not saying you're wrong to want that. I just think you might have to lower your standards a bit. You can't expect people to completely forget you're a prince. When they first meet you, that is the only thing they know about you. You just need to give them a chance to get to know the real you before you reject them out of hand. Why not turn your position into an asset, rather than a liability? You could have anyone you want!" He turns to look at Kenessa. "How do you think I managed to convince Kenessa to court me? She probably wouldn't have looked at me twice if I wasn't going to be king someday."

Kenessa smiles sweetly at her husband. "Is that what you think, darling? Surely you don't believe I'm that shallow." They beam at each other for a few more seconds, and I'm just about to gag on my toast when she turns to me. "Unlike these two, I understand what you're saying, and I think you've got it exactly right. There's no need to settle for someone who's just a pretty face. I'm sure the right man for you will come along before you know it."

I nod, but I'm not convinced. I'm always going to be a prince, and I doubt I'll ever find a man who doesn't care about that. So many people in my life act like the only thing that matters about me is my title, and not just when it comes to courting. Everyone has ideas about how a prince should act, should feel, should *think*, and they just assume I do act and feel and think those things, even if I don't. Then when I inevitably mess up or say the wrong thing, because I'm not perfect, someone's always disappointed in me.

I don't say any of that, though, partially because I know they'll just dismiss my concerns, and partially because I have this irrational fear that saying it will make it come true.

Some of what I'm feeling must be showing in my expression, because Samis pats my shoulder. "Don't look so glum," he chides. "You're only twenty-five years old! I'm sure you'll meet your man soon enough, like Kenessa said. And, if it's too difficult, you can just ask Mother and Father to find someone for you."

I shudder involuntarily. "Don't even joke about that. You know how I feel about arranged marriages."

Samis nods, a hint of a smile on his face. "Well, what better way to avoid marrying some man you've never even met than actually going out there and meeting people? I know things didn't work out with Petris, but I've got a few other friends I can introduce you to. Who knows—maybe you'll find that one or two of them is more than just a 'pretty face,' as Kenessa says. Even if they aren't, it's not the end of the world! There's nothing wrong with having a little fun while you're still young. Before you get married, of course," he adds hastily as Kenessa glares at him. "The same goes for you, Emma, by the way. I know you'd rather spend your time working, but everyone needs a distraction now and then."

I figure this is as good a chance as any to change the topic away from my love life and onto less fraught grounds. "Speaking of which, Emma, what is this project you've been working on lately? I don't think you've ever actually told me."

"I don't know if I'd call it a project, exactly," Emma replies. "There's been an outbreak of wasting fever in two of the settlements just outside the city walls. I'm working with the palace healers to see if we can track the source and prevent it from spreading any farther."

"How bad is it?" Kenessa asks. "Should we be worried?"

"There's no reason to be worried at the moment, no. It's only a few isolated cases so far, and nobody's died just yet. Hopefully, it'll stay that way." She turns to Samis. "None of you mention this to Mother or Father, by the way. I don't want them to get upset, like they did when *someone* told them I was doing that census of the prison inmates."

Samis holds up his hands in mock surrender. "I've told you a million times, that was an accident. My lips are sealed. I promise."

The two of them bicker for a while longer, with Kenessa and I jumping in occasionally, before we all decide it's time for the four of us to go about our days. Just as I'm about to leave, though, Samis stops me and Emma.

"I almost forgot to tell you. Mother and Father are having dinner with the Learas tomorrow night, and they want us all to be there. I didn't think they were supposed to be here until summer, but apparently I was wrong."

Kenessa scratches her cheek. "Can someone please tell me who exactly the Learas are? Your mother has mentioned them quite a few times, but I felt too awkward to ask her."

"Catherine Leara is Mother's friend," Samis explains. "They grew up at the Zeteyoni court together, and I'm told they were inseparable. When Mother came to Soeria to marry Father, she asked Catherine to come too, but Catherine stayed in Zeteyon and married a viscount. She and Mother have stayed in touch, though, and her daughter Riella spent some time here in Cedelia studying foreign affairs and diplomacy a few years ago—Darien, you and Riella are friends, right?" He waits for me to nod before he continues. "Anyway, it seems like she's finally taking up Mother's offer, because the whole family is coming to live here in

Cedelia. I'm betting Catherine and her husband are hoping to play matchmaker and marry their kids off to some rich and powerful Soerian nobles. After all, *some* people are willing to use their connections to our family to find a good match." He looks at me meaningfully, and I ignore him, just as meaningfully. "In any event, Mother wants us all to have dinner together so we can reacquaint ourselves. It'll be us plus the four Learas—Catherine, Aloran, Riella, and ..." He pauses, then turns to me and Emma. "Do either of you remember the son's name?"

I shake my head, and Emma shrugs. Kenessa says something to Samis, but I tune the three of them out, thinking about what Samis said earlier. *I'm sure you'll meet your man soon enough.*

If only I could let myself believe that he's right.

# CHAPTER THREE

B y the time I get to the dining room the next night, Samis, Emma, and Kenessa have already arrived. My parents, King Tolmir and Queen Merandia of Soeria, are here too, which is less of a surprise; I don't know where I got my lack of punctuality from, but it certainly wasn't either of them.

"Ah, there you are, Darien!" Mother says as I enter the room. "I was wondering whether to send a servant to come and fetch you."

I walk over to the couch where she's sitting. "How could I miss it? You've only been talking about this dinner for the last month."

"I'm sure you'd react the same way if you were seeing Ivy for the first time in years, my son." She turns around and fingers my lapel. "I'm guessing she chose this outfit for you?"

I glance down at my clothes—a white, silk shirt, a high-collared, dark-blue jacket with gold buttons, and gray pants that are so dark they might as well be black—before looking back up. "What, you don't think I'm capable of choosing my own?"

Her only response is a hint of a smile.

"Fine." I sigh. "Yes, she did pick it out. But I helped."

Before Mother can respond to that blatant falsehood, a page steps into the room and bows. "Your Majesties, may I present Viscount Aloran Leara and Viscountess Catherine Leara, and their children." The page bows again and withdraws, and the Learas enter before the rest of us move to greet them.

Ignoring the others, I head straight for Riella, a lightness to my step that wasn't there before. She and I may not be as close as Mother and Catherine, but I'd still say I'm closer to her than to anyone besides Ivy, Samis, and Emma. She's only been gone for a couple years, but I've missed her quite a bit. When she first came to court about ten years ago, Mother thought it would be a good idea to have us take history lessons together, and it wasn't long before we became friends. I was upset when she went back to Zeteyon so she could get some hands-on experience running a large estate, but I always knew she'd be back before too long. Of course, I didn't think she'd bring her whole family with her, but I'm sure Mother doesn't mind.

Riella spots me as I come close, turning away from the rest of the group and gives me a wide smile and a hug when I stop before her. "It's good to see you again, Darien," she says. She leans back, her light brown hair tied up neatly into a bun, and her eyes sparkling with mirth as she lowers her voice. "Don't tell my parents I said this, but I was starting to get tired of being out in the country. There's just nothing to *do* there, you know?"

"I mean, that's why you came here in the first place, isn't it?" I ask, my smile matching her own. "To tell you the truth, I know how you feel. Things were getting too boring without you around."

"Oh, don't worry, I think we can fix that before too long." There's a mischievous glint in her eyes. "Tell me, have you gotten out of the palace at all since I left? Or even out of your study?"

"I'll have you know I went to Lady Gerreso's ball just last night, thank you very much," I inform her. "I met some people, even danced a bit."

"Keep it up and you'll turn into Samis in no time," she says with a wink. "Speaking of meeting people, though, let me introduce you to my brother Tag. I think the two of you will get along wonderfully." She gestures to Tag, who had been standing behind her so quietly that I didn't even realize he was there.

He steps forward and stands beside his sister, a tiny smile on his face, and for a moment I forget how to breathe, or talk, or move, or do anything but stand there with a dumb expression, because Tag is without a doubt the most beautiful man I've ever seen in my life. He's clean shaven, with deep chestnut-brown hair that's wavy and perhaps a bit longer than mine, and his eyes are the same earthy color. Not exactly the most striking combination, but somehow it fit him. No, not just *fit* him—he makes Petris, who I thought was quite good-looking, seem average in comparison. His body is somewhere between lean and muscular, and his well-cut clothes accentuate his features. *Why in the world has nobody thought to introduce us before now?*

The strange thing is, Tag doesn't look like the kind of man that I usually go for. He's not very tall—perhaps half a foot shorter than me—and his lips are thin, not full. But there's just something about him, something that I can't quite put my finger on. Whatever it is, I'm already hooked.

With a jolt, I realize I'm gawking and try to pull myself together. "It's nice to meet you, Tag. Welcome to Cedelia."

Fortunately, neither Tag nor his sister seems upset at my reaction. In fact, he flashes that tiny smile again. "Thank you, Your Royal Highness," he says. "It's a pleasure to meet you, too."

He begins to bow, but I reach out a hand and stop him.

"Please, call me Darien," I say, and he takes my outstretched hand, his grip warm and strong. "I hope you enjoy your time here at the palace."

"In that case, thank you, Darien," he says, his smile a bit wider than it was before. "I'm sure I'll enjoy it quite a bit."

I'm almost lost in his eyes when I realize Riella is speaking again, "See, I knew you two would like each other," she says, and my mind starts to race as I try to figure out if there's a hidden meaning behind her words. "Darien, I was hoping that you could introduce Tag to life at court, if it's not too much trouble? I'm sure you'll be a much better companion for him than Samis or Emma."

*Is she doing what I think she's doing?* If she is, I suppose I'm willing to go along with it for now. I don't like being manipulated, but right now I can't help it. I don't know that I *want* to help it. "That sounds like a great idea, Riella," I say, studiously avoiding looking at Tag so I don't get distracted by his beautiful eyes again. "It would be my pleasure."

"Excellent! I'm glad to hear it."

I think she's about to say more, but Mother calls me over to greet the viscount and viscountess, while Samis, Emma, and Kenessa come over to speak to Tag and Riella. With some difficulty, I tear myself away from the attractive man before me, then join my parents and the elder Learas.

As I chat with the viscount and viscountess, I'm struck by just how different they are from each other. I've met the viscountess a few times—despite what Mother said earlier, it hasn't been that long since they've seen each other—and every time she's been friendly and vivacious, a true extrovert if I've ever seen one, like Samis. Her hair, the same color as Tag's, is relatively short, and her green eyes sparkle with mirth. I've never met her husband in person before—at least, not that I remember—although Riella has told me about him. Apparently, he's an introvert like me, only he's taken it to another level. I once gently prodded Riella as to why he never came to visit her like her mother did, and she told me he hates traveling and is usually content to stay at their estate in Zeteyon. Actually, now that I think about it, she mentioned Tag was the same way; maybe that explains why nobody's introduced me to him before.

In any event, Riella's description of her father seems to be pretty on the nose. The entire time we're talking—if you can call it that—he seems mildly discomfited, with the corners of his mouth pulled down into a half-scowl and his arms crossed in front of his chest. I might be offended if Riella hadn't told me he does the same thing to everyone. When my parents and the viscountess start reminiscing about their younger days, he shows no interest in conversing with me or them, and in my boredom, I'm powerless to stop my eyes from wandering back to Tag more than once. Hopefully the viscount doesn't notice.

*Although, if he does, at least he probably won't say anything about it.*

After a minute or so of awkward silence between me and the viscount, a bell sounds—our cue to go sit at the dinner table. Shaking my head to clear my mind, I choose a seat near the middle of the table, with Riella to my right and Samis to my left. Tag sits across from me, and it takes all my willpower not to stare at him. *Is Riella really trying to set us up, or is that just wishful thinking?*

Fortunately, Riella is just as extroverted as her mother and has no trouble carrying the conversation. At first, I try to engage with her, but soon I'm paying just enough attention to avoid being impolite, my focus repeatedly wandering to the gorgeous man across from me.

Finally, after the remains of the second course have been taken away, I take a few quiet breaths, hoping I can tamp down at least some of my anxiety, and clear my throat. Tag turns his head away from Emma, who's describing her newest project to the viscountess. "I know you've only been here for a few days," I say to him, "but what do you think of Cedelia so far?"

"From what I've seen, it seems like an interesting city." He grins at me, and I wonder if he can hear my heart begin to pound like a drum. "I already have a list of places I want to go. Historical sites, mostly. Riella promised me she'd show me around when she has time."

I perk up even more, if that's possible. "You like history?"

"I do," he confirms. "Nowhere near as much as my father does, though. I think he's more excited than I am, which is rare."

I glance at the Viscount, whose dour expression doesn't seem to have changed at all in the last hour. "I can believe that." I turn back to Tag. "Are you excited to live here in the palace?"

"You could definitely say that." His grin fades slightly. "Although, to be honest, I'm a little nervous too. This"—he gestures widely at the room around us—"isn't exactly what I'm used to."

"Oh? In what sense?"

"I'm not sure how much you've heard from Riella about our home, but it's pretty much in the middle of nowhere. I mean, there are vine-yards around and a few villages, but nothing so grand as this."

"I've heard. I'm guessing it's a lot quieter. And less crowded, too."

He nods. "Exactly. I mean, just being here in the palace ... we've only been here a day, and I swear I've never seen anything like it in my life.

The food, the music, the clothes, everything. I have a feeling it's going to be rather stressful just trying to keep track of who everyone is and how I'm supposed to act. Riella warned me it would be intense before we left Zeteyon, but I didn't really believe her until we actually got here." He blushes ever so slightly, and his voice softens. "I feel like I have so much to learn."

"Well, we can fix that, can't we?" I silently thank him for giving me a perfect opening, even as I wonder if it was intentional or an accident. "I was serious when I said it would be my pleasure to show you around. We'll get you up to speed in no time."

He gives me a sweet smile that makes my heart pound even harder. "Thank you, Darien," he says, and, for just a second, I see a glint in his eyes—the same one I saw in Riella's eyes when she introduced the two of us. It's there and gone in a flash, but somehow seeing it even for that brief moment gives me hope. "I'd like that very much."

# CHAPTER FOUR

Later that night, when dinner is over and I'm safely back in my rooms, I let out a quiet breath and sink onto a couch. My heart is still pounding madly, as though I've just run to the city walls and back. I stare at the ceiling, my mind racing just as fast as my heart. The thoughts that flit through it like butterflies are simultaneously hopeful and pessimistic, because underneath everything is that little voice that tells me this is all good to be true.

*Riella wouldn't try to set the two of us up if she didn't think he'd be interested, too, would she?* She's mentioned him a few times over the years and told me a little about him—mostly that he's kind but shy and dislikes traveling almost as much as their father—but I never got the sense that she saw him as a potential romantic interest for me up until today. *Am I building castles in the sky?*

I go back and forth, back and forth, until I've got myself so twisted around that I don't know which way is up. The doubt won't leave no matter how much I tell it to shut up.

Some part of me is surprised at the strength of my response. I've never reacted this way to any other man, especially one whom I've just met. Maybe it's because I've spent so long trying to find someone, with so many false starts and failed attempts—like last night, for instance. If anything, Petris was better than most; usually it takes far less time for me to realize they're after my title.

But with Tag, I didn't get that sense at all. Besides, this just feels ... *different*, somehow, even if I can't explain why. Maybe I'm wrong, trying to convince myself that this is the time when it'll finally work out for me because I want to believe it. If I am wrong about Tag, though, I'm not sure I could do anything about it right now, other than try to keep myself far away from the extremes of unwarranted hope and disabling despondency.

Yet, doing that takes quite a bit of energy, which is why I spend the rest of the night and a good portion of the next few days in a bit of a haze. My thoughts turn to Tag more often than I'd care to admit. When I close my eyes, I see him sitting across from me at the dinner table, smiling that perfect smile at me, and my heart races like a thoroughbred's.

Once my mind clears up enough that I feel reasonably rational—a few days after the dinner—I decide it's time to actually *see* him again. I suppose I could keep waiting and hope that he makes the first move, but I think I might actually go crazy if I wait any longer, so I write him a brief message:

> Tag,
> I hope you're adjusting to life at the palace well. I'm looking forward to fulfilling my promise to show you around the court. If you're available, I'd love

to have lunch with you—tomorrow, perhaps? If not
then, I'm happy to find another time.

Sincerely,
Darien

After reading it over a few times to make sure I haven't accidentally
said something stupid, I hand it off to Joram, my steward. Meanwhile,
I sit back and pretend to review a petition while my mind is completely
elsewhere.

After one of the most anxiety-filled half-hours of my entire life, Joram
returns to my study with a bow and presents me with Tag's reply. My
hands are shaking as I take the message; fortunately, Joram is much too
discreet to comment on it. Opening the message takes longer than it
should, and my trepidation increases with every additional second.

Once I've finally managed to get it open, I read it quickly.

Darien,
I would love to join you for lunch tomorrow. Just let
me know where and when, and I'll be there.
Looking forward to it,

Tag

It's a short message, but I read it again, just in case I completely
misread it the first time. Once I've finally managed to convince myself
I'm not missing anything, I breathe a quiet sigh of relief.

"Joram, please tell my kitchen staff that I'll be taking lunch tomorrow in my rooms," I say without looking up. Unlike my hands, my voice is even and steady. "And tell them to send enough food for two."

The next day, the hour or so before lunch is torture. *What if I'm over-thinking this whole thing?* Maybe Samis is right, and the viscount and viscountess brought him here so he can find some rich Soerian to marry. Maybe I angered Riella somehow when she was here before, and this is her way of getting back at me. Maybe this is all some sort of fantasy, and all four of them are still at the Leara estate, far away from here. No remote possibility seems too outrageous right now.

Fortunately, one of those fears—that this is all a hallucination induced by my desperation to find a good man to court—is dispelled when Joram lets Tag into my antechamber at the agreed-upon time, announcing him with a bow before leaving the two of us alone.

I get up to greet Tag, my heart pounding, and I wonder why it's so difficult to just act normal. He looks even better than he did a few days ago, if that's possible. A simple but well-cut brown coat that matches his eyes and hair covers a white linen shirt, while his deep-blue pants provide some contrast and remind me of the ocean. The shirt and coat seem almost perfectly designed to show off his arms and chest, which both look like works of art. I make a mental note to send a thank-you gift to the Learas' tailor, whoever they are.

I start when I realize I've been staring at him for an amount of time that is rapidly approaching impropriety. "Please, come in." My voice is slightly higher than normal—although, it may not matter, since he may not be able to hear it over the sound of my thrumming heart. "Thanks for coming on such short notice."

If I didn't know better, I'd say that he starts at the sound of my voice too, as though he's been checking *me* out.

"Of course, Darien." A small smile plays on his face as his eyes meet mine, an involuntary grin that I doubt he even knows is there. "Thank you for inviting me. Riella's told me so much about you, and I've been looking forward to getting to know you better."

"Really, it's my pleasure." *In more ways than one.* "I hope you don't mind, but I asked my steward to set up a small table for lunch. I figured there's no reason to sit at a full dining table when it's just the two of us. It'll be more intimate."

As soon as the words are out of my mouth, I cringe. *Damn, I didn't mean to say it like that.*

His eyebrows rise, but I plow on, doing my best to immediately forget my gaffe. "Plus, the view from the window is quite nice. I think you'll like it."

"That sounds wonderful," he replies, still giving me that soft smile. "Please, lead the way."

I show him to my dining area, and we take our seats at the table while I speculate on whether I'll be able to make it through the next few hours without going completely insane. "So," I ask, "now that you've had a chance to look around, what do you think of the palace?"

"It's beautiful. At least, what I've seen so far is. It's definitely bigger than I was expecting." He lowers his voice and leans forward slightly. "Don't tell anyone, but I got lost on the way to your rooms. I had to ask a servant for directions."

I smile, despite myself. "If it makes you feel any better, I still get lost occasionally."

He looks at me as though he's not sure whether I'm being serious or joking.

"It's true! I swear whoever designed this place was secretly trying to make it a maze instead of a palace."

"Okay, okay, I believe you," he says, chuckling. "I'm glad I'm in good company, at least."

Try as I might, I can't help but wonder if there's a deeper meaning to his words. *If only…*

There's a pause in the conversation while servants place the first course, a chilled potato-and-leek soup with cheese and bacon mixed in, before us. After a bit of silence, I resume our conversation by saying, "I have to confess, Riella has told me a little bit about you."

"Oh, really?" He looks up from his soup, his eyebrows slightly raised. "What did she say?"

"Not that much, if I'm honest." *She* definitely *didn't mention how attractive you are.* "Mostly that you're more introverted than she is and that you didn't mind living in the country."

"That sounds about right. Riella was always more excited about the prospect of living in a city than me. She was so excited when our parents agreed to let her study here a few years ago. But me, on the other hand … I guess I got used to living out in the country, and I wasn't sure I was ready for the hustle and bustle of court." He glances down, and his voice softens. "Hopefully you won't be offended, but I'm willing to admit I wasn't really looking forward to leaving home. Like I said the other day, there's just so much I don't know."

"I'm not offended," I reassure him. "Life at court can be confusing at times, and not just because the palace is a maze. I can understand why you might prefer to be away from all the chaos. If you don't mind my asking, though, what brings you to court? Not that I'm upset you're here or anything like that, you understand."

He looks at me, that when that small smile grows back on his face, all I can think about is how beautiful he is. "Back when Riella and I came of age, my parents started talking about moving to Osella so we could be introduced to the Zeteyoni court," he continues. "I guess they thought we could start networking with other people our age, maybe get positions of influence in the government, or whatever. But they didn't follow through—my mother never said it outright, but I think she hated growing up there. Obviously, Riella ended up coming to study here instead, and that turned out well, so when Her Majesty offered to have the rest of us join Riella, my parents jumped at the chance. I didn't really want to come, but Riella convinced me it's for the best." His eyes catch mine, just for a second, and I'm not sure whether it's intentional. "So far, I think she's right."

*Be still my beating heart.* "I'm glad to hear that," I say, meaning it. "And if there's anything I can do to make your time here any better, please let me know, and I'll do my best to help you."

"Thank you, Darien," he says, a hint of that sweet smile still on his face. "I really appreciate it."

For a long moment, we sit silently, looking at each other, and I can't help but wonder if he's as nervous as I am. Just thinking about the prospect makes me even more anxious, which isn't helpful. I open my mouth to say something—I'm not quite sure what—to break the silence, but I'm interrupted by the arrival of the main course: roasted duck in plum sauce with a side of mushrooms and yellow squash. It smells wonderful, and we both dig in immediately.

"This is delicious," Tag says between mouthfuls. "I'm sure there are things I won't like about living at court, but something tells me the food won't be one of them."

I can't help but snort at that. "Just try to avoid having breakfast—or any meal, really—with Samis. He prefers to dine family style, and if you're not careful, he'll finish everything before you can blink."

Tag laughs wholeheartedly, and the sound warms my heart. "I'll keep that in mind," he says. "Thanks for the warning."

"Of course," I say, and he gives me a wide smile in return. Seeing it gives me confidence, and, before I realize what I'm doing, I gently reach out and touch his hand with mine.

But just as I brush his skin, he pulls his hand back so we're no longer touching. He only moves a bit, and not rapidly, like he'd touched a flame, but it's enough. My confidence dissipates, leaving me short of breath, like I've just climbed the tallest mountain in Soeria. I do my best to console myself, to convince myself that I haven't just made a huge mistake. It could have just been bad timing on my part. Or maybe I completely misread the situation, and I'm wrong about everything.

"I'm sorry," I tell him. "I didn't mean to make you uncomfortable."

"It's fine. I just ... wasn't expecting it, that's all." He flashes a grin at me. "Now then, you were saying something about Samis?"

We continue chatting for a little while longer as I silently question everything I've ever done in my entire life. Once we've finished eating and the conversation has run its course, I guide him to the entrance to my suite and bid him farewell. "I really enjoyed eating lunch with you," I tell him. Granted, I say that nearly every time I have a meal with someone important, even if it was a disaster, but this time I really mean it. "We should do it again sometime."

He bows ever so slightly. "I enjoyed it too," he says. "I'm sure we'll see each other again soon."

He stands here for a moment longer, and, for just the briefest millisecond, I think I see a glint in his eyes. It's not quite like the one I saw in his eyes at dinner a few days ago, but it's not that different either.

Yet just as soon as it was there, it's gone, making me question whether I even saw it in the first place. With a final wave goodbye, he turns and walks away, leaving me to replay and analyze every second of the last hour or so, and wonder if I'm going to lose my mind before the week is out.

# CHAPTER FIVE

T ry as I might, I can't stop myself from spending a good portion of the next few days thinking about that spark of *something* I saw in Tag's eyes as he left my suite. I've seen it twice now, and my gut tells me it's a good sign.

But every time I almost convince myself that I have a chance with him, I remember the way he moved his hand away the moment I touched it. It might have been a coincidence or an involuntary reaction on his part. But, when it comes to courting, I've previously gotten my hopes up and been let down so many times, and I refuse to let that happen again. Not if I can help it.

Of course, none of this obsessing is particularly good for my mental health, so in an effort to distract myself from thoughts of Tag, I throw myself into my royal duties with a vigor I'm not sure I've ever matched before.

Unfortunately, it doesn't take me long to realize that sitting at a desk and reading papers isn't exactly the most mentally stimulating activity, and it's hard to focus on such tasks when my thoughts are determined to be elsewhere. *I need to find something else to do.*

What follows is a series of increasingly desperate attempts to find a better distraction. First up is Ivy, who seems rather surprised to see me when I find her throwing knives at a straw target in the small training courtyard near the guards' barracks. That doesn't stop her from challenging me to a competition. At least, that's how she describes it, but I suspect it's really just a way for her to show off her admittedly superior skills. There may be things that I'm better than her at—emphasis on *may*—but knife-throwing is definitely not one of them.

True to form, the 'competition' is over in barely fifteen minutes.

"That was even worse than usual, and you've set a pretty low bar," she says as we retrieve the knives from the target. "Are you sure you're alright?"

"I'm fine," I tell her, wincing as I rotate my shoulder. She gives me a look that clearly says she knows that I'm not, in fact, fine, so I add, "Listen, I promise if I ask someone for advice, you'll be the first on the list."

"You know that you can always talk to me about anything, right?" She waits for me to nod. "Good. That's all I need." She gestures back to the practice target. "Now then, if you're not going to tell me what's bothering you, shall we get back to it?"

"Is this really how you spend your free time?" I ask, more to delay any further embarrassment than for an answer. "There have to be better ways to spend your time that don't involve deadly weapons."

She shrugs, tossing a knife in the air and catching it handle-first. "Maybe there are, but it doesn't hurt to be prepared. Sure, it's probably more useful for you to learn about history and diplomacy and all that, but someone has to be prepared to protect the country. The way things are going, we may need people who know their weapons sooner rather than later."

My ears perk up at the last sentence. "'The way things are going'? What does that mean?"

"Honestly? It's probably nothing. You know I like to spend time with the soldiers in the city garrison, and a few of them seem to think their services will be needed soon." She shakes her head. "But I wouldn't worry about it if I were you. They're probably just restless, and if there is something wrong, I'm sure the King and his advisors are on top of it." She turns back to the target. "Now, hurry up and lose to me already so I can make fun of you some more."

Feeling vaguely disquieted, I do as she asked, stepping up and throwing my knife at the straw target. The knife almost misses the target, bouncing off to one side uselessly. The next throw, and the one after that, go just about as well as the first one did, and it's not long before my unease is replaced by annoyance. *How is it this hard to throw a stupid knife at a man-sized bundle of straw?*

Finally, after three rounds of complete embarrassment, I give up. I could still use a distraction from my thoughts about Tag, but perhaps one that's not quite this humiliating. To add injury to insult, I can already tell that my arm will be sore when I wake up tomorrow. At least I didn't miss the target *every* time.

My next attempt at distraction is Emma, who's almost as surprised to see me as Ivy was. But when I ask her if I can help with her attempts to track the wasting fever cases in the outlying villages, her surprise quickly gives way to regret.

"Sorry, but there's really nothing you or I can do at this point," she says. "Maybe if you were a healer, but you're not. Plus, I don't want to risk you getting sick." She gestures at the large stack of papers in front of her. "Unless you want to help me search through these census records that I found in the library to see if there's any information on prior outbreaks? I doubt we'll find anything helpful, but it's better than doing nothing."

That at least sounds less painful than knife throwing, but it also sounds just as boring as the petitions I should be reviewing right now, so I politely decline and move on to my next attempt.

If Ivy and Emma were surprised when I talked to them, Samis is absolutely shocked. "Let me get this straight," he says slowly. "You want to take my place at a *council meeting*? Is this some kind of joke?"

I assure him that I'm being serious, but he laughs anyway.

"If you really want to, then, by all means, be my guest. Just remember that you asked me, not the other way around."

I know I probably shouldn't ask, but my curiosity gets the better of me. "It can't be that bad." I pause. "Can it?"

He just laughs even harder. "Don't worry, you'll find out soon enough!" He pats me on the shoulder and leaves me with that, still chuckling as he walks away.

I stare at his back for a few moments, trying to figure out if he's just messing with me, before I turn to go. His reaction was ... concerning, to say the least, but I still think he might have been playing a prank on me. *Only one way to find out.*

When I arrive at the council meeting an hour or so later, most of the councilors are already there, seated around the long, rectangular table—those ranked highest are closest to me, while those of lower rank are seated at the far end of the table. As soon as they notice me walking in, they stand and bow to me as deeply as etiquette calls for based on their title and position. The highest-ranked councilor, Duke Zoran Arondel, barely nods his head, while the lowest ranking, Lord Mokurot, bends so far his head nearly hits the table.

I take my seat, feeling slightly self-conscious. I haven't attended a meeting since before I came of age, but from what Samis has told me, I think I'll be able to handle it. Assuming I don't fall asleep a few hours in, that is.

Once I've taken my place at the head of the table, the others resume their seats. If Father were here, he'd be sitting where I am, but Samis told me he's eating lunch with the ambassador from Jirena Sadai, so I get the dubious honor of being the focus of everyone's attention. At least I don't have to explain to Father why I'm here. I'm sure he wouldn't say anything—at least not in public—but I doubt he'd be very happy to see me taking Samis's place, even if it's only for one meeting. *Well, what he doesn't know won't hurt him.*

As soon as everyone is settled, I motion for the discussion to begin.

"Your Royal Highness, I have an update on the situation with Zeteyon," says Colonel Deor Belling, a high-ranking officer in the Soerian Army and the commander of Cedelia's garrison. Their short black hair frames an angular face, and they sit ramrod straight in their chair, the very epitome of military discipline. I don't interact with them very much—I've never really had much of an interest in the military outside of my historical research—but from what I've heard, they're exceedingly competent at their job, which is reassuring given its importance. "Your Royal Highness is aware that we have an alliance with Zeteyon thanks to the marriage between the king and queen, correct?" They barely wait for me to nod before continuing. "I can report that the border conflict between Zeteyon and Khoria shows no sign of ending, although it seems doubtful at the present time that it will erupt into a full-scale war."

That's not great, but I suppose it could be worse. "Has my uncle requested our aid?" I ask. I know Father would rather avoid getting involved in any conflict if at all possible, and I wholeheartedly agree with him on that, at least.

Fortunately, Belling shakes their head. "No, Your Royal Highness. So far, King Zeikas has kept us out of it. However, on your father's orders, I have instructed our ambassadors in Osella and Pyaran to offer to act as mediators. Given our relationship with Zeteyon, it seems unlikely the Khorians will accept our offer; still, we should be prepared to consider what further instructions to give them on the off chance they prove to be amenable to mediation."

"I understand." No doubt coming up with those instructions will take up quite a bit of Father's time. "Does anyone else have anything to add on this topic?"

At that, Countess Nynavia Voeli, a long-time member of the council and the head of the royal treasury, clears her throat. She's one of the few councilors I interact with outside of formal events, thanks to a shared interest in history; in fact, she helped me track down the account of the Battle of Cavain that I showed Samis a few days ago.

"Do we expect to be called into this conflict at some point in the future?" she asks Belling. "I presume the army is prepared for that eventuality, but I have no doubt that it would require a rather large expenditure."

"It's a possibility, I suppose, but a remote one," Belling replies. "As long as the conflict remains at a relatively low intensity, I doubt King Zeikas and the Zeteyoni government will feel the need to get us involved. However, I should note that for the near future, we will be unable to call on the Zeteyoni army to come to our aid should we require it."

Voeli nods and leans back in her chair. "Excellent," I say. "Thank you for the report, Belling. Now then, moving on—"

"Excuse me, Your Royal Highness," interrupts Archduchess Pyria Rolsteg, a tall woman with long, auburn hair seated next to Duke Arondel. Although she's rather high ranking, her family is new to the nobility, at least compared with most of the other people at this table. If I'm remembering correctly, her great-great-grandfather, Vrax Rolsteg, was a merchant who made enough money selling arms during the War of Dissolution to buy a title. Since then, the Rolstegs have used impressive dowries to marry into almost every noble family in Soeria.

"I apologize for interrupting," Rolsteg continues. "But if I may ask—Belling, you said we won't be able to call on their army? Does that mean we're on our own should someone attack us? Should we be worried?"

I do my best to keep my expression neutral even though I feel a slight chill. Rolsteg certainly *seems* concerned, but something about the way she said it—a whisper of a hint of hopefulness in her voice, perhaps—has put my guard up. If I didn't know better, I'd say she's excited at the prospect of Soeria being left to defend itself alone. But that would be absurd—after all, it's not like she would gain anything from it. It's far more likely that I misheard her. Or I'm already losing my ability to pay attention, less than ten minutes in.

It must be the latter, because Belling's expression hasn't changed one bit. "Theoretically we are, but I doubt it will be a problem," they say. "We have no reason to expect that we will require their aid anytime soon. Perhaps if the situation persists for an extended period of time, or if one of our neighbors starts acting aggressively, we may need to start worrying. But until and unless that happens, there is no reason for distress."

Rolsteg nods. I search her expression for a hint of disappointment, but I see none, so I let my guard back down. With the military report complete, Voeli speaks next, giving me and the Council an update on the kingdom's finances. She does a good job of keeping her remarks to a minimum, thankfully.

Any hope of getting out of this meeting early is dashed, though, when Arondel follows with a report on the beginning of the planting season and the state of the crown lands. Unlike Voeli, he speaks for quite a long time, and so does everyone after him. In fact, it seems like just about everyone in the room besides me, Belling, and Voeli feels the need to give a long-winded speech on some random topic. What's worse, most of those speeches turn into never-ending debates.

At first, I try my best to follow the discussion, and even jump in with a suggestion or a comment here or there, but it soon becomes a struggle just to stay awake. By the time the meeting ends—nearly four hours after it started—I have a newfound appreciation for Samis. *He has to go through* this *three times a week*? *How does he not sleep through the entire thing*? Not for the first time, I'm grateful for whatever stroke of luck made me the second child, not the heir. If I had to put up with those meetings all the time, I might just run away and go live out in the country somewhere.

To be fair, attending this meeting wasn't a *complete* waste of my time, because the discussion—while boring—was just important enough that I was able to stop thinking about Tag for a little while. Now that it's over, though, my thoughts immediately return to him in full force. It might be funny if it wasn't so sad.

Fortunately, I have one idea left, and if it doesn't succeed, I'm not sure what I'll do. With my fingers crossed, I head toward my favorite room in the entire palace.

As always, when I enter the library, I'm struck by the majesty of the place. Stone bookshelves line the walls, while the center of the room is mostly taken up by tables where scholars can sit and read. There are usually a good number in attendance, perusing historical records from the Empire days or searching for rare books, and today is no exception. Thanks to decades of amassing books and scrolls from all over the world, we have one of the best collections in the country, perhaps second only to the one at the university in Qiros, near the border with Jirena Sadai. It doesn't hurt that the palace survived the dissolution of the Empire mostly unscathed—thanks in no small part to my great-great-grandmother's military prowess—while other places didn't.

Unlike in other parts of the palace, the light in here comes entirely from glowbulbs. If someone tried to light a candle in here, regardless of their rank, Vellington, the head librarian, would have them thrown out so fast their head would spin. The glowbulbs, like their name implies, don't actually burn, but just give off a constant glow. Some genius inventor came up with the idea right before the Empire dissolved, presumably to the great relief of librarians everywhere. Apparently, the process to make them is quite difficult, so they're mostly limited to us and the rest of the nobility.

Just walking in here makes me feel nostalgic. When I was younger, I retreated here when I was exhausted from interminable diplomacy lessons or weapons training with Ivy. Nowadays, it's the perfect place for historical research, which I do two or three times a week. I even have a small space on the upper floor that I've informally claimed for myself. I suppose I could have just officially declared it mine, but I hate pulling rank, especially for something as unimportant as this. The space is toward the back, so there's no reason for most people to go there, and over the years I've finally convinced the librarians to leave me alone when I'm there.

Apparently, it's not as secluded as I thought, because as I get closer, I see someone's sitting in my alcove. I can't tell who it is from this far away, but the tables near the entrance aren't particularly full, so whoever it is must value their privacy. I debate leaving them to their own devices and just finding somewhere else to sit, but I'm curious as to who it is.

When I do finally get close enough to see, I'm not sure whether to laugh or cry. It looks like Tag is absorbed in whatever he's reading—I can't see what the book is from here, but I can tell that it's absurdly large—and I almost turn and walk away before he can look up and notice me standing there. But just like at the dinner where I first saw him, his presence drags me toward him like a moth to a glowbulb, and I am powerless to resist.

Perhaps I shouldn't have worried that he would notice me, because he's so focused on reading his book that even when I come within a few feet of him, he doesn't look up. After a few awkward seconds of just standing here, I clear my throat to get his attention. He jumps and turns, but when he sees it's me, he gives me an easy smile that makes my heart soar.

"Darien!" he exclaims. "I'm sorry, I didn't know you were there." He brushes a stray lock of hair back into place, and my heart does a little flip. "Is there something I can do for you?"

"Don't worry, you're fine," I tell him. "I'm sorry for startling you, so I guess we're even. I just came here to read something. Seems like you had the same idea."

"Yeah, that's right. The rest of the library seemed pretty busy, and I didn't think I could lug this huge book all the way back to my room. This little alcove looked so inviting, and the view of the garden from the window is wonderful." He nods to the seat across from him, a light blush reddening his cheeks. "Do you want to join me? I don't want to intrude if you've got other plans, but I wouldn't mind some company."

I desperately try to keep my expression neutral. "I'd be happy to join you." I take the seat he indicated. "If you don't mind me asking, what are you reading?"

"Oh, this?" he asks, blushing for some reason. "It's a treatise on how best to run an estate. Ways to lower the fiscal burden on workers without impacting profits, that sort of thing." His eyes become unfocused, as though he's looking past me. "I know Riella will inherit our family's estate someday, but she's always been more immersed in the big picture than the details, so I'll probably end up helping her put some of her ideas into practice. I know it's a small estate, especially compared to all this, but we still have a duty to the people who live and work there. The way things are now ... well, I wouldn't say things are bad for them, but they could always be *better*. I know things won't be as good as they were under the Empire, not for a while, but I'm always looking for ways to improve the tenants' lives." He gestures to the gigantic tome on the table. "The author of this book did case studies on various estates that tried to do things differently—what their objectives were, how they tried to implement them, and how they worked out in the end. Like in Weigar, when the local lord—" He pauses, and his eyes snap back to mine. "I'm sorry. I tend to get carried away when I'm talking about something I find interesting. I'll get back to reading instead of talking your ear off."

"No, please continue." It doesn't sound like the most interesting topic I've ever heard, but listening to him talk about something he's passionate about is much better than sitting in silence and letting my mind wander. "What happened in Weigar?"

He looks at me, his eyes slightly squinted as he bites his bottom lip. "You're sure you want to hear about it? I don't want to impose if you'd rather do something else."

I just nod, not trusting myself to say anything.

To my pleasure, his face lights up a bit. "Well, there was a mysterious disease that began killing townspeople, and none of the local healers had any idea what to do about it. But one of Lord Upton's advisors had a theory that the disease was spread by rats, and..." He continues talking, and I listen closely enough to respond adequately, but mostly I'm just enjoying being around him. *I wonder if he feels the same way.*

We keep discussing the book for minutes that turn into hours, and before I know it, the sun has set. Tag trails off as he sees me looking out the window, and when he turns to see for himself, he chuckles softly.

"I told you I tend to get carried away," he says with a guilty smile. "I hope you didn't have any plans for this evening."

"I didn't," I assure him. "And even if I did, I wouldn't be upset. I had a good time with you."

"I'm glad to hear that," he says with a grin that turns into a wide yawn. "I can't believe I talked through most of the afternoon. I think I'm going to go back to my rooms and rest a bit." He stands up, yawning once more. "Goodnight, Darien. We should do this again sometime."

"We should," I agree. "But I have one condition."

"What would that be?"

"Next time, I'm picking the book."

He laughs. "I think I can handle that," he says, his eyes twinkling. "Well, I should be going. I'll see you later."

"Goodbye, Tag. Have a good night."

He nods and walks away, leaving me sitting at the table, wondering if there's any chance that he feels the same way about me that I'm starting to feel for him.

# CHAPTER SIX

The air outside isn't quite freezing, but it's close enough to make my teeth chatter. By this time of day, any light or warmth that the setting sun has yet to share is blocked by the city walls and the densely packed buildings that populate this part of Cedelia. I'm still not sure why Samis insisted that we meet in the city instead of just talking things out in the palace; when I asked him, he just shrugged and said, "You need to get out more." I didn't have the willpower to argue with him, so here I am.

Still, the cold doesn't completely deter me. It's been a few days since I saw Tag at the library, but I've been thinking about him quite a bit since then, and hopefully the shock of the cool air on my face will help distract me. Besides, despite what Samis seems to think, I do enjoy getting out of the palace on occasion, especially when I need to clear my mind. And my mind could certainly use a good clearing right now.

My boots click loudly as I walk down the cobblestone road toward a tavern called the Crystal Sword. Behind me, following at an unobtrusive distance, is one of the palace guards. Her presence is more of a precaution than anything else, as her skills likely won't be needed tonight. I'm dressed like any other noble, so there's no reason for anyone to single me out as a prince—not that anyone would really want to attack me even if they knew, but it's better to be safe than sorry. Plus, there are torches lighting up the street, so there aren't many shadows where pickpockets might lurk.

In retrospect, I should have known that Samis would realize something has been off recently, and once he gets a bit between his teeth, there's no stopping him. Even when we were much younger, Samis was always convinced that every problem had a solution if he just tried hard enough to find it.

I'm not sure I'm headed in the right direction—Samis comes here far more often than I do—but eventually I spot a building with a large sign depicting a silver sword that appears to glitter in the half light. As I approach the tavern, I see another palace guard seemingly lounging outside, which means Samis is already here. The guard bows to me slightly as I walk by, and I acknowledge him with a nod as I walk through the entrance.

As soon as I enter, my nose is assaulted by contrasting smells. The scent of roasting meat mixes with smoke from candles and a large fireplace and, underlying it all, is the musk of people enclosed into a relatively small room. I wouldn't say it's *unpleasant*, exactly, but it is certainly a shock to the senses.

It's still early in the evening, but the common room is already starting to fill up. At one table, a group of four people who look like well-to-do merchants or minor nobles are playing cards, while others are eating dinner or drinking ale. Samis sits near the back, his table slightly separated from the rest of the common room, presumably for privacy. He sees me and waves me over with a big grin.

I've barely sat down when he slides me a mug of ale. "You actually showed up," he says. "And here I thought I was going to have to be all by myself for the rest of the night."

"I'm sure you would have found some way to entertain yourself without too much trouble." I take a sip of the ale; it's better than I was expecting—hoppy and strong without being too bitter. "In fact, I'm betting you were thinking about joining that card game."

"Maybe I was," he says, laughing. "I still might." His laughter fades. "But, first, tell me: what in the world is going on with you? It must be serious if you're willing to sit through a council meeting, of all things."

I'm saved from having to respond by a server who stops at our table with two plates of food—roast chicken and cabbage, with a generous hunk of bread still steaming from the oven. It smells amazing, but I always lose my appetite when I'm nervous, and tonight is no exception. Samis, on the other hand, digs in immediately. I'm not surprised that he ordered before I got here, but I am surprised he waited long enough so that his food would arrive around the same time I did. I pick at my food while Samis demolishes his, and I try to figure out what to say to him.

Eventually, he stops eating just long enough to say, "You didn't answer my question."

I swallow over a sudden lump in my throat. "You know Tag Leara, right?"

Samis pushes away his empty plate. "Of course I do. I was there when you met him not a week ago, remember?"

"Yes, *obviously* I remember. I just wanted to make sure you knew who I'm talking about. You meet new people all the time, after all, and I doubt even you can remember all of them."

He doesn't rise to the bait. "In that case, yes, I know who he is." His eyes narrow. "He's not giving you any trouble, is he?"

"No! Nothing like that. I mean, not in the way you're probably thinking, at least."

"What does that mean? Either he's bothering you or he isn't. Which is it?" A look of realization passes across his face before I can answer. "You want to court him, don't you? Is that it?"

*Here goes nothing.* "Yes," I confess. "I don't know what it is about him, but I felt a spark almost as soon as we met."

"Good for you!" He reaches across the table and clasps my shoulder with one hand, grinning. "I knew you'd find you like someone eventually, and from what I've seen he seems like he'd be a good match for you. So, what's the problem, then?"

I glare at him. "For starters, I don't even know if he's interested in me. I mean, I think he is, but what if he's just being polite? Or what if I just think he's interested because I want it to be true? And..." I bite my lip; I know Samis just wants to help, but it's hard to shake this irrational fear that saying it out loud might make it come true somehow. "What if he is interested in me, but only because of my title? You know I don't want to court someone who doesn't care about me as a person. But I feel more strongly about him than I ever have about anyone else, even if I can't explain why. He doesn't seem like the others, but what if I'm wrong? If it turned out that he was only after my position, I don't know if I could bring myself to turn him down."

"I still think you're setting an unreachable goal for yourself there." Samis holds up a hand to forestall my response. "I know you think I'm wrong. It doesn't matter. If that's how you feel, that's how you feel. I'm not going to tell you to compromise your principles and start courting someone just for the sake of it—that's Mother and Father's job, not mine. I *will* tell you one thing, though." His eyes hold mine, as though he's making sure I'm paying attention to his every word. "Tag might be interested in you, or he might not. Maybe he is, but only because you're a prince. I don't know either of those things, and clearly neither do you. But I *do* know that the easiest way for you to find out is to *talk to him yourself.*"

I roll my eyes at him. "Right, so I'll just walk up to him and ask, 'Are you interested in courting me? And if so, would you still be interested even if I wasn't a prince?' I'm sure that'll go over just great."

As usual, Samis doesn't seem to be affected by my sarcasm. "You're a smart man, Darien. You'll figure something out."

*If only I was so certain.* "Well, in any event, thanks for listening to me. I really do appreciate it, you know, even if I don't end up taking your advice."

"Of course, Darien. That's what siblings are for, right?" He grins, then gestures to the full plate in front of me. "Also, are you going to eat that?"

# CHAPTER SEVEN

I wake from half-remembered dreams the next morning with a pounding headache and a conviction that I'll never drink ale again—or at least, not for a while and definitely not as much as I did last night. My only consolation is that Samis must be feeling the same way too, unless he's found a way to magically rid himself of a hangover and never told me. I wouldn't put it past him.

It's not until I've gotten dressed and shuffled over to my dining area to eat breakfast that I realize there's something else stuck in my mind alongside the nausea and dizziness. *Samis was right. I just need to tell Tag how I feel, and hope he feels the same way.* It seems so obvious now, in the light of day—although I do wish the sun would do me a favor and be just a little less bright today—and I'm determined to act before I lose my nerve.

Of course, I'm not going to march to the Learas' chambers right now and declare my feelings for him, like Samis suggested. Even if I wasn't hung over, I'm not sure I want to go about this too assertively. I think—*I hope*—Tag will be interested, but I still can't forget the way he pulled back when I touched his hand a few days ago. Besides, he doesn't seem like the kind of person who would respond well to that kind of directness. I'm afraid that if I go up to him without any warning and put him on the spot, he'll just turn me down out of reflex. But if I wait too long, I might miss my chance. No, I need to figure out a way to get him alone—and in a good mood, preferably—without spooking him.

I ruminate on this problem as I finish breakfast and continue to think about it even after I've retreated to my study to work on today's papers. My thoughts go in circles for what feels like hours, barely paying attention to the pile of reports and petitions in front of me while I come up with options, only to discard them a moment later.

*I could ask Riella if he's said anything about me to her.* No, that's *too* indirect. Not to mention rather awkward. I can do better.

*I could ask him if he'd like to attend a ball with me or something.* Not a bad idea, but he might just think I'm introducing him to court like I promised. Plus, I know I'll have enough trouble telling him how I feel when it's just the two of us; I can't imagine doing it when we're around hundreds of strangers.

*I could get Ivy to befriend him and learn his innermost secrets.* She could probably do it. But deceiving him probably isn't the best way to start a courtship, and it would take too long anyway. *What to do, what to do...*

Nothing feels right, and I'm about to give up and go about the rest of my day when I remember something Samis said last night, and, just like that, the perfect answer slams into me like a sledgehammer. *That's what siblings are for.* A plan—one that's simple yet shrewd—builds itself in my mind with stunning speed. I sit here, barely moving, trying to figure out if there's something I missed, some factor I'm not seeing that could doom this new plan, but I can't think of any. After all, if my guess is right, I'm not the only one who wants us to start courting.

It doesn't take long before adrenaline hits, and as soon as it does, I immediately go off to find Ivy, my hangover forgotten in the rush. I need her assistance. Plus, if she can't help me for whatever reason, I can at least vent my frustrations by throwing some of her knives at the straw target she uses for practice. It's basically a win-win situation.

She's in her rooms when I get there, which is good because I'm so energized right now, I feel like I might burst. In fact, we've barely sat down before I start talking.

"Can you do me a favor? I promise it isn't too onerous."

She leans back in her seat and tilts her head slightly. "You're not going to ask me to stab anyone, are you?"

I gape at her, my train of thought briefly interrupted. "No, Ivy, I'm not going to ask you that. Not right now, at least." She just nods, so I continue. "You know Riella Leara, right? I think you and she have met before."

"That's right. I wouldn't say we're, like, *best friends* or anything, but I certainly know her. Why do you ask?"

*So far, so good.* "Would you mind inviting her to join you at some event or activity or something within the next couple of days? I don't really care what it is, but preferably something in the morning, or maybe around lunchtime."

She thinks about it for what feels like hours. "I ... suppose I can do that," she finally says. "Actually, now that I think about it, there's a visiting Verreenese scholar who studies different martial arts techniques. She's planning on giving a demonstration two days from now at noon at their embassy. I could invite Riella to come with me."

I let out a relieved breath. "That would be wonderful. Thank you."

"Of course. But can I ask what the point of all this is, exactly?"

I debate whether or not to tell her, already feeling self-conscious about the whole thing. "I can't tell you why just yet. I don't want to jinx it. I promise you it's nothing nefarious."

"I'll take your word for it, I suppose. But you owe me one."

"Don't worry," I tell her. Even though that's only the first part of my plan, it still feels like a weight's been lifted off my shoulders. "I think I know how I can repay you."

The next afternoon, I send a message to Riella, asking her to stop by my study when she gets a chance, and about half an hour later, Joram lets me know that she's arrived. I tell him to send her in, my heart pounding.

"What do you need, Darien?" she asks as she walks over to my desk. "The messenger just said you asked to see me, but he didn't tell me why."

I gesture to the papers on my desk. "I have a report from our ambassador in Raktos. She mentioned something called a *ghoriam*, and I had no idea what she was talking about. I figured it would be best to just ask you rather than go research it for myself."

Riella's eyes light up. She loves studying foreign affairs almost as much as I love history. "I can see why you might be confused," she says, taking a seat on the couch across from me. "It's not really a common thing, even in Raktos. In short, a *ghoriam* is someone who advises a noble, but it's a bit more complicated than that. They tend to be around the same age as whoever they're advising, so they're usually more of a companion than an advisor. More than that, though, they're supposed to always tell the truth, even if it's not what the noble wants to hear, and they can't be punished for it. At least, that's how it works in theory. But in practice..."

I tune her out, paying just enough attention so I don't arouse her suspicion. The question I asked her isn't really that important. I just needed some pretense to talk to her that wouldn't risk me running into Tag in the process. Meanwhile, I'm focusing on not giving away too much when I get to the real reason that I asked her to come here—and also on trying to keep my anxiety down. *This should work*, I remind myself. *But if it doesn't, it probably won't be too much of a setback.*

At least, I hope it won't be. Either way, I'll find out soon enough.

After what feels like an interminable amount of time, Riella wraps up with, "So, that's probably why the ambassador brought up the subject. Does that answer your question?"

"It does," I confirm. "I get it, now. Thanks, Riella. I appreciate it."

She nods and stands to go, but before she can get to the door of my study, I call out to her, trying to sound as though a thought has just come to me.

"Sorry, but I almost forgot—would you have any interest in going riding with me tomorrow around lunchtime? I was planning on going with someone else, but now he can't make it. I haven't really gotten to catch up with you since you got back to court, and I know you love riding."

She stops and turns back toward me, frowning lightly. "I would love to, but I told Ivy I'd go to an event with her tomorrow afternoon—some lecture on how to stab things better, I'm assuming. Perhaps another time, though?"

I let my face fall a bit. "Oh. That's too bad." I pause for a moment, pretending to think. "In that case, could you maybe ask Tag if he'd like to go instead? I really was looking forward to getting out of the palace for a little while, and I don't want to go by myself."

She gives me a real, genuine smile. "That's a great idea! I don't think he has anything going on tomorrow, but I'll ask. I'm sure he'd love to go with you."

A wave of relief washes over me at her words, and I let a bit of it show. "Excellent. If he does want to come, tell him to meet me at the stables tomorrow at eleven."

"Of course. Hopefully he's available—I'm sure the two of you would have a wonderful time together."

*A wonderful time, huh? She really has no idea just how much I hope she's right.* I thank her, holding back a sudden onrush of exhilaration. With that, we say our goodbyes, and as soon as she's gone, I lean back in my seat and exhale deeply, feeling a small smile creep onto my face. *Part two, check.*

# CHAPTER EIGHT

I arrive at the stables a few minutes before noon the next day, my mind racing like one of the thoroughbreds. I'm a bit early for once, so I'm not surprised to find that Tag hasn't arrived yet. If you ignore its size, this stable is exactly like any other. The air is suffused with the earthy scent of hay and horses, and grooms bustle about, mucking out stalls and ensuring the horses are fed.

When I arrive, one of the grooms is already preparing my horse, Laya, while another readies one that I assume is Tag's. As always, when I see Laya, I calm down a bit. Out of all the horses in the palace stables—and there are quite a few—she's my favorite and has been ever since she came here as a foal nearly ten years ago. She was gifted to me by Countess Voeli when I came of age, although I'm guessing Voeli wasn't aware that Laya was completely deaf when she gave her to me. Voeli certainly seemed upset enough when she eventually found out. She even offered to take Laya back and replace her, but I never considered accepting her offer, not for a moment. Even when Samis said he'd be happy to find me a better riding horse, I told him in no uncertain terms that I was keeping her. She's one of the sweetest, gentlest creatures I know, and I love her.

Also, training her was an excellent excuse to spend some quality time without having to interact with people, so that was definitely a plus.

I don't want to get in the grooms' way, so I sit on a bench to one side and close my eyes, trying to calm myself further before Tag shows up. *It'll be alright. You can do this.*

It isn't very long before I hear a familiar voice. "Hello, Darien. It's good to see you again."

I open my eyes to see Tag standing at the entrance to the stables. Somehow, he looks even better than I remember. His outfit is simple, something like what I would have chosen for myself had I not agreed to let Ivy choose for me in return for her part in my plan. On him, it looks perfect. Black riding boots with silver inlays are paired with snow-white breeches, a shirt of the same color, and a brown jacket to round it all out. Whether or not he intended it, but the effect it all has on me is undeniable, to the point where I almost can't believe how good he looks. If someone were to ask me right now to describe the man of my dreams, I'd just point to Tag.

I realize I'm staring at him and force myself to look away for a second before my eyes return to his. *At least he's probably used to it by now.*

Instead of looking put off, though, he smiles, just a little bit.

"It's good to see you too," I say, my ears getting warm despite the temperate weather. "Shall we?"

He nods, and I gesture for the grooms to bring Laya and Tag's horse, who he calls Kemi, over to us.

"Are we going somewhere in particular?" Tag asks as we mount our horses.

"We are," I reply with a grin. "Just follow me."

He gestures for me to take the lead, and I guide Laya out of the stables, then through the castle gates and into the city proper, along the wide tree-lined road that runs from the palace to the eastern gate of the city. Stalls line either side of the path under the shade of the trees, and the air rings with the sound of merchants selling food and clothes and jewelry. Since it's the middle of the day, I didn't feel the need to bring guards, so it's just me and Tag; nobody appears to pay any special attention to us, which is just the way I like it. I'm sure it's not unusual to see well-dressed riders this close to the palace, and nothing marks me out as anything more than just another noble.

It doesn't take long to reach the city wall, an imposing structure of brick and stone that's almost as old as Cedelia itself. An officer guarding the gate salutes me as we pass through, crossing out of the city and into the market town that encircles the wall. Here, ramshackle wooden buildings abut the stone, crowding against one another like weary travelers huddled for warmth.

Tag and I follow the main road through the market town and beyond, as the densely packed buildings give way to open farmland. After a mile, we branch off onto a smaller side road—more of a trail, really—which eventually meanders into a forest.

Slowly, the path begins to increase in elevation, becoming a moderate incline. Just before it becomes too steep for the horses to go any further, it levels out. At the same time, it leaves the forest behind, opening to a wide meadow. We've doubled back so we're facing west, toward Cedelia. About a hundred feet away from us, the meadow drops off and abruptly becomes a cliff. Between us and the cliff is an ocean, not of water but of flowers, an explosion of color, the frothy waves and soft sand in this case are delicate petals and broad green leaves. I let out a sigh of relief; I wasn't sure if the flowers would be in bloom just yet.

Tag and I dismount and tether our horses to trees at the edge of the forest, before turning back to the sea of flowers. "It's beautiful," he says, a touch of awe in his voice. "How did you find this place?"

"Ivy and I, and a couple of our friends stumbled on it when we were kids." *I knew he'd like it here.* "They don't really come out here much anymore, but I still do sometimes. It's a good place to just get away from everything."

"I can see why. It's incredible. So ... *peaceful.*"

I nod in agreement, but all I can think is that it's even more incredible with him here.

I lead him over to a large, flat-topped rock near the edge of the cliff, where we take a thick blanket out of the saddlebags, spread it out, and arrange the picnic I asked the kitchens to prepare on top of it. As we're setting up, I look from him to Cedelia and can't decide which view is better. A sense of longing blooms in me, as warm and bright as the flowers around us, and I almost tell him how I feel right then and there. But the feeling passes almost as quickly as it came. *There's no need to rush.*

The food provided by the kitchens is simple, yet tasty—hard cheese, bread baked this morning, sausages, and a few apples. After we've eaten our fill, Tag and I each take one of the remaining apples and walk over to give them to the horses. Laya sees me coming almost immediately and stops grazing, her ears flicking up toward the sky.

"She's deaf," I tell Tag, who's looking at me slightly askance. I'm ready to explain why I ride her—it wouldn't be the first time someone didn't understand—but he just nods and gives me a bright smile that sets my heart aflutter.

When we get back to the blanket, I pull out a bottle of wine. I forgot to bring glasses, so we drink straight from the bottle, passing it back and forth every so often, chatting about everything and nothing. Once the wine is gone, we both lie on the blanket, close enough to touch, staring at the sky. Even though the air is a bit chilly, the sun is warm, and I bask in its glow, hoping the good weather is an omen. Tag's hand is next to mine, and I swear it's closer than it was just minutes before. I turn my head so I'm looking at him, my eyes drinking him in, as though his beauty is all I need to sustain me. *It's time.* I take a deep breath, ready to share my feelings with him, and hopefully find out his.

But before I can, he rolls onto his side and props his head up in his hand. "I'm glad you let me come with you," he says, the corners of his mouth turned up in a grin that lights up his eyes. "I hope Riella didn't force you to bring me. She told me it was your idea, but I got the sense she was just saying that to make me feel better."

"Don't worry about that," I say, my heart thumping against my ribs with every beat. "I'm glad you're here. I enjoy spending time with you."

He doesn't reply immediately, and I take the chance to just look at him. His beautiful eyes sparkle with an emotion I can't quite place. His lips are still quirked in a tiny grin, showing just a hint of bright, white teeth; I doubt he even knows he's grinning. He fills my senses, my vision and smell and hearing, and I want so badly to add *touch* to that list. I've never wanted him more than I do right now. I've never wanted anyone more than I want him at this moment.

I open my mouth a second time to tell him how I feel, but once again, he speaks before I do. "Thank you for bringing me here. It's so beautiful, and..." He looks down for a second before his eyes return to mine. "And there's something I need to tell you."

My heart starts beating even faster, which I didn't think was possible. "What is it?" I don't dare to let myself guess what he's going to say.

He gazes down at me, his expression unreadable for a few seconds. Then before I have time to wonder what he's thinking, he closes the meager distance between us and gently kisses me on the lips.

As soon as his lips meet mine, my mind nearly shuts down, like I've been struck by lightning. My heart, already racing, pounds faster than it ever has before, and my nerves tingle with sparks. Even though part of me is screaming to kiss him back, to pull him close and never let him go, I can't move. All I can do is think about how good this feels and enjoy the softness of his lips against mine.

Before I can move at all, let alone respond in kind, he's pulling away. He moves slowly at first, then quickly, a stricken look crossing his face. "I'm so sorry," he says. "Please, forgive me. I shouldn't have—"

The sight of his distress is enough to finally allow me to move again. Instead of letting him finish that sentence, I do what I should have done before: grab the back of his head, bring his face to mine, and kiss him deeply. I almost feel him melt in my arms, just as I feel my own nerves melting away.

After a little while, he pulls away again, this time with a big, unreserved smile. He wraps his arms around me and lays his head on my chest, his hair tickling the bottom of my chin. I gently stroke it with my hand, luxuriating in the feel of its silkiness against my skin.

When I find my voice, I say the first thing that comes to my mind. "What took you so long?"

He lifts his head and rests his chin on my chest. I want to kiss him again, but through sheer force of will I manage to hold off while he answers my question.

"Trust me, I wanted to," he says. "I wasn't sure how you'd respond, and I was afraid. I fell for you the moment we met, but I didn't dare hope you would return my feelings. I just couldn't believe that a prince would be interested in *me*, of all people." He looks away, blushing. "Plus, I heard a rumor that you went to a ball the night before we met and spent the entire time dancing with one man. I didn't know if you and he were courting."

I'm not sure whether to laugh or cry. *I suppose it's not really Petris's fault.* "I don't blame you for thinking that. But just so you know, he and I were never courting. We met that night, and I haven't seen him since."

Tag takes my hand in his and kisses it lightly. "I believe you, Darien. Still, it took me some time to realize that you two weren't an item. Then, even after we started spending time together, I thought maybe you were just being polite to me or taking pity on me because I'm new here. The idea that you might actually feel the same way just seemed too good to be true."

"I can understand why you might have thought that." I squeeze his hand and look deeply into his brown eyes. "But I'll have you know that *I* fell for *you* the first time we met, too. You just looked so perfect, and the more I got to know you..." I can't hold it in any longer, so I lift my head up and kiss him again, reveling in the feel of his touch. "It was never pity, or politeness, or anything of the sort. I wanted to spend time with you because I like being with you. It's as simple as that."

His laugh is light and unburdened. "I really hoped that was the case, but I couldn't be sure. I wanted to find out, but I had no idea how I was going to work up the courage to ask you. Today, though..." His eyes shine, and he gives me a wide smile that melts my heart. "Today, you just looked so amazing, and between that and the wine and this whole scene,

I just couldn't help myself." A look of pleased realization passes across his face. "That's why you brought me here, isn't it? Was this your plan all along?"

"Maybe," I reply, trying to sound mysterious. He makes an amused sound in his throat and tickles my side, and I give in almost immediately. "Okay, fine, yes! But it worked, didn't it?" Now he's laughing too. "Seriously, though, I didn't plan for you to kiss me, although I'm certainly glad you did. Actually..." A tiny bit of embarrassment creeps into my voice. "I was about to tell you how I feel, but you beat me to it. Thanks for saving me the trouble of having to make an awkward speech."

He laughs even harder. "You're welcome. Always glad to help out." He gently caresses my cheek with the side of his hand. "Now that we've established that we both like each other, what comes next?"

Anxiety worms its way into my mind despite my elation. *Here goes nothing.* "I was hoping that we could start courting officially, if you're interested." That little voice in the back of my mind starts to rumble, but I stomp it down before it can say anything. "I really like you, and I want the whole world to know it."

"I would love to court you, Darien. I really would." His grin fades, and he looks down, as coldness washes over me, like the sun has just dipped behind a cloud. "But you're a prince. Whoever you court is going to be put under a microscope, every last detail of their life scrutinized endlessly. You know I'm not very outgoing, and the idea of being in the spotlight all the time ... I just don't know if I could handle the pressure."

Strangely, his words have a calming effect on me, even though it's not the answer I wanted. *If he only wanted me for my title, he would have said yes immediately.* I put a finger under his chin and gently lift his head until his eyes meet mine. "I'm not going to lie to you and tell you that courting a prince is easy," I tell him. "But I *really* like you, and I want to be with you. I don't like being in the public eye either, and I promise I'll do my best to keep the spotlight away from you. Plus, it might turn out to be easier than you expect. Nobody really cares what I do, not when Samis is there to soak up all the attention."

"I really like you too." I can tell from his voice that he means it. "But aren't princes supposed to court other royals?"

I reach up and brush a stray lock of hair away from his face. "Typically, yes. But then, Kenessa—you remember her, right? Well, she's the daughter of a duchess, so it's not like I'd be the only one breaking the mold. Still, you're right. Courting me would be more complicated than if you were courting someone else. But I don't want to give up on you just because things *might* go wrong in the future. Especially not when we both struggled to get to this point in the first place."

He thinks about it while I hold my breath. Finally, after a few anxiety-filled moments, he says, "I don't want to give up on you either, so I say let's give it a shot."

Relief floods through me as he leans down and kisses me again.

"But ... if it's alright with you," he continues, "can we hold off on making our courtship official for now? I'm still happy to be with you unofficially, and I know we won't be able to keep it a secret forever. I just want to get more acclimated to living here before the entire court finds out."

"That's fine with me." I lightly stroke his cheek with my thumb. "As long as I get to be with you, I don't care whether anyone else knows about it just yet."

"It's a deal." He leans down and lays his head back against my chest. "And to think, I was afraid that you'd get mad at me if you found out how I feel. Can you imagine how terrible that would be? Only in the palace for a few weeks, and already on the prince's bad side."

"I don't blame you for being afraid. But you could never get on my bad side." I plant a kiss on the top of his head. "Even if you were to, say, kiss me out of nowhere without any warning."

"When you didn't kiss me back, I thought I was done for," he says, momentarily somber until his grin returns. "Still, I suppose I can forgive you, even if you did nearly give me a heart attack." He laughs again. "But that's not even the worst part. If only one of us had been willing to take the chance earlier, we could have done this weeks ago and saved us both a lot of heartache."

I take his hand and gently press it against my lips. "I'm sorry I didn't react at first. I was surprised." He looks sufficiently placated. "I'm also sorry I didn't just come right out and say how much I like you before today. I know a way I can make it up to you, though."

"Oh?" he says, raising one eyebrow.

I think he already knows what it is, though, and he doesn't seem surprised when I pull him close and kiss him deeply, again and again and again.

We lie on the blanket for hours, kissing and chatting and holding each other close, as afternoon passes into evening. I wish we could stay like this forever, but eventually the sun begins to sink lower in the sky, and it starts to get cold, so we decide to get back to the palace before it's too dark for the horses to find their footing on the path through the forest.

By the time we get back to the large square that abuts the palace, it's almost sunset. The sun is blocked by the building, but the sky that we can see is blue and yellow and orange and pink and red, a beautiful end to a beautiful day. Almost as beautiful as Tag.

He catches me looking at him and winks at me. My heart, which had almost returned to my body, takes flight again.

Shortly, we reach the stables, and dismount under the last rays of the setting sun. We walk together into the palace, so close we're almost touching. When we reach the point where we must go our separate ways, I stop him in the middle of the hallway. I look around quickly; there are a few servants farther down the hall, but none particularly close.

"Listen, Tag..." Some of my anxiety comes back, although it's a mere shadow of what I felt earlier today. "Would you like to come back to my rooms with me? We can spend the night together, if you want to."

"I promised Riella I would dine with her tonight," he says with a regretful sigh. Before my heart can fall too far, he adds, "But I'm free tomorrow night. Perhaps we could see each other then?"

I reach out and cup his face in one hand. He nuzzles my palm and kisses it lightly. "I would love that."

He looks into my eyes as though he's searching for something. He must like what he sees because he beams at me. "Then I'll be there. I promise."

It's enough for me. I pull him close, and we kiss twice—the first time slowly, and the second quickly. Then he turns to leave, and I return to my rooms, still feeling like I'm floating on air.

# CHAPTER NINE

M y good mood persists through the rest of the day and into the
next. Even after I eat a light breakfast and walk to Mother's
study, I feel like my feet aren't really touching the ground. I know this
feeling won't last forever, but I'm going to enjoy it while it does.

The door to Mother's study is open when I get there, but I knock anyway to announce my presence. Mother, sitting at a teak writing desk near
one of the windows, looks up at the sound. "Good morning, Darien,"
she says. "You're up early."

She's not wrong. For the second night in a row, I couldn't sleep,
although for a different reason this time.

"Good morning." I walk into the room and kiss her lightly on the
cheek. Her room is nowhere near as utilitarian as mine. Paintings hang
on the walls and vases full of fresh-cut flowers sit on windowsills, while
light streams in from large windows along one side of the room, lending
a rich, rosy glow to the cherrywood-paneled walls. A small piano sits in
the back. Quite often, when I come here for one reason or another, she's
playing, and I hear her before I even get close. "I figured you'd be here."

"And you were right." She gestures to a chair nearby, and I sit down. "To what do I owe the honor?"

I try my best to appear unconcerned. "I was just wondering—how did you and Catherine Leara end up becoming friends?"

She gives me a piercing look. "That's an odd question. Why do you want to know?"

It's a simple question, one that I expected her to ask, but I still hesitate before I answer. Despite what I told Tag yesterday, some people will disapprove of me courting someone who's ranked so much lower than me. Most of the council will be in that group, and probably Father too. If I'm lucky, Mother will tell me something, *anything*, that I can use to argue that Tag is an acceptable suitor.

Still, I promised Tag I wouldn't tell anyone about us yet, so I just shrug and say, "Like I said, I was just wondering. I know she's important to you, and I feel bad that I don't know much more about your friendship beyond the basics."

Apparently, that was a good enough answer for her. "Catherine's grandmother Elsera served as an advisor to my grandmother while the latter was queen, and then to my father after he became king. Elsera was born into a very old family. A branch of my own family, in fact—although they branched off many, *many* years before Elsera and my grandmother were born. Well before the Empire fell, even." She crosses her arms. "Unfortunately, when I was young, your grandparents only allowed me to fraternize with other children of 'appropriate' rank. While Elsera's branch of the family wasn't particularly influential or rich, they were related to royalty, which lent them a certain amount of prestige. It was enough that Catherine and I were encouraged to become friends from a young age. Most of the other children I was allowed to play with were terrors—spoiled brats who were used to getting whatever they asked for—but Catherine and I got along quite well, and the rest is history, I suppose."

Okay, that's good—the part about Catherine's family being good enough to meet my grandparents' apparently high standards, at least. "If her family was so prestigious, why did she bring Tag and Riella here instead of going back there?

Mother smiles tightly. "Oh, that was never going to happen. Catherine may be many things, but conceited is not one of them. She never really fit in well at a court that was obsessed with rank above all else. Even so, I don't think she ever got quite used to living out in the country where nothing ever happens. She certainly seemed happy enough to accept my invitation to come here for an extended stay." She uncrosses her arms and looks me directly in the eye. "Now what's this all about, really? I know you love history, but this is obscure, even for you."

"Nothing! Truly, I mean it." I try to sound innocent. "She clearly means a lot to you, and I guess I just wanted to understand why. You certainly talked about her quite often before they got here, but you never really mentioned how you two came to be friends in the first place."

She looks at me for a few seconds before saying, "I suppose that makes sense."

I silently breathe a sigh of relief.

"How are you getting along with Tag?" she continues. "Catherine told me that you offered to introduce him to life at court, and I hear that the two of you are becoming quite close."

Just like that, my guard is back up. "We are," I say carefully. "I've been spending some time with him over the last few weeks. In fact, we just went on a ride together yesterday."

"Excellent!" If she does know, she's doing a good job of not showing it. "I know you're already friendly with Riella, but from what Catherine has told me, it sounds like you and Tag should have no trouble becoming friends as well."

I can't tell whether there's a hidden meaning behind her words.

"Now, I don't want to be rude," she continues, "but I do need to get back to work. So, unless there's anything else?"

I shake my head. I suppose I could try to surreptitiously figure out whether she knows about me and Tag being more than friends, but if she *does* know, there's really nothing I can do about it anyway. I bid her goodbye and take my leave, feeling better than I did before.

Later that evening, I'm alone in my chambers, waiting with increasing anticipation, when a quiet knock sounds on the door. I'm there in a flash, and when I open the door and see Tag's beautiful face staring back at me, I quickly pull him in and close the door behind him.

I've no sooner turned back to face him when he's pulling me in for a deep kiss, his tongue brushing against mine. Then he leans back for a second, and I look at him, trying to drink this scene in, everything, so I can burn a perfect image into my memory. I can't believe how incredible he looks, even in casual clothes—a loose, white nightshirt, and plain tan pants that are doing an excellent job of showing off his legs. His short hair is messier than usual, but, somehow, it's endearing. I almost like it better this way.

I cup his face in one hand, gently caressing the silky-smooth skin of his cheek, and brush a solitary loose curl of his hair back with the other. He smiles at my touch, and, for a moment, it's like the world around us has vanished, as though he and I are the only things that matter. "So, now that I'm here," he says quietly, "what would you like to do?"

"I've got a few suggestions," I whisper into his ear, before I pull him close and kiss his perfect lips. I've wanted others before, felt as though I'm a firework about to explode, but I've never *needed* anyone like I need him. All the other men that came before him pale in comparison. I wrap my arms around his waist, feeling him open up to me, and slowly move my hands lower on his back. Now that I have him, I don't want to let him go.

He looks up at me, our faces barely inches apart, and it's clear he knows what I'm thinking. Then he's kissing me again, lightly at first, slowly getting firmer and deeper. His lips are softer than moonlight, and the touch of his hands on my bare skin is as gentle as silk. Before I know it, my hands are grabbing his shirt and pulling it off him. The sight of his muscular arms, chest, and stomach depletes the vestiges of reserve that still remain in my mind, leaving only desire in their wake.

My shirt is quickly gone too, then my pants, and soon his naked body is pressed against mine, nothing daring to come between us. The warmth of his skin is a welcome contrast from the cool night air. I try to get as close as I can to the fire that seems to rage inside him, not caring whether I get burned. Our kisses become hungrier, more passionate, as we both throw caution to the wind.

Somehow, we make it over to the bed, and I push him down, taking a second to admire the way he looks against the white sheets. He smiles at me, his perfect, white teeth framed by rosebud-red lips, and I can't hold myself back anymore. I fall onto the bed next to him, and the last coherent thought I have before I fully give in to my desire is that I've never been happier to lose control.

When I come back to myself, I'm lying in the bed with Tag, cuddled up next to him. My heart is beating at a normal rate for what feels like the first time in weeks, and I'm more content than I've ever been before. For a minute or so, we lie here, holding each other, both of us silent. I don't know about him, but I don't want to shatter the moment by speaking.

We lie there for a few minutes more, before Tag finally breaks the silence. "You know," he says, "if I had known this would happen, I would have kissed you without warning the first night we met." As if to emphasize his point, he kisses me again, his warm, soft lips against mine.

"That would have been nice," I say, when he finally allows me to speak. "But better late than never." My fingers lightly trace his bare hip. "Besides, I'd say it's turned out pretty well so far."

He laughs and kisses me again. "I can't disagree with that."

A lock of his hair has fallen out of place, covering his left eye; I gently push it back into place. "Will you stay with me tonight?" I ask quietly. "Now that I finally have you, I don't want to let you go."

He snuggles even closer to me, if that's possible. "Of course I will. I don't want you to let go of me either."

I'm all too happy to oblige him, so I hold him close, feeling his heart beat in time with mine, until we fall asleep in each other's arms.

# CHAPTER TEN

The next few weeks are a whirlwind of happiness and discovery. Tag and I spend just about every night together, although most days we're apart. We don't quite go to extreme lengths to avoid being seen together—I *am* supposed to be introducing him to court, and he says it wouldn't be the end of the world if someone saw us eating lunch together or something like that—but we do at least try to keep our unofficial courtship from being widely known.

Still, I doubt we can completely avoid people finding out, even if we try our hardest. I'm sure my servants have figured out why I've been dismissing them early almost every night, just as I'm sure the Learas' servants—and maybe even Tag's parents or Riella—have noticed Tag's bed has barely been slept in recently. But Tag seems okay with it, and I follow his lead. If all goes well, everyone will find out about us soon enough. I can't wait to show him off, but, in the meantime, I'm happy to go along with his request.

When we do meet during the day, I take it upon myself to show him the parts of the palace that he hasn't seen yet and the rest of Cedelia.

He's already been to the palace gardens and the library, but there's so much more to explore. One day, I take him to the circuit near the edge of the city so we can watch the horse races. Another day, I take him to the tallest tower in the city, an old watchtower that dates back to the early days of the Empire, where we can see the entire city spread out before us. Later, in a moment of either complete brilliance or sheer idiocy, I take him to the courtyard where Ivy practices her knife-throwing. I'm secretly pleased to discover he's no better than me at it.

As we spend more and more time together, I find myself falling for him more and more. Perhaps it's just because he's new to court, but he doesn't have the unspoken arrogance that I associate with most of the people who live here in the palace, outside of my own family and a few others. It's refreshing to be around someone who doesn't think they're better than everyone else just because they live in the same building as Father, or because they have a title that's been passed down in their family for generations. When I'm with Tag, I feel a sense of comfort, of belonging, as though I've known him for years—and, more importantly, as though he's known me for years. It feels like he likes me for the person that I am, not for the person I should be.

Beneath my happiness and excitement is a deep, deep sense of relief. Tag is a wonder, someone I hoped—but never really expected—I would find. I know it's still early and there are any number of things that can go wrong, but for the first time in my life, I'm really starting to believe things can turn out well, that someone can love me for who I am and not just the family I was born into. It's a wonderful feeling.

One Saturday morning, about two weeks after Tag and I started secretly courting, I receive a message from Father. There's a slight quiver in my stomach as I open it, trying to figure out what I've done to attract his attention.

*Come to my study as soon as possible. I need to discuss something with you.*

It's rather terse, but I'd be far more surprised if it wasn't. *I wonder what he wants this time?*

Try as I might, I can't come up with anything. Samis and Father meet to discuss the affairs of the kingdom, or whatever else, pretty much every day around dawn. Among the many things they share is a propensity for getting business done early in the morning, while the rest of us are still asleep. But I usually only get invited to his study when I've messed up somehow. As far as I know, I haven't made any major mistakes recently.

Unless ... maybe he found out about me and Tag somehow? That could be it, but I can't imagine why he would summon me if that was the case. It's not like we're doing anything wrong, after all. Still, the possibility is enough to cause me no small amount of disquiet during the short walk to my parents' chambers.

When I arrive, a servant guides me to a large study, where my father, King Tolmir Garros of Soeria, sits at a small table by an arched window. In the morning light, he looks like an older replica of Samis, although his hair is longer and lighter, and he has a goatee where Samis is clean-shaven. A few wrinkles line his face, but there are fewer than I would expect for someone who reached the age of fifty not too long ago. Even from here, I can feel a sense of intensity, of vitality, coming from him, like a fire gives off heat.

Yet, being the king is a stressful job, and I can see the signs if I look closely enough. His hair has always been light, but now it's closer to white than it is to brown, and there are lines at the corners of his mouth that I assume come from nearly thirty years of grimacing at bad news delivered by his advisors. But, as far as I can tell, he's showing no signs of slowing despite his increasing age. It wouldn't surprise me if he's the same way after another thirty years have passed.

Next to Father at the table is one of his closest friends and advisors, Lord Alrudden Kerion, High Chancellor of Soeria. A neat stack of papers sits in front of Kerion; no doubt reports that he's decided require Father's attention. Like Mother and the viscountess, the two of them grew up together, and I know Father values Kerion's opinion, so it's no surprise to see him here. In contrast with Father, Kerion is the sort of person who would go unnoticed in a crowd. Though, his analytical mind is second to none. Father may be the face of the kingdom, but Kerion is its brain and hands, taking care of the myriad details necessary for ensuring the country runs smoothly.

I patiently wait by the door for a minute or so, still unable to figure out why I'm here, before Father notices me and waves me over. "Darien, please join us."

Kerion nods to me as I take my seat next to him.

"Alrudden, you're almost done, correct?" Father says.

"Actually, I have two more minor items to discuss before we move on, Your Majesty," he says, and Father motions for him to continue. Kerion dips his head slightly before he resumes speaking. "Evidently a shepherd in a town just over the border with Verreene has declared herself to be a descendant of the last empress and the heiress of the Idrian Empire. I'm told she tried to gather an army and march on the capital. Fortunately, the Verrenese army captured her without too much bloodshed, and the rabble dispersed quickly after that. They did manage to cause damage to some Soerian lands before their defeat, though."

"Send someone we trust to inspect the affected area and come up with an estimate of how much gold it would take to repair the damage," Father says. "I'll discuss compensation with the Verrenese ambassador next time I see her."

Kerion nods; I have no doubt he'll carry out Father's orders to the letter as soon as this meeting is over.

"And the second item?" Father prompts.

"Your Majesty may recall that we discussed an outbreak of wasting fever in the villages surrounding Cedelia some weeks ago?" Kerion barely waits for Father to nod before he continues. "It appears that our efforts to keep the outbreak contained have been unsuccessful, as three cases have been reported in the city proper."

Father mutters a quiet oath. Then, at a normal volume, he says, "Are any of the cases in the city serious?"

Kerion shakes his head. "Thankfully no, Your Majesty. But we don't know whether the disease has spread, and there may be additional cases in coming days."

Father mulls this over for a moment. "See to it that any who fall ill in the city are placed under quarantine. We don't want the disease to spread any further. Send some of the palace healers to see what they can do for those who are already sick." He turns to me. "I suppose that just leaves you, then. Alrudden and I were talking about you before you came in."

"I see," I reply, my pulse beginning to pick up. The two of them discussing me is never a good sign. "What were you talking about, exactly?"

He smiles, but there's no humor in it. "It's no secret that I'm getting up there in years, Darien."

I don't even blink at his bluntness. I'm more than used to it by now.

"Hopefully," he continues, "I still have many good years ahead of me, but I might not. I'm certain Samis will have no trouble stepping into my shoes once I'm gone. Emma will do well, too, assuming she ever discovers how to multitask instead of focusing her energy on one activity at a time. You, on the other hand..." He lets his words hang in the air for a moment. "When that time comes, I expect you to aid Samis any way you can, should he require your assistance."

*Is this really what he wanted to discuss?* Suffice to say I've heard this before. He's always favored Samis and Emma over me, for as long as I can remember. Not openly, and not exceedingly, but I know where I stand. "I understand, Father."

"I'm not sure that you do." His words are quiet, yet sharp as a knife. "You see, when I say *any* way you can, I mean it."

Bile rises in the back of my throat. "What would you have me do that I'm not currently doing?"

This time, when he smiles, it looks real, which scares me more than I care to admit. "The same thing every prince or princess your age should do, of course: get married and raise heirs. The council has been increasingly insistent that it's well past time for you to get married, and I've finally decided that they're right. To that end, I instructed Alrudden to begin the process of finding a match for you a few weeks ago."

Gray dread mixed with red anger settles over me, starting at my head and working its way down to my toes. *This can't happen now! Not when I finally managed to get Tag!* "Do I at least get to have a say in who you're going to set me up with?" I struggle to keep my voice even; if I keep it together, maybe I can convince him that Tag is an option. "Or are you just going to choose someone for me?"

Father looks at me like I've just said something insane, and my heart drops. "Do you think I had any say in the matter when my marriage to your mother was arranged by your grandparents? No, you'll do as you're told, for the good of your family—and, more importantly, your *country*." He glares at me for a moment longer, then shakes his head. "In any event, the point is moot. When Alrudden and I first discussed the matter some weeks ago, I instructed him to communicate with the governments of our neighboring countries, to see if any of them have any interest in forming an alliance through a marriage between you and a foreign prince. They—"

"Wait a second," I interrupt. I know I shouldn't, but I can't help myself; this is quickly turning into my worst nightmare, and I feel like I have to do *something* or I'll burst. "You're only considering foreign princes? Why does it have to be a prince? And for that matter, why are you even sending these messages in the first place? If I'm going to be forced to marry someone, why can't it be someone who's already here? Are you really trying to tell me there's *nobody* here that's acceptable? Why not just pick someone that I already know?"

Father's eyes hold mine, daring me to look away. His brows are drawn down and his mouth is compressed into a thin line, as though he's barely containing his anger. Which makes sense because no one ever challenges him once he's made a decision. "You may not have learned this from the reports you spend all your time reading, but our position is tenuous. Perhaps if we were still just one part of a large empire, we could get away with being less than vigilant. But you just heard Kerion talk about that Verrenese shepherd who declared herself the next empress, did you not? What do you think would happen if—*when*—some fool king or queen decides to do the same thing, and chooses to attack Soeria? Do you really doubt that Raktos or Verreene or Jirena Sadai would move in at the first sign of Soerian weakness?" His gaze bores into me like an auger through wood. "The *only* reason they haven't done so already is because of our alliance with Zeteyon—which only came about through my *arranged* marriage to your mother, by the way. And thanks to your uncle's pointless bickering with the Khorians, we can't rely on that to keep us safe anymore. Besides, that alliance won't last forever, and we need to be prepared."

Every word he says is like a tiny earthquake to my being. "But... I don't..." I pause and take a moment to corral my thoughts. "Belling told me that we don't have to worry about the Zeteyoni army being unavailable," I finally say, knowing it won't matter to him, and that I have to try anyway. "They said it shouldn't be a problem."

Father's gaze is as sharp as an assassin's dagger. "Belling may be right. They usually are. But I am the king, not them, and *I* am the one who bears ultimate responsibility when it comes to keeping Soeria safe. If arranging a marriage for you makes the country even *slightly* more secure, it is a small price to pay."

Heat flushes through me, and I have to stop myself from shaking with anger. "I'm supposed to marry someone I've never met before, just because that's what you did? That will somehow fix all our problems? Why didn't you make Samis marry some foreign princess instead? *He's* the one that's going to be king, not me!"

"You're entirely correct," he says. I thought my saying that would make him angry—maybe I even wanted to make him angry—but he speaks calmly, as though we're discussing the weather, and not my impending doom. "I don't mean anything against Kenessa personally, but your brother should have married a princess instead of her. Allowing him to marry her was a mistake, and I will not make that mistake again." His voice is soft, but there's hardness underneath it, like steel covered with silk. "Now then, do you have any more irrelevant objections, or may I finish?"

I have quite a few objections, but I know that it wouldn't do me any good to voice them, so I stay quiet. *Maybe I can still fix this somehow.*

"The reason why I'm mentioning this to you now," he continues, "is that I received a message from Jirena Sadai this morning. Their queen has a brother who is willing to consider marrying you. His name is Arbois, and he's about your age. Evidently, the Jirenians want to move quickly, since he was planning to leave the Jirenian court in Segaron a week or so after the messenger left. I expect he'll presumably choose comfort over speed, which means he'll be here perhaps two weeks from now. We'll have to—"

"Wait, you've already found someone?" I stare at him. "And you didn't even think to tell me about this until now? You could have at least mentioned something before you invited this Arbois person to come to the palace!"

Father frowns, but he otherwise seems undeterred by my distress. "Truth be told, I did not officially invite Arbois just yet," he says. "They decided to send him here on their own initiative. Of course, I was planning to invite him within the near future anyway. If anything, their impatience is a benefit. We would be lucky to gain an alliance with them quickly, before the effects of your uncle's folly can truly be felt."

A spike of fear as cold as ice blooms in the pit of my stomach. *No. This can't be happening. It can't!*

"As I was saying before I was rudely interrupted," Father continues, "we'll have to agree on terms for the marriage treaty, but I have no reason to doubt that the negotiations will go smoothly."

The anger I was feeling starts to slip away, leaving behind a numbness that starts at my toes and works its way up, even as I struggle to keep it from enveloping me completely. I try desperately to figure out a way out of this, but there's not much I can do if Father is determined.

Still ... there *is* one card left that I can play. It's a long shot, but I would never forgive myself if I didn't at least try. *Hopefully Tag will forgive me, though.* "I understand how important it is to you that I make a good match." I lift my head and look him in the eyes, trying to project confidence. "But I've already found a better suitor than this Arbois—Tag Leara. He and I have been courting for almost a month now. He's already here, so you wouldn't have to wait weeks to make an agreement. And he's foreign, too. So, there's really no reason for Arbois to even come here, is there?"

"You mean Catherine's son? Why would he be an acceptable match?" There's more than a hint of anger in Father's tone. "Do you expect me to go to the council and tell them that you turned down a prince for someone whose family's highest title is viscount?"

I open my mouth to respond, but he holds up a hand to forestall me, and I remain silent.

"You need not tell me that you like each other, as I am certain you were about to do," he says. "As much as you may wish to deny it, that has no bearing on the choice of whom you marry. The important considerations are that the Leara family is of low rank; they have little in the way of money, lands, or influence; and, most importantly, you marrying him would gain *nothing* for Soeria. You need to marry someone who brings an alliance with them, preferably a powerful one. That person may or may not be Prince Arbois, but it is certainly *not* Tag Leara."

"Are you so sure? Tag's mother was born into a branch of the Zeteyoni royal family. I'm sure you know how haughty Mother's parents are, and apparently Catherine was of high enough rank that they allowed her to be one of Mother's companions. Maybe that'll be enough for Uncle Zeikas to continue the alliance between our two nations."

"Did he tell you this?" Father asks, his voice soft as silk once again. "Because if he did, and you believed him, then you're not nearly as smart as you think you are."

I bite down my own rising anger and try to remain civil. "No. Mother told me."

Father sits there without saying anything for a while after that. His expression softens as his brows furrow. I get the feeling that he's calculating something, weighing the possibilities before coming to a decision that could change my life forever. Meanwhile, I hold my breath and dare to hope. *Please, Father...*

Finally, after what feels like several eternities, he shakes his head. "No. We already have an alliance with Zeteyon, and it's proven to be quite unreliable. If your uncle isn't willing to keep to his obligations when his own sister is involved, I sincerely doubt he'll change his tune should you marry someone whose connection to his family is tenuous at best. No, we must look elsewhere to ensure Soeria's security."

My heart falls farther with every word, and when he's finished speaking, I feel as though it's beating somewhere deep in the earth beneath me. Some of my distress must be showing on my face, because, for just a moment, Father's strong façade cracks, and I see the weariness and pain that I'm certain has built up over the long years.

"Understand that I'm not doing this out of spite or malice, son," he says quietly. I wouldn't say his tone is *gentle*, exactly, but it's certainly less severe than it was before. "Making difficult decisions like this one is my burden to bear, and it gives me no pleasure to see you this way. Whether you like it or not, you have a burden to bear too, a price to pay that others will never face. Be thankful that your burden isn't greater."

I feel empty, like I've used up all my strength fighting a battle I was doomed to lose. "What am I supposed to tell Tag?" It comes out as a whisper, barely audible.

Any gentleness in Father's tone is gone in a flash. "What you tell him is no concern of mine. Although, perhaps you should tell him the truth: that the choice of who you marry matters not only to you, but to the entire country, and that the latter is by far the more important of the two."

Part of me wants to argue with him, to convince him somehow that he's wrong. Part of me wants to scream at him, to tell him that I'm not going to give up on Tag just because he thinks it's what Soeria needs. Part of me wants to curl up in a ball and cry, to pretend this isn't happening, that my worst nightmare isn't coming true before my very eyes.

But I know that all of those would be pointless and might even make things worse. Instead, I just whisper, "Am I done here?"

He waves at the door, his attention already back to his work, and I hurry out of the room, trying desperately not to cry.

# CHAPTER ELEVEN

I barely manage to get out of Father's study before tears start flowing. My vision starts to blur, and I stumble to one side of the hallway, hoping no one is around to see me. I lean against the wall, dropping my head into my hands. *How can he do this to me?*

As much as I hate to admit it, as much as I wish I could rail against this newfound injustice, deep down I know that this is my fault. I should have known this would happen. But instead, I let myself believe I had a chance at love, that I could be with someone who cared about me. All Father did was remind me how naïve I was. I'd forgotten that I'm nothing more than a pawn in a vast game, a prince without a self, nothing more than my title, and there's no one to blame but myself. I should have listened to that little voice in my head, the one that told me there's no escaping the inevitable, because deep down I knew it was right all along.

When my tears have lessened enough that I can see again, I push away from the wall and walk away from Father's chambers, my head hanging low and my shoulders slumped. It wouldn't be fair to Tag if I tried to hide this from him—even though it will break his heart to hear the truth. Even though it will break my heart to say it.

But I know that waiting any longer will just make it hurt more, so I trudge to the rooms the Learas share, my feet weighing a hundred pounds each.

I'm granted a slight reprieve when the Learas' steward tells me Tag is practicing archery in one of the palace courtyards. It takes a few more minutes to walk over there, but I still haven't figured out how to tell him when I reach the courtyard, so instead of catching Tag's attention immediately, I stand out of sight and watch.

Tag and a few others are shooting at targets lined up against a wall to my right. Off to one side, Earon, the weapons instructor watches, occasionally giving them suggestions. The archers' attention is focused on the flight of their arrows, so none of them so much as glance in my direction. With a pang in my chest, a pang that's raw and sharp, I watch as Tag raises his bow with one hand, pulls the arrow back, and fires in one smooth motion. The arrow he shoots flies true, hitting the target in the middle of the torso, right where the heart would be.

The sound of the arrow *thwack*ing into the target shakes me out of my reverie. I walk up to Earon, who bows to me deeply without taking his attention from the archers. Careful not to distract them, I quietly ask Earon to tell Tag that I would like to speak with him. It's probably a bit strange for me to come here myself, rather than sending a messenger, but right now I'm not sure I care. *It's not like it will matter whether anyone finds out about us when we're about to break up anyway.* Either way, Earon doesn't say anything about it. He just nods and delivers my message while I retreat into the shadows of a nearby hallway.

A short time later, Tag joins me, sweating from exertion but no less beautiful for it. He smiles when he sees me. "Darien! What a pleasant surprise." He peers into my eyes, and his smile fades away. "What's wrong?"

I turn my head away, a cowardly way to avoid having to see the effect my words have on him. "Tag, I..." I trail off, seemingly unable to form the words.

"What is it?" he prompts. "Is everything okay?

My vision starts to blur again, and almost before I know it, Tag's arms are wrapped around me, holding me close.

"It's okay," he says. "I don't know what's bothering you, but whatever it is, we'll face it together."

*Together.* That word cuts through the fog in my mind, and I unwrap myself from his embrace and push him away, just enough so I can look into his eyes. "I just spoke to my father." I try and fail to keep my voice from quivering. "He wants to arrange a marriage between me and some foreign prince, even though he knows I can't stand the thought of marrying someone I've never met before. He told me he's been sending out feelers to other countries to see if any of them have any interest. Apparently, there's a prince in Jirena Sadai who's interested in negotiating for my hand, and he'll be here in a couple weeks. I told him..." Now that I've started, it's like a dam has broken, and the words pour out of me in a rush, and I consciously make myself slow down. "I told him that you and I are courting. I'm sorry, Tag. I know you wanted to keep it quiet, but I had to take the chance that he'd see it my way."

Tag looks at me with an unreadable expression. "I see," he says, his tone carefully guarded. "And what did he say?"

"He ... he said that it doesn't matter, because you're not a prince."

His face falls in an instant, and, for a second, I can see the hurt he must be feeling, before he covers it up. Seeing it gives me more pain than I would have thought possible. "I'm so sorry," I tell him, my voice cracking. "I wish it could be otherwise, but I don't think there's any way to convince him."

He looks at me, his eyes starting to tear up as well. "What does that mean for us?" he whispers.

*This is it.* I force myself to look at him, even though it hurts almost more than I can bear. *It's the least I can do, right*? "I .... We ...." Every time I try to say it, something stops me, like I'm choking on my own words. It feels like my heart is breaking in two, like I'm being shattered into pieces. I know what I have to say, but I just can't make myself say it. Not when I'm this close to getting what I always wanted.

After a few more eternity-long seconds of silence, something snaps in my mind, and I shake my head, as though I can push away the fog that's clouding it. "I don't care what he thinks." This time the words come out easily, like a river flowing downstream to the sea. "I really like you, and I don't want to throw away what we have for someone I've never even met before. If there's even a chance you and I might work out in the future, then I want to keep courting you, no matter what Father says."

Tag blinks rapidly a couple times, then gives me a watery smile. He reaches out and cups my face in his palm, gently stroking my cheek with his thumb. "Oh, Darien. I really like you, too, and I'm more than willing to see where this goes." His smile, already ephemeral, fully fades away. "But can we really stay together if your father is opposed to it? What if he decides you have to marry this prince he told you about?"

"I...." I want so badly to tell him that it will work out, that everything will be alright, but lying to him would just make things even worse later.

"I don't know. I can't imagine he'd be happy if he found out we're still courting. But maybe the negotiations will fall through, and I'll be able to convince him you're an acceptable match somehow." I have no idea if that's even possible, but there has to be a way. "I won't lie to you and say it's likely. But as long as there's any chance, I'm willing to give it a shot."

He glances around to make sure there's nobody near us, then silently wraps his arms around me again and lays his head against my chest. "This is why I was hesitant to start courting you," he murmurs. "I don't like the idea of watching from afar while you court someone else, even if you're only pretending."

I want to reassure him that he has nothing to worry about, but before I can say anything, he lifts his head and looks into my eyes. "But now that I've got you, I'm not going to give you up without a fight. So, I suppose I can put up with it."

Relief washes through me. "Thank you," I whisper.

"Don't mention it." His smile comes back for just a second before it vanishes again. "Is there anything we can do now? Or do we just have to wait until this prince shows up and hope that things don't work out?"

I'm about to tell him that there's not much we can do when a thought comes to me. "Actually, there is one thing we could try," I tell him. "But I don't think you're going to like it."

Samis raises his eyebrows as he takes his seat across from me at the table. The Crystal Sword isn't nearly as packed as the last time I was here, but there's still a hum of noise, a low rumble of chatter like the sound of wind rushing through grass. "Is everything alright?" He sounds concerned, but there's a lightness to his tone that tells me he's not being entirely serious. "I have to admit, I thought you might have been joking when you suggested we meet here."

I don't blame him for being surprised. Normally I would have just talked to him in the palace, but I didn't want to take the chance that someone would overhear us. Fortunately, there's no one sitting nearby, but I lower my voice anyway. "No, Samis. Everything's not alright."

He leans forward, his eyes locked onto mine. "What's wrong, then? You know you can talk to me about anything, right?"

"Of course I know." *If it were up to me, we'd have talked about this long ago.* "First of all, I need to tell you that I'm courting Tag Leara."

Samis breaks out into a wide grin. "That's wonderful! I'm glad you finally took the initiative." He winks at me. "How long have you two been courting?"

I wince. "About a month."

His grin fades. "I see. Is there a reason why you didn't tell me before now?"

"Tag asked me to keep it quiet," I reply, somewhat defensively. "Just for a little while, until he gets more used to living at court. I promised I wouldn't tell anyone. We were going to tell you eventually."

He looks at me for a long moment, then sighs. "I suppose I can't be too angry at you for keeping your promise. It would be a bad start to the courtship if you broke his trust early on. But then, why are you telling me now? And why do you say everything's not alright? I thought this was what you wanted."

"The reason I'm telling you now is because I need some advice, and Tag agreed that this was the best way." I take a moment to gather my thoughts as he nods for me to continue. "You know how strongly I feel about him. Everything was going fine until a few days ago. But then ..." I inhale and exhale slowly, trying to breathe out all my anxiety and fear. It doesn't work. "Father told me he wants to arrange a marriage for me."

Samis pauses mid-bite and looks up, unease in his eyes. "I see," he says slowly as he gently puts his fork back down on his plate, half his dinner uneaten. "It's a nasty business, arranged marriage. Never liked the idea, and I never will. Do you know if he has someone in mind?"

"Apparently, the Jirenians are sending a prince to Cedelia as we speak."

"Ah. Now I can understand your concern. The question is, what can we do about it?"

*Direct and to the point, like always.* "How did you convince Father to let you marry Kenessa? I know he was against it, but I never quite figured out how you did it."

"It was simple, really—I told him that he could probably force me to marry some other woman if he tried hard enough. He would have had to make the palace guards drag me to the altar, but I suppose he could have done it in the end." The image that his words conjure in my mind is simultaneously hilarious and horrifying. "But I *also* told him that even if he did that, he couldn't force me to have heirs. I suppose the thought of you becoming king after me was enough to make him give in."

I wrinkle my nose. Doing something similar probably won't work for me, given that I'm not planning on having biological heirs anyway. "Very funny. What about the council? Did they support you?"

He snorts. "Are you kidding? The heir to the throne marrying the daughter of a lowly duchess? If anything, they were more opposed to it than Father was. But it's not like they have the final say when it comes to who I—or you, or anyone else—choose to marry, even though they act like they do sometimes. Besides, you know how Father is—after I managed to convince him to let me marry Kenessa, he brought the council around rather quickly."

That's hardly surprising. The council can be obstinate, but when it comes to sheer determination, they've got nothing on Father. "Well, I'm glad it worked out for you, but I think you're right—I doubt the same strategy would work for me."

"Probably not." He shifts in his seat, biting his lip. "If I'm being honest, it might be harder for you convince them. If there's one thing I've learned from those blasted meetings, it's that things have changed since I married Kenessa, and not for the better. I'm not surprised that Father is trying to make an alliance with the Jirenians."

My scalp prickles. "What do you mean?"

He opens his mouth as if to say something, then closes it and shakes his head before speaking again. "It's nothing. Forget I said anything." He leans even farther forward, his eyes burning with an inner light. "The point is, no matter what happens, I'm on your side. If you want to be with Tag, I don't care if Father and the council are both against it. You—and Emma, for that matter—deserve to spend your life with someone you love, not someone Father's chosen for you."

That answer wasn't exactly reassuring, but I know I'm not going to get any more details right now, so I just let him change the subject. "Thank you, Samis. I really appreciate it."

"I'm sure you do." He smiles, still ignoring the remains of his meal. "Don't worry. I'm sure everything will turn out fine in the end."

I return his smile with one of my own, but it's weak, and doesn't last very long. *If only I was so certain.*

# CHAPTER TWELVE

"Do I really have to be here for this?" I grumble. "Aren't I going to see him more than enough over the next few weeks?"

Mother gently squeezes my arm, ignoring Father's glare. The three of us, as well as Samis, Emma, and Kenessa, are ensconced in a small audience hall, waiting for the guest of honor to arrive. I don't come in here very often, but I know it's not uncommon for Father to receive high-ranking foreign guests in this room.

"You should be here when he arrives," Mother says, her voice soft. "After all, you might be marrying him before too long."

I shudder at her words. It's been about a week and a half since my chat with Samis in the Crystal Sword, and I still haven't figured out how I can fix this situation without angering anyone. "Not if I have anything to say about it."

"I know you're not happy about this, but you should at least give him a chance, Darien. Besides, even if you don't end up marrying him, you'll still want to be a good host. Who knows, you might even *like* him."

*I seriously doubt it.* I'm about to tell her that, but Father glares at me again, and I decide it's better to remain silent.

I glance at a large grandfather clock standing against one wall for what feels like the millionth time in the last ten minutes. *Arbois should be here any second.* As far as I know, he arrived in Cedelia yesterday, and stayed with the Jirenian ambassador last night. The delay isn't uncommon—nobody wants to be introduced to the king while they're still dusty from the road—but it certainly isn't helping with my anxiety. Meanwhile, I haven't seen Tag since last night; he wasn't in my bed when I woke up this morning, and I'm guessing he's making himself scarce. The fact that he has to isn't really helping either.

As though Arbois was summoned by my thoughts, I hear voices outside the door. A page opens it and steps in, bowing first to my parents, and then to the rest of us.

"Your Majesties, Your Royal Highnesses, may I present His Grace, Prince Arbois Valeran of Jirena Sadai."

My heart jumps into my throat and stays there.

The page steps aside, and Arbois sweeps in behind him. He looks older than I expected, though it could just be his neatly trimmed beard throwing me off. His hair is short and light blond, almost white, and he's perhaps a few inches shorter than me. His face is nothing special—perhaps his nose is a bit larger than average, but that's about it. On the whole, I'd say he's neither particularly attractive nor unattractive. *At least Tag won't feel like he has competition.*

Arbois walks up to us confidently, his head held high, and stops before my parents. "Your Majesties," he says with a slight bow. "Thank you for inviting me to Cedelia."

"You are welcome in our home," Father says, his genteel tone so different from the one he usually uses with me. "I trust your journey was not too arduous?"

"I encountered no troubles on my way here, Your Majesty. Not that I expected any, of course. It surely would have been different had I come in the winter." He laughs as though he's just said something funny. "Although the winters here are nothing compared to those in Jirena Sadai. I mean no offense, Your Majesty."

Father doesn't look offended. From what I've heard of Jirena Sadai, Arbois's words are an understatement. "I'm glad to hear it. Please, Prince Arbois, allow me to introduce my family," Father says, before he indicates Mother. "My wife, Queen Merandia of Soeria, formerly a princess of Zeteyon."

Arbois bows a bit lower than he did to Father before taking Mother's outstretched hand and kissing the back of it. "I'm pleased to meet you, Your Majesty."

Mother returns his greeting, her expression one of careful politeness. I wish I knew what she's thinking; she's hardly giving anything away with her formal smile and respectful nod of her head.

Next, Father turns to his right. "My eldest son, Prince Samis, his wife, Princess Kenessa, and my daughter, Princess Emma."

Arbois repeats the same bow-and-kiss routine with Kenessa and Emma before shaking my brother's hand. To the inexperienced eye, Samis looks welcoming, but I notice the subtle signs of his exaggerated formality, as though he's keeping Arbois at a distance. *Good to know I'm not the only one who doesn't want him here.*

Finally, Father turns to me, and my heart begins to pound even faster. "My second son, Prince Darien."

Arbois looks at me for a second before bowing much deeper than he did for anyone else. *Is he mocking me?*

When he straightens up, he takes my hand with a broad smile and shakes it. "The reason I'm here, of course. Pleased to meet you, Darien."

It takes every single ounce of civility in me to smile back at him. I know I should be putting on a good face, making him feel welcome, but somehow even *pretending* to be nice to him feels like cheating on Tag. "I'm pleased to meet you as well," I say, somehow managing to keep my voice even. "I hope you enjoy your stay in Cedelia." *I hope it's a very short stay.*

I'm not sure if I'm biased, or if it's just a trick of the light, but, for a bare moment, I see an appraising look in his eyes, as though I'm a prize racehorse and he's calculating how much money I'm worth. "Thank you, Darien," he says, his hand still clasping mine, almost possessively. "I've been looking forward to this for quite a while."

I manage to make it through the rest of the welcome session without embarrassing myself, which is a huge victory in my book. After a torturous twenty minutes, Arbois leaves to get settled in his rooms while the rest of us go about our day. My break won't last long, though, because we're supposed to all have dinner together tonight. Even as I leave the audience hall, I'm already dreading it. I'm sure Father will insist that I talk to Arbois, in the mistaken hope that I'll forget about Tag and fall for Arbois instead.

But the truth is that even if Arbois were just another visitor, instead of a prospective suitor, I probably still wouldn't want to get to know him. Something about the way he looked at me, like I was being examined from head to toe, doesn't sit well with me. I'm hardly unbiased—I already have reason to dislike him before we even met—and it's possible that I'm overreacting, but I don't want to spend any more time with him than absolutely necessary.

I'm so caught up in my thoughts that I barely notice when Samis catches up with me. "Darien, stop walking so fast," he says, his voice low. "I want to talk to you."

His words shake me out of my reverie. "What is it?"

"I know you're upset about the whole situation. But if you want to stay with Tag, you need to think this through. Why would Arbois come here *himself*, this early in the negotiations, when he could have sent a representative? Normally suitors of his rank don't show up in person until after an initial agreement has been drafted, but we haven't even started negotiating yet. I don't know exactly what it is, but something seems strange about all this. He's here for a reason. He *wants* something, and I don't think it's you. At least, not you as a person. I mean no offense, of course."

Somehow, I'm not offended. "Alright, then. If you're so sure that he wants something, then what is it?"

He shrugs. "I don't know yet. Maybe he's trying to make someone back home jealous, or to make contacts here so he can open a new market for Jirenian goods. Maybe the Jirenian treasury is running out of money, and he's hoping he can get a large dowry before we find out that they're destitute. Or maybe it's something else entirely. Whatever it is, you and I need to figure it out, because maybe if we give it to him, he'll quit the

negotiations and go back to Jirena Sadai. I assume that's what you want."
He pauses, his expression deadly serious. "But you cannot find out what
he wants if you ignore him, or if you get on his bad side. You need to gain
his trust."

I swallow a lump in my throat that wasn't there just a few seconds
before. "I'll try my best to be civil to him. But *gaining his trust*? I don't
know if I can do that."

"You have to," Samis says, like it's the simplest thing in the world. "It
might be the only way you can get rid of Arbois before Father decides
it's time for you to marry him."

He turns and walks away without waiting for a response, leaving me
standing by myself, feeling more alone than I've ever felt in my life.

The remaining time before dinner flies by far too quickly for my liking.
A couple hours before I'm supposed to go to the dining room, I send a
message to Ivy, asking if she wants to help pick out my outfit. I think she
can tell I want her commiseration more than her fashion advice, though,
because she listens to me patiently while I complain, as she has several
times in the last week or so.

With less than half an hour to go before dinner, she finally chooses
some clothes for me without making me try on a dozen different options,
as she normally would. She even offers to 'rough up' Arbois for me, but it
doesn't take me very long to shoot down that idea. Something tells me it
wouldn't end well if Arbois stormed out of the palace and back to Jirena
Sadai with a stab wound or two.

At the appointed time—and not a second earlier—I make my way down to the dining room. Everyone else is already there waiting for me, and I try my best not to feel self-conscious as I walk into the room with their eyes all on me. Shortly after I arrive, everyone makes their way to the table, ready to eat.

Of course, I'm seated next to Arbois. Thankfully, he's engaged in a conversation with Father, and they continue to converse as we take our seats, and the first course is served. I'm not quite sure how I feel about being ignored by him—on the one hand, I'm afraid I'll slip up and accidentally reveal to him that I don't want to marry him, but Samis's admonition to gain his trust is still fresh in my mind, and I know I'm going to have to talk to Arbois at *some* point in order to do that. I just need to build up my confidence a bit first.

I get my chance after the second course has been served, when Father is distracted by something Samis has said. I turn to Arbois and say to him, "How do you like Cedelia so far?"

He gives me a polite smile. "I must say, it's rather beautiful. I've actually been meaning to come here for quite a while—there are a few historical sites of interest that I want to see while I'm here."

"Ah, so you're interested in history then?" I inwardly breathe a sigh of relief as he nods. History seems like a safe subject to discuss, especially if he enjoys it too. "What made you want to study the subject?"

He chuckles as though I've just made a joke. "How could I not, living in Segaron? The city is steeped in history, you know. It's difficult to turn one's head without seeing some monument or ancient building. Not that I mean to insult Cedelia, of course. But Segaron *was* the capital of the Idrian Empire for centuries. Sometimes, I feel like I can almost hear the Imperial cavalry parading in the courtyard of the Palace of the Moon. You have heard of the Palace of the Moon, yes?"

"Of course I have," I say, pushing down a twinge of annoyance. "It was the emperor's residence, wasn't it?"

"It was, until my family conquered it. Calling it a palace is a bit of a misnomer—it's really a fortress, but I suppose the former sounds better. In any event, it's quite large. I daresay this entire building we sit in, as grand as it is, would fit in the main courtyard. The walls are gray, and in the winter, ice freezes on them. Some say when the moon is full, light reflects off the ice and makes the walls shine too—hence the name." He smiles at me. "You'll see for yourself sometime. I'm sure we'll return to Segaron once we're married."

"Perhaps." I know I should be polite, but I can't stop myself from needling him a bit. "I'm sure Segaron was a sight to behold back in the days of the Empire. But is it really the same now?"

"Of course it is." He says it like he's telling me the sky is blue. "The Empire may be gone, but its legacy remains. The war destroyed much of the city, but not all of it, and what was destroyed has been rebuilt since. I doubt even the last empress would notice the difference, were she alive today." His eyes focus on a point over shoulder, as though he's looking through me. "And who knows what could happen? Perhaps someday the Empire—or something like it—will return, and Segaron will be the Imperial capital once again. Oh, it might take decades, and it would require a steep price in blood and steel, but it *could* happen. All it would take is someone with the right vision and enough ambition to see it through... That's just a pipe dream, of course. But you'll see how glorious Segaron—really, all of Jirena Sadai—is for yourself soon enough."

Before I can respond, Mother asks him about his journey, and he turns away from me, which is fortunate because I had no idea what I was going to say. I turn back to my food, only to find that my appetite has completely disappeared. Instead of hunger, a cold sensation creeps through me, starting at my toes and working up toward my head. I already knew I might have to marry him whether I wanted to or not, but now, for the first time, it seems *real*, not just an abstract possibility.

Without really thinking about it, I push my chair away from the table and stand up. The rest of the party's conversations stop as everyone looks in my direction, making me feel even more self-conscious.

"Are you alright, Darien?" Samis asks, the concern in his tone clear.

"I'm fine, thank you," I reply, making a half-hearted attempt at a smile. "I just need to get some air. I'll be back in a few moments."

I walk away from the table without waiting to hear if anyone responds, but I can't avoid the feeling of their eyes on me as I make my escape.

"He doesn't sound *too* bad," Tag says later that night, tapping his foot against the floor. "Although, perhaps I should be worried. If I remember correctly, you have a track record of falling for men when you dine with them for the first time."

"That only happened once. I promise." I squeeze his hand lightly, and he grins at me. "In all honesty, though, you don't have to worry about me falling in love with him. Like Samis said, there's something ... *off* about him, something I can't quite put my finger on." I pause, then sigh. "Or maybe I'm just grasping at straws, searching for a reason not to like him. Either way, I'm not interested in courting him."

"Don't worry, I believe you." He stands up and wraps his arms around me, and when he speaks again, his voice is as soft as his touch. "You know, in a way, I'm glad he's not outright terrible. It seems like you're going to have to be around him, whether you like it or not. At least this way, you won't have to suffer too much."

"I suppose that's true." I kiss him lightly on the nose. "But in the end, it doesn't really matter. As long as I have you to come back to, I can handle being around him for a little while."

Tag's expression turns nervous, and just like that I'm cold all over again, like I've been dipped in ice water. "What's wrong?" I ask him.

He silently extricates himself from my grip and returns to his previous perch on my bed. "I've been thinking about that myself," he says slowly. "Do you think it's a good idea for us to spend so much time together while Arbois is here?"

"Of course I do. Why wouldn't I?"

"What if we get caught? I know we're technically not doing anything wrong, but I don't think your father would take it well if he found out we're still courting. We could get into serious trouble."

I sit on the bed next to him and wrap him in my arms. "Don't worry about that. We won't get caught. And if we do, it won't be a problem."

"It won't be a problem for *you*. You're a prince. You can get away with things like this. I know you don't intend to marry Arbois, but the rest of the court doesn't know that. If people think I'm the reason the negotiations failed, whatever reputation I have will be completely destroyed."

I can't deny that he's right, but I don't want to admit it. "You think we should just avoid each other completely until he leaves?"

"No! Of course I'm not saying that. I just think we should stop sleeping in the same bed every night." He leans in and gently kisses my cheek. "Trust me, I don't like it either. I could never give you up completely. We'll still see each other sometimes during the day, or in the evening. It only has to last until he's gone."

I feel my stubborn opposition draining away. "If you think that's for the best, then I'll follow your lead. But are you sure it's what you want?"

He looks me directly in the eye, his jaws set and his eyes shining. "Is it what I *want*? Of course not. I want to spend my days and nights with you, and in a perfect world, that's exactly what I'd do. But we don't live in a perfect world, Darien. Even if the chance of us getting caught is small, the risk is great—for me, at least. As much as I want to, I can't ignore that."

I look into his earth-brown eyes. I can see he's telling the truth, that he really is worried about the consequences. "Alright, you've convinced me. I hate the idea of being away from you, but I can see why it's necessary."

He leans against me, and I gently stroke his hair. "I'm sorry," he says. "You know how I feel about you. If we're lucky, Arbois will leave soon, and we can go back to the way we were before."

# CHAPTER THIRTEEN

Tag and I agree to only see each other a few times over the coming two weeks, and only during the day or in the evenings, never at night. When in public together, we're careful not to show too much affection for each other. I decide that if anyone asks, I'll tell them that I promised Riella I would introduce Tag to the court. Fortunately, either nobody notices the brief looks and quiet smiles Tag and I give each other, or they don't care.

Still, it grates on me that I can't openly be with Tag like I want to be. Of course, that's mostly because I like being around him, but it's also because I know that if I *do* end up marrying Arbois, I won't be able to be around him at all. Unless Arbois is okay with me having a lover, which I sincerely doubt. Part of me resents the fact that I have to spend what could be my last unmarried days away from the one person who's managed to make me feel like love, real love, is a possibility, even though I know it's not Arbois's fault.

For the first day or two after Tag and I decide to keep apart, I debate with myself about whether to keep my distance from my new suitor, or to suck it up and try to spend time with him. On the one hand, I want to figure out *why* Arbois came here so early in the process, rather than just sending some Jirenian official to negotiate on his behalf. But on the other hand ... the more time Arbois and I spend together, the more likely he is to take my polite attention as actual interest, and I don't want him to stick around thinking I'm keen to court him. Plus, I'm afraid if I let myself get closer to him, I'll start to feel guilty, and then it will be harder for me to send him away empty-handed. If I keep him at a distance, I can avoid the pain that might result in either of us getting too attached to the other.

This is what I do—until the third day when curiosity wins me over and I send a messenger to Arbois's rooms, inviting him to tour Cedelia with me on horseback, with a few city guards accompanying us. After all, Samis is right. If I can find out what Arbois wants, maybe I can convince him to leave before a marriage treaty is signed. Breaking Arbois's heart is a risk I'm going to have to take. If it means I get to be with Tag in the end, then I'm willing to accept the guilt.

I figure Arbois and I can talk as we ride, and maybe he'll open up about himself. If I'm lucky, he'll even give me some hint as to what it is that he's looking for.

But to my dismay, although the weather is pleasant and Arbois is perfectly polite as we ride around the city, he's also distant. He seems happy to hear me talk about myself or Cedelia, but every time I try to bring the conversation around to him, he deflects, as though this is simply a business transaction to him rather than the prelude to a life together. Which I suppose it is, in a way. Occasionally, when he comments on the size of Cedelia or the grandeur of its buildings or something like that, he'll let a hint of arrogance bleed into his words, but no more than what I would expect from someone in his position, and with no detail that suggests why he's here or what he wants. I suppose it's not too surprising—Jirenians aren't exactly known for being the most forthright people, and, so far, Arbois seems no exception—but it is a bit annoying. Still, it's only our second time meeting each other, so I comfort myself by thinking that maybe he's just nervous.

Yet, our second and third dates—a concert put on by the palace orchestra and a lunch with the Jirenian ambassador and her staff, respectively—don't go much better. If you can call them dates.

"It's like he doesn't even have a personality," I vent to Ivy the day after the third 'date,' stretched out on a sofa in her chambers while she sits in a chair nearby, sharpening one of her knives. "Seriously, isn't the point of this for us to get to know each other? I mean, if we *were* going to end up spending the rest of our lives together, I'd at least want to get an idea of what he's like before we get married. Am I crazy?"

She visibly struggles not to roll her eyes. Even though he's only been here for a week, this isn't the first time I've complained to her about Arbois, and I doubt it will be the last. "You're not crazy, Darien," she says, in a tone that says the exact opposite. "But come on, the answer is staring you in the face. Isn't it obvious?"

I just shake my head, and she frowns disapprovingly.

"All the times you've seen him so far, you've been surrounded by other people. Does it really surprise you that he's not willing to tell you all about his hopes and dreams when he doesn't have privacy? You need to do something one-on-one, with just the two of you. I bet if you do that, he'll be much more willing to talk."

I was afraid she'd say that. "You're right. I just...." I trail off.

"What is it?" she finally asks. "You know you can tell me anything, right?"

"I know, and I love you for it. It's just that ..." I pause, trying to figure out how to say what I'm feeling without giving away too much. Despite what she said, I can't tell her *everything*, so I just say, "You're right, I need to get him alone. I just feel like at least if there are other people around, I can pretend he's visiting for some other reason, and I'm showing him around the court or whatever. But if it's only me and him, then it would all feel more ... real, somehow, like I'm giving in to Father and accepting the fact that we're going to get married."

"Darien, look at me."

I do as she requests. Her gaze is sympathetic, but there's a steel in her eyes that's as hard as the knife she's sharpening. "I understand how you're feeling, and I get why you're upset. But if you want to get rid of him, you need to figure out what he wants and give it to him."

"You sound like Samis," I grumble.

"There are worse people to sound like." She reaches over and pats me gently on the arm. "Now if you'll excuse me, I'm about to go train with Earon. So, unless you'd like to join me...?"

That's all the excuse I need to get going, so I leave her chambers with a quick goodbye, planning to head back to my room to review petitions and figure out how to get Arbois to divulge his secrets.

But before I can get more than a few steps away from Ivy's rooms, a thought comes to me, and I come to a stop in the middle of the hallway. *She's right—I need to figure out what Arbois wants, and it's clear he's not willing to tell me. But maybe....*

I stand there, barely aware of my surroundings, as an idea forms in my mind. Just like that, I shake my head and start walking again, in the direction of the rooms that Arbois is occupying while he's in the palace. I walk with purpose, not because I'm sure of myself, but because if I slow down, I might realize what a terrible idea this is.

I let out a sigh of relief as I approach the door to Arbois's antechamber. The door is closed—which is good, considering what I'm about to do—but I can hear people talking inside, two of them. *Perfect.*

I inch ever closer to the door, but I can't quite make out what they're saying, so with a brief look around to make sure no one can see me, I quietly move until my ear is pressed against the rough wood.

Now the voices are clear. "... be patient, Your Grace," one of them says. It's not Arbois; whoever it is, their voice is deep and rumbling, like distant thunder. "It may take a while, but there's no reason to expect that your strategy will prove to be unsuccessful."

"As I've told you several times before, time is of the essence." That voice definitely belongs to Arbois. The note of politeness I'm used to hearing from him is gone, replaced a distinct hint of disdain, but I'm still certain it's him. "Every minute—every *second*—of delay increases the danger I face. The longer it takes, the more likely it is she'll find out what I'm doing and try to stop me. Lest you forget, that would be just as disastrous for you as it would be for me."

*Someone's trying to stop him from marrying me? Why? Or is he talking about something else?* I press my ear even harder against the door. I can hear Arbois and the other person slightly clearer, but it doesn't help me understand what they're talking about any better. "If it were in my power to make things go faster, I would do so, Your Grace," the other voice intones. "But even so, I have no doubt that everything will go as planned."

"I hope you're right, for your sake as well as mine. I have not come this far to fail now. Understood?" There's a pause, then Arbois continues with, "Now, if you'll excuse me, I have business to be about."

Footsteps sound like they're approaching the door, so I jump back. I only have a second or two to compose myself before the door opens and Arbois steps out, his mouth turned down into a grim expression. *Does he know I was listening?*

But when he sees me, his eyes light up. "Darien!" he exclaims, any traces of the disdain I heard earlier gone. "What an unexpected surprise! To what do I owe the honor?"

I try harder than I ever have in my life to put an innocent smile on my face. "Your timing is excellent, Arbois. I was just passing by, and I just..." I rack my brain frantically, trying to think of an excuse for why I'm here that won't make him suspicious. "I thought I would ask if you wanted to come to dine with me tonight. Just the two of us, I mean."

He looks at me for a few eternity-long seconds, then claps his hands together and says, "That sounds like a wonderful idea! I'd be happy to join you."

My knees go weak with relief. *He believes me, then.* "Excellent. Shall we say seven o'clock?"

"That sounds perfect." He grins at me; maybe I'm imagining things, but it almost looks like a leer. "I'm already looking forward to it."

My heart and my mind are still racing from my close call with Arbois as I return to my rooms. Much as I try, I can't figure out what Arbois and the other person were talking about. *Who is he so afraid of, and why would she try to stop him*? I know Arbois's sister is the Queen of Jirena Sadai, but she was the one who sent him here, wasn't she? Maybe there's someone else she wants him to marry. But then, why would he have come to Cedelia in the first place? I may be a prince, but any benefits Arbois would gain from marrying me wouldn't really matter if he burns all his bridges back home.

I spend the remaining time before dinner thinking about it, my thoughts going back and forth in circles until I don't know which way is up. Maybe he's trying to sabotage the negotiations somehow, and he doesn't want his sister to find out? I *am* trying to do something similar myself, after all, but that seems like wishful thinking on my part. Or perhaps he wasn't referring to his sister? Maybe he's worried about a jealous lover he spurned? It's entirely possible, but I really have no idea if it's actually true.

For that matter, who was he talking to? It might have been his steward—I've never met the man, but Samis has, and, apparently, he's rather large, so the deep voice would make sense—but I really have no idea. Clearly, it's someone that Arbois trusts enough to let in on his plans, but that doesn't really help much.

Despite my constant overthinking, I don't come up with any concrete answers, just more questions. With about fifteen minutes to go before dinner, I make myself stop so I can get dressed and mentally prepare myself, and by the time Joram announces Arbois's arrival, I've calmed down enough that Arbois won't notice anything amiss. *At least, I hope he won't.* Either way, there's not much I can do about it right now, other than maybe try to get some information out of Arbois while we eat.

Speaking of whom, Arbois looks perfectly relaxed as he saunters into my dining room, giving me a strong handshake and looking me directly in the eye when he's announced. "I'm glad you invited me, Darien," he says as we take our seats. "I do so want to get to know you."

"And I you. I trust you didn't have any trouble finding your way to my rooms?"

"Not really. I had my steward ask for directions from one of the servants beforehand." He laughs, but it sounds forced. "You know, it's just struck me that I've been here for nearly a week, and this is the first time I've actually been inside your suite. It's a bit strange, given the circumstances, isn't it? I might think you were trying to avoid me if I didn't know better."

He looks at me expectantly while I frantically try to think of an answer that doesn't come *too* close to the truth.

"Of course I'm not trying to avoid you," I finally say. "I just thought you'd be more interested in seeing the rest of the palace than my boring chambers."

"I suppose that makes sense. I must say, your library is wonderful. I've been able to do quite a bit of research there."

He looks like he's about to say more, but the servants choose that moment to deliver the first course—a salad with apples, walnuts, and salty cheese, and glasses of blood-red wine—and we both start eating.

While we're eating, I consider how I can broach the topic that's on my mind. But the silence grows, and nothing really comes to me, so I guess

I'm just going to have to improvise. *Here goes nothing*. "How are you enjoying your stay in Soeria so far?"

"I like it quite a bit," he replies, looking up from his food. "Your family has been nothing but hospitable."

"I'm very glad to hear it. Of course, it's the least we can do, considering how far you've traveled to get here."

He nods. "Yes, it was a rather long journey, wasn't it? But my time here is already proving to be quite productive, so I suppose it was worth it."

I have a feeling that's as good of an opening as I'm going to get. "Productive? Perhaps I'm out of the loop, but last I heard the negotiations haven't been finalized just yet."

"You're right about that. Of course, concluding our marriage is my primary objective, but I do have other business in Cedelia. Just because the treaty hasn't been signed yet doesn't mean that my time here hasn't been worthwhile."

Now I'm genuinely intrigued. "Really? What sort of business?"

"Nothing that would concern you," he says, waving a hand dismissively. "Oh, I forgot to mention earlier—in addition to the library, I've also enjoyed the palace gardens quite a bit. Jirena Sadai is quite cold this time of year, and..."

I try not to let my disappointment show as he continues telling me about the differences between our two countries. His opacity isn't surprising, but it is starting to get rather annoying.

The second and third courses come and go as we continue to chat about inconsequential things. He seems personable enough, and it takes me a little while to realize that he's studiously avoiding talking about our potential future together. I'm not sure whether that's a good thing or a bad thing—I don't really *want* to have a future with him, after all—but either way, it doesn't bother me too much at this point. Maybe he just doesn't want to jinx it.

It's not until the main course has arrived that things start to get interesting again. "So, Darien," he says, in between bites of his roast beef, "you consider yourself to be a historian, even if an amateur one, correct?"

"I do," I reply, suddenly cautious. *Where is he going with this?*

"Well then, tell me something: how do you think history will record the two of us hundreds of years from now?"

I take a moment to think about it. "I'm... not quite sure. I suppose it depends on what happens in the future, doesn't it? We both have quite a bit more living to do, I should hope."

"I certainly hope so too. Still, I believe that if you wish to understand someone, you must look at their beginnings." He waves a hand in my direction. "Don't get me wrong—certainly many people achieve quite a bit later in life. But even if they do, their base, their *foundation*, is laid down relatively early on. You and I have very similar foundations, I should think."

"Oh really?" Now I'm even more confused than I was before. "In what way?"

"Isn't it obvious? Surely you can see the parallels. Both of us are princes, nearly as highly ranked as we can possibly be in our respective countries, and yet neither of us is destined to become king. You have your brother and I have my sister, and unless fate intervenes, it is their lines that will hold the thrones forever, not ours."

"I can't deny that's true," I allow. "But is our position really all that matters about us?"

"Of course it is. We may wish to believe otherwise, but when it comes down to it, you and I are nothing more than our titles, and that's all we'll ever be. Sure, we may try to pretend otherwise, but we'll never succeed in being anything other than princes. All we can hope to do is to use our positions—our birthrights—for our own benefit, instead of letting *them* use us." He pauses for a few moments with a solemn expression on his face before his polite smile returns. "I must say, your chef is quite excellent. This roast beef is perhaps the best I've ever had. In fact..."

Once again, I tune him out while he chatters about the food and how good it is. This time, though, I'm much more rattled than I was before. His words repeat themselves in my mind: *You and I are nothing more than our titles, and that's all we'll ever be.* I try to make them go away, to think of something else, but they stick there despite my efforts, and I can't dislodge them no matter how hard I try.

# CHAPTER FOURTEEN

The remainder of the dinner is uneventful, and by the time Arbois leaves my dining area, I'm no closer to figuring out what it is he wants here in Cedelia. It's a bit disheartening—until I figure it out, there's no way to get rid of him without angering Father, the Council, Arbois himself, and likely the entire government of Jirena Sadai in the process.

Of course, two heads are better than one, so the next morning I find Samis, hoping he can give me some insight into how to resolve the situation. I manage to catch him in his study after breakfast and tell him all about my dinner with Arbois and the conversation I overheard yesterday.

When I finish, Samis leans back in his chair, deep in thought. "That *is* interesting," he says slowly. "You're right about one thing, by the way—Arbois's steward does have a pretty deep voice. He certainly could be the other person you heard."

*Well, that's one mystery solved.* "Do you have any idea why Arbois is so intent on marrying me, though? Or who would want to stop him?"

"No idea. Like you said, I can't imagine he'd be here without his sister's express approval. Perhaps he meant the ambassador? But I can't imagine why she'd want to stop you two from getting married, or what she could do to him if she really is against it."

We're both quiet for a few moments, pondering the puzzle that is Arbois.

"What about you?" I finally ask. "Have you gotten anything out of him?"

He shakes his head. "No, and I doubt I'm likely to get him alone anytime soon. I've tried, but it seems he spends most of his time in the negotiations for the marriage treaty—when he's not with you, that is. Although..."

I wait for him to continue, but he just sits there silently, staring off into space. "Although what?"

He thinks for a moment longer, then says, "Father and I are supposed to have dinner with him and some of the council tonight. I'll see to it that I'm seated next to Arbois. Maybe I can corner him and get him to say something that we can use." He shrugs. "It's better than nothing, right?"

"That sounds like a plan." I mean, not a particularly *good* plan, but it's not like I have anything better at the moment. "Do you want me to come too?"

"Thanks for the offer, but I think it would be better if it was just me. Maybe I'll have better luck on my own. If it doesn't work, then next time we can try to take him on together." He stands up and comes around to this side of the table, standing next to me and patting my shoulder gently. "Don't worry, Darien. You may not believe it, but time is on our side right now."

I try to keep Samis's words in mind to calm myself down as I go about the rest of my day. *'You may not believe it, but time is on our side right now.'* He's definitely right about the first part; I can only hope he's right about the second part, too. It would be easier if I was involved in the actual negotiations, but as far as I know, only Father and Arbois himself, and perhaps Kerion, are present for those. I'm not sure if the limited attendance is at Father's request or Arbois's, but either way, the result is the same.

To be honest, it's not a surprise that I'm not involved in the negotiations. Normally, both sides send a representative in their place, for the early stages at least. Which is why it's surprising that Arbois is already here—he could have had the Jirenian ambassador, or perhaps an advisor to his sister, come in his place. Maybe he has a strong opinion about the amount of my dowry, or his future title, or how much aid Jirena Sadai will be required to give Soeria if we're attacked. But if Samis's hunch is right—and I have no reason to doubt it is—then he's here for some other reason entirely. The sooner we find out what it is, the sooner I can get rid of Arbois and go back to being with Tag.

Unfortunately, when I see Samis the day after his dinner with Arbois, it seems he didn't have any better luck than I did. "I barely even got a chance to talk to him," he says, with a heavy sigh. "And when I did get a chance, I couldn't get a single useful word out of him. Oh, he was happy to chat about Segaron, or how much he enjoys Cedelia at this time of year, but as soon as we even approached talking about why he's here, it was like talking to a wall. A polite wall, to be sure, but a wall nonetheless."

"Yeah, tell me about it." *At least it's not just me.* "Why didn't you get much a chance to talk to him? I thought you were going to finagle it so you were sitting next to him."

"I did. But Rolsteg was on his other side, and she kept peppering him with questions about Jirena Sadai the whole night. I swear I've never seen her so animated before. It was strange." He shakes his head. "But what's done is done. There will be more dinners. Maybe I'll invite him to dine with me and Kenessa sometime, just the three of us. Unless you have a better idea?"

I ponder the problem for a moment. "You know," I say slowly, "if there's anyone who knows what Arbois wants besides Arbois himself, it's Father, right? He spends more time with Arbois than the rest of us combined. Plus, maybe Arbois gave something away during the negotiations that will reveal why he's here. I could ask him if he has any insight."

Samis raises his eyebrows. "I thought the whole point of this was to get rid of Arbois *without* Father finding out?"

"I mean, I'm not just going to march in there and tell him everything. I can be subtle when I want to, you know."

"It's your funeral, I suppose. But you'll have to wait—Father's leaving to visit Fort Alesen for a few days with Belling, Rolsteg, and a few others. Apparently, he's really got a bee in his bonnet about this whole thing with Uncle Zeikas and the Khorians, and he wants to make sure our defenses are in good shape."

"Yeah, tell me about it." I suppose it makes sense that he'd go to Fort Alesen if he really is worried about Cedelia's defenses; it's the closest major garrison outside of the one in the city itself. "Do you know when he'll be back?"

Samis shrugs. "Three or four days from now, maybe. I'm actually supposed to join him there tomorrow—if you like, I can send you a message when we return."

I suppose that's the best I can hope for, so I tell Samis that's fine, then take my leave, trying to convince myself that it's not already too late.

Three days later, I'm reviewing petitions in my chambers when I receive a message from Samis, letting me know that he and Father have returned to the palace. I debate whether to go talk to Father right now, but it doesn't take me long to decide I'll have better luck if I wait until he's had a chance to rest. Besides, if I show up in his study so soon after he returned and start asking questions, he might wonder *why* I'm asking.

So, I wait until the next morning, anticipation slowly building, and by the time I knock on the door to Father's chambers, I'm already starting to sweat. *You can do this, Darien. All you have to do is talk to him without giving away too much. It won't be nearly as daunting as it sounds.*

I'm so wound up that I almost jump when the door opens, revealing Father's steward, Ebira, a short, gray-haired woman who's been giving me the same steely gaze for as long as I can remember. "May I help you, Your Royal Highness?" she asks, her voice high and clear.

I swallow, hoping she doesn't notice how nervous I am. "I was hoping to speak to Father, if he's not too busy."

"Of course, Your Royal Highness," she says with a slight bow. When she looks back up at me, there's an expression on her face that I don't often see—one of uncertainty, underlaid by worry. "Unfortunately, His Majesty was taken to the infirmary last night, and as far as I know, he is still there."

I stare at her for a second or two. I don't know what I was expecting her to say, but it certainly wasn't that. "What happened?" I finally ask. "Is he sick?"

"His Majesty was not feeling well last night. I believe he only had minor complaints at first, but his condition worsened over the course of the night, and Her Majesty insisted that he be taken to the infirmary around midnight."

Unease starts to bubble up in the back of my mind, and I do my best to push it down. I know Father wouldn't have gone to the infirmary unless his symptoms were serious. Although we don't always get along, I'd still be upset if something bad were to happen to him. Plus, for all his faults as a father, he's a good king, and the last thing Soeria needs right now is instability. Maybe he just ate something that didn't agree with him.

"Thank you for updating me, Ebira. I'm going to go see how he's doing."

She bows deeply, but I barely notice it as I turn to go.

After a few minutes of walking, distracted by increasingly apprehensive thoughts, I reach the infirmary, a relatively large room with beds spaced around three walls. Bright sunlight streams in through large windows on the fourth wall. Healers dressed in white robes sit beside occupied beds, tending the sick as best they can. There seems to be more patients here than usual, but I don't even bother looking to see if Father is in any of the beds. Instead, I walk straight through the room, to a small door set in the far wall. Beyond this door is a smaller, more private area; it's where Father will be.

As I expected, Father is lying on a bed in the back room. Mother sits at his side and a healer stands next to him. Father's eyes are closed, and I can tell just by looking at him that he's ill. There are dark circles under his eyes that aren't usually there, and his skin looks waxy and pale. But his chest rises and falls evenly, and he seems to be resting peacefully, so maybe it's not too bad. *Hopefully Mother or the healer can give me some good news.*

Mother's facing away from me, so she doesn't see me immediately when I walk in. I quietly walk up to her.

"How is he? What happened?" My voice is quiet, but she still jumps at the unexpected sound.

When she turns to me, her face is resolute. "He seemed fine when he got back from Fort Alesen, but after dinner last night, he told me his stomach was bothering him." Her voice is as quiet as mine, but there's more than a hint of worry in it. "I thought it might have been something he had eaten, but he said he'd been feeling a bit off since earlier. A few hours later he started vomiting, and I insisted he come down here." She nods to the healer. "Arille gave him an infusion of ginger and some sleeping herbs, and the vomiting stopped. He's been asleep since then."

I nod my thanks to Mother before turning to Arille. "What do you think it is?"

She hesitates before answering, and my stomach drops a bit. "As I told Her Majesty, I'm not quite certain. But I do have a theory."

"Well?" I ask, trying to keep the impatience I'm starting to feel out of my voice. "What is it?"

Arille sighs. "I will tell you, Your Royal Highness, but first I must warn you that this is only a theory, and that until we have further information, there's no reason to jump to conclusions."

I nod impatiently and motion for her to continue.

"I believe His Majesty may have wasting fever. There has been a minor outbreak in the city recently, and we've even had a few cases in the palace itself. So far, His Majesty's symptoms are consistent with what we would expect, and it's certainly possible that His Majesty caught the disease from someone in the palace. If that is the case, there isn't very much we can do, other than wait and make His Majesty as comfortable as we can."

I had hoped I might get some good news before the end of the day, but contrary to Arille's prediction, Father's condition hasn't improved by the time I go to bed. When I go to the infirmary first thing the following morning, he looks even worse. Yesterday, he looked somewhat normal—it was obvious he was sick, to be sure, but it wasn't *this* bad. Today, his face is yellow and sagging, and he wheezes with every inhalation.

Seeing him like this rattles me to my core. I always knew Father was just as susceptible to illness as the rest of us are, but I don't know if I ever truly believed it. *I'm sure he'll be fine*, I reassure myself. *Arille said he'd be alright*. My thoughts sound hollow, even to me.

Today, instead of Arille, there's a healer I don't recognize in the room. Mother is still sitting by his bedside in the same chair as she was yesterday, as though she hasn't moved. It's entirely possible—she looks haggard, and I doubt she slept at all last night. When I tell her I'll sit and watch Father for a few hours so she can get some sleep, she only argues a little before giving in. Then it's just me, Father, and the healer in the chamber.

Once she's gone, the room is silent except for Father's wheezing breaths. For the most part, he's still, as though he's sleeping normally. But occasionally he'll stir and mutter something that doesn't make any sense. The first few times this happens, I try to puzzle out what he's saying, but it eventually becomes clear that it's just nonsense, a product of delirium. Every so often, Arille leaves, and another healer takes her place, but I don't really feel like introducing myself to the others right now.

The rest of the time, while Father sleeps and the healers silently keep watch, I'm left alone with my thoughts. Unlike the infirmary—which, apart from Father's wheezing breaths, is silent and outwardly calm—my mind is roiling with negative emotions like a stormy sea. There's shock—*how could this have happened so quickly, when he was fine just a few days ago?*—and fear for what this means for my family and Soeria if Father doesn't recover.

What I *don't* feel is grief, and that makes me feel even worse. It's almost like a symbol is lying in the bed in front of me instead of my own flesh and blood. Maybe it makes sense, in a strange way, since Father has always put Soeria ahead of me—ahead of everyone, including the rest of his family, including himself. I should feel some sort of anguish or despair or heartache, but no matter how hard I try, I can't summon them.

I sit here for what feels like hours, losing track of time, slowly growing more and more consumed by my thoughts, until Mother eventually returns. The bags under her eyes have lessened now, but she moves slowly, her arms hanging limply at her sides as she walks. Emma follows behind her, looking much the same.

Neither of them seem interested in talking, so we sit in silence. Every so often, whichever healer is on duty examines Father, looking progressively grimmer each time they do. Father doesn't seem to be getting any better, and my mood gets worse and worse as the day goes on. After the sun sets, a servant brings me, Emma, and Mother dinner, and we eat in silence, too. The food tastes like ashes.

Eventually, long after the sun has set, Mother insists Emma and I get some sleep. I don't have the energy to fight her. I return to my rooms and barely manage to undress before I collapse on the bed.

When I wake, my eyes gritty with sleep, it feels like almost no time has passed. For a bleary moment, I wonder if it's morning, but there's no light streaming in through the curtains on the windows, so it must still be night.

In my fatigued state, it takes me a moment to realize there are voices outside my door. I can't tell what they're saying, and I'm almost too tired to care. But one of the voices sounds insistent, so it must be important. I get up with a sigh. I feel wearier than I ever have in my entire life; it takes far more effort than it should just to get up and walk to my bedroom door.

When I open it, I see Joram talking to someone, but he's blocking whoever it is from my sight. "—needs to sleep, Your Royal Highness," he says quietly. "Whatever it is, it can wait until morning."

*Your Royal Highness—well, that certainly narrows it down.*

A tingling sensation starts at my toes and works its way up my body as I step forward and see Kenessa. Her brows are drawn down in anger, but the way the corners of her mouth quiver just a bit betrays her fear. A prickle of raw dread runs through my mind.

"Thank you, Joram," I say, "but it's too late. I'm already awake." I turn to Kenessa. This close, I can see tears running down her cheeks. "What's wrong? Is it Father?" I swallow. "Is he...?"

She shakes her head, and I feel relief for the briefest of moments before I realize that there must be some other reason why she's here in the middle of the night. She opens her mouth, but no words come out. "Breathe, Kenessa," I say quietly. She does as I ask, inhaling and exhaling slowly. "Now tell me what's wrong."

Her eyes lock on mine. I see alarm in her gaze as clear as day; just seeing it makes my heart plummet down to my toes.

"It's Samis," she says, her voice uneven. "He's sick, too."

# CHAPTER FIFTEEN

"Tell me what happened," I say to Kenessa as we walk toward the rooms she and Samis share. In the short time it took me to get dressed, the sun began to rise, and now soft morning light filters in through the hallway windows. All the fatigue I was feeling before is completely gone. "Is it the same illness that Father has?"

"I ... don't know," she replies. "He seemed fine most of the day, but when we sat down for dinner, he said he was feeling nauseous. He could barely eat anything at all. It didn't seem as bad as what your father had, so he thought maybe it was just a cold. In any event, he didn't want to bother you or your mother with it. I told him to lie down, but a few hours later he could barely even get out of the bed."

*Samis ignoring food? That* is *concerning*. "He hasn't gotten worse since then, right?"

She nods. "That's right. But he hasn't improved, either."

"And you're sure it isn't a cold?"

"I suppose it might be, but I'm still worried. If it wasn't for your father, I'd say Samis would be right as rain in a few days, if it even took that long. But if he has whatever illness your father does..." She doesn't have to finish the sentence. "I didn't know what to do. I'm sorry for waking you up, but I had to tell someone, and you were the first person who came to mind."

"It's alright," I reassure her. "Maybe you're right, and he just has a cold. Or perhaps he ate something that disagreed with him." It sounds unlikely, even to me, but I have to cling to whatever hope I can find, or I'll collapse right here in the hallway. "Even if he and Father do have the same illness, Samis is young and healthy. I'm sure he'll be fine."

"I hope you're right, Darien. I really do."

We reach the doors to her rooms, and she pauses for a moment, calm visibly settling over her like a shroud. "Alright," she says. "Let me take you to him."

She leads me through their rooms and into their bedroom. The sunlight coming through the windows isn't very bright, but even so, I can tell Samis doesn't look good. His skin is sallow, waxy, and yellow—perhaps not quite as bad as Father's, but it's obvious that something is wrong with him. It's an arresting sight, and I feel like I have to struggle to put one foot in front of the other, as though my mind is trying to tell me to run, to ignore my sick brother, like everything will be fine if I can just not see it.

But I can no more ignore Samis than I can forget my own name, so I walk up to him, an increasing sense of dread flowing through my mind.

Samis opens his eyes as Kenessa and I approach. "Hello, Darien." His voice is labored. "Sorry to get you out of bed. I know you've had a long day."

I sit on the edge of his bed, taking his hand in mine; it's cold and clammy. "Don't worry about it, Samis. You know I'm always here for you."

He smiles weakly and starts to respond, but before he can, he starts coughing.

I wait for his coughs to subside. "Is there a reason why you haven't gone to the infirmary yet?" I ask gently.

"Don't want to scare Mother and Father."

I almost smile despite myself. *Typical Samis, always thinking of others instead of himself.*

"I'm sure I'll be fine," he continues, "and they've got more than enough on their minds already."

Looking at him, I'm not nearly as certain. "All the same, we might want to send for a healer to take a look at you. We'll do it quietly, so we don't alert Mother and Father. Just as a precaution."

He coughs again a few times; each one is like a drumbeat, pounding in my ears. "If it will make you feel better, then by all means, go ahead. Just make sure not to bother them."

"I will," I say. He didn't even try to fight back. "Kenessa, I'm going to go send someone to fetch a healer. I'll be right back."

She nods, all traces of her previous lack of composure gone, and I go find a servant, instructing him to go to the infirmary and bring back a healer without alerting either of my parents. Then I return to Samis's bedroom and listen to him talk with Kenessa for a while, although for the most part their conversation goes in one ear and out the other. One thought cycles through my mind: *They will get better. They have to.*

About ten minutes later, the servant returns with Arille. She takes one look at Samis before asking me and Kenessa to leave the room so she can examine him; I'm guessing she doesn't really need privacy but doesn't want us hovering over her. So, Kenessa and I sit in Samis's antechamber in heavy silence, both of us evidently afraid to break the spell.

A short time later, Arille exits the bedroom. Kenessa is on her feet in a flash, barely waiting for her to shut the door.

"Well?" Kenessa asks, a touch of impatience in her tone. "What is it? Is he going to get better?"

Arille's unease is betrayed by the way the corners of her mouth are turned down just a bit. "All the evidence points to both His Majesty and His Royal Highness having wasting fever. For the most part, their symptoms are in line with what we would expect. I understand that the two of them recently visited Fort Alesen?" She waits for us to nod. "After His Majesty fell ill, I checked with one of the palace clerks, who informed me that there have been several cases of wasting fever in Fort Alesen, all of them reported within the last day or so. It is certainly plausible that they both contracted it there. While we cannot be entirely certain that wasting fever is, in fact, the cause, there are currently several other patients in the infirmary with similar symptoms who are known to have visited areas where the disease is present, so it seems likely."

"Wait a second," I say. "Should the rest of us be worried about catching it from them?"

"As far as we are aware, patients with wasting fever are not directly contagious to others. Most likely, it is transmitted through drinking contaminated water. As long as Your Royal Highnesses stay away from the outlying villages, you should be fine. Even if it *is* contagious, you have both already spent a good amount of time in close contact with those who have already fallen ill, so it's a bit too late to be worrying about that.

However, if you are concerned, there's no harm in isolating yourselves for a few days to be certain."

Kenessa shakes her head vigorously. "No. Absolutely not. I appreciate your suggestion, but I'm not going to abandon Samis while he's ill. If I get sick too, then so be it."

"Of course, Your Royal Highness," Arille says with a slight bow. "I understand completely."

Kenessa takes a deep breath; I'm guessing she wasn't expecting Arille to agree with her quite so easily. "In the meantime, is there anything you can do?" she asks, her voice restrained. "Can you cure them? Or at least treat them somehow?"

Arille shakes her head again. "I'm sorry, but if wasting fever is indeed the cause of their illnesses, there isn't much we can do. Of course, they may still get better—it is far from uncommon for the disease to resolve on its own after a few days. But as much as I wish otherwise, all we can do is wait, and try to make them comfortable."

With that, Arille returns to Samis's bedroom, and after we've had a chance to compose ourselves, Kenessa and I join her and sit with Samis while he sleeps. Every so often, he wakes and talks to Kenessa and me for a few minutes before he falls back asleep. Arille keeps a watchful eye on him for a few hours, until another healer takes over.

Like with Father yesterday, I hold out hope for good news, but it gets harder with every minute. As the hours pass, Samis's condition doesn't improve, and my hope slowly but steadily slips away. By noon, nearly seven hours after Kenessa woke me, he's noticeably worse, and we decide that we can keep this from Mother no longer. I volunteer to be the one to tell her. At least I can check on Father while I'm in the infirmary. It almost hurts to leave Samis while he's in this state, but Mother deserves to know.

Yet, the moment I walk into the infirmary, all thoughts of Samis flee my mind. Father's face looks sunken and sallow, even more jaundiced than yesterday, and his breathing is ragged, like his lungs are fighting against him. Seeing him this way nearly takes my breath away, too. I don't need a healer to tell me he's unlikely to get better anytime soon.

Mother and Emma are sitting by Father's bedside with near-identical grim expressions on their faces. Neither of them looks up; in fact, Mother's eyes never even left Father's face for the barest second at the sound of the door. I expected her eyes to be dull, but instead they're bright and hard. It's only after I've started telling her about Samis that she looks away from Father, although her expression doesn't change at all.

Once I'm finished talking, she glances from me to Father indecisively, not responding for a few seconds. Then she turns back to me and says, "I'll go to Samis. You stay here and send a messenger if there's even the *slightest* change in your father's condition."

I nod, afraid to say anything, and she leaves me to sit with Emma and the dying husk of my father.

I spend the rest of the day going back and forth between Samis's bedroom and the infirmary, constantly afraid something will happen to

Father while I'm with Samis and vice versa. They each get progressively worse, and any hope of recovery slowly vanishes with each passing minute. Occasionally, Samis still wakes and talks to whoever's in the room with him, but his voice becomes weaker and weaker each time.

Sometime around midnight, Mother insists I get some sleep, even if it's a few hours. I'm far too numb to disobey. When I get back to my rooms, exhausted mentally and physically, the only thing I want is to sleep.

But then I open the door of my bedroom, and it takes a few moments for me to register the fact that Tag is sitting on the edge of my bed. I'm not sure if he's a hallucination, but if he is, he's a welcome one.

He looks up when I walk in, and immediately stands up and comes over to me, stopping a few feet away. "I'm so sorry about your father and your brother," he says quietly. "I came by earlier, but Joram told me you were in the infirmary, and I didn't want to bother you, so I just figured I'd wait here instead." He takes a deep breath. "I know you're probably tired right now, so if you want me to go I can—"

I don't let him finish the sentence. Instead, I close the distance between us and wrap my arms around him, holding him like I'm lost at sea, and he's my life raft. He holds me back, his touch gentle, enveloping me in his warmth. Without warning, there are tears running down my cheeks, and I cling to him even closer. "Please stay, Tag." My voice breaks when I say his name. "*Please*. I need you."

Somehow, I'm sitting on the bed with Tag's arms still wrapped around me.

"I'm here, Darien," he whispers. "I'm right here, and I'm not going anywhere. I promise."

I let him hold me while I cry. He doesn't let go of me for a second, even when the tears are gone and exhaustion is all that's left, and I fall asleep in his arms.

For the second day in a row, I wake before dawn. I feel like I didn't sleep at all, but my boots have been removed and Tag is out cold next to me, so I must have, even if only for an hour or two.

In my exhausted state, it takes me a few moments to realize what woke me up. Finally, my eyes focus on Joram, who's standing off to one side of the room. His head hangs low, his shoulders slumped, as though the weight of the world rests on his shoulders. Whatever hope I had left is extinguished like a dying flame just seeing him like this.

When he sees I'm awake, he motions for me to follow him. I get out of bed, taking care not to wake Tag, and leave my bedroom. I briefly question whether it's a problem that Joram saw us sleeping in the bed together before I decide I couldn't care less right now.

"What is it?" I ask Joram quietly. I think I already know what he's going to tell me, but I still have to ask. "Is it Father?"

"Your Royal Highness..." Joram's voice is uneven, perhaps the first time I've ever heard it so. "The queen is here to see you."

My mood, already terrible, drops down another notch. "Is..." There are only a few reasons I can think of as to why Mother would leave Father and Samis right now, and none of them are good. *Maybe this is all just a bad dream.* "Is Father alright? And Samis?"

Joram hesitates. "You should speak to the queen," he finally says.

I can tell I'm not going to get anything more from him, so I walk into the antechamber, as though I'm sleepwalking. Mother is there, her eyes red and puffy and her lips pinched into a grimace. She looks worn, as though she's aged ten years in the last few days.

"Darien..." She trails off and swallows. "I have to tell you something."

My vision grows blurry, and I blink a few tears away, the first of what I'm guessing will be many. "Tell me. Please."

She looks me in the eye, her gaze nearly as dull and empty as I feel. "Your father is dead."

# CHAPTER SIXTEEN

Mother's words hang in the air as a wave of dizziness crashes over me, and my chest tightens to the point where it feels like I'm going to be crushed into the ground. "Are you certain he's..." I can't finish the sentence.

"Yes. I'm certain." She hesitates briefly. "He went peacefully, if it's any consolation."

The sense of hopelessness I'm feeling grows. I try to push it away, but only succeed in lessening it a bit. "What about Samis? How is he?"

At the sound of his name, she winces, just the tiniest bit. "I ... don't know," she says. "I was with your father until he ... until a few minutes ago. I'm going to Samis's rooms now. I just..." She takes a deep breath. "I wanted you to hear it from me."

"Thank you, Mother. I appreciate it." Tears sting my eyes, but I blink them away. *I can grieve* later. *Right now, Samis needs me.* "I'll come with you."

I start to walk forward, but Mother hesitates.

"I know you want to see your brother," she says softly. "But maybe you should stay here and get some sleep. There's nothing you can do to make him get better. If he doesn't, you will become king, and—"

"Stop." It comes out more forcefully than I intend. "Samis *is* going to get better. He has to. And if he doesn't..."

Mother just looks at me and nods. I know she's thinking the same thing I am. *If he doesn't get better, I at least want to say goodbye to him.*

With that settled, I ask Joram to inform Tag of what's happened when he wakes, and then I follow Mother out of my rooms and into the hallway. We plod down to Samis's rooms. Each of my steps feels like a struggle, as though a weight is hanging around my neck. The hallways are dark and quiet—not unusual for this time of night, but, somehow, I feel like there should be something ... different about them, something to reflect the fact that the world's falling apart. *Father is dead. Samis might die, too. If he does, I become...*

I shake my head. *No. Don't even think it, Darien.*

There's a heavy pall in Samis's rooms, as though the air has been suffused with death. Outwardly, everything seems normal, but there's a stench of sickness that tickles my nose, barely noticeable but there all the same. Our quiet footfalls on the carpeted floor sound like bangs in the suffocating silence. Mother goes into the bedroom immediately, but I pause before the door, my legs shaking, as though the thing that I fear the most won't be real if I don't see it.

It takes a good minute for me to gather enough courage so I can step inside. When I do, the first thing I see is Kenessa sitting in a chair next to their bed. She has the same exact look Mother had yesterday when I went to see Father for the last time, and as soon as I see it, I know the same outcome is inevitable. Emma sits on the other side of the bed, her eyes hard and her jaw set. Her posture is erect, and her chin is held high as she watches Samis's chest rise and fall. She looks as though she's already lost one battle and she's determined not to lose the second, as though she can pull Samis back from the brink of death with her bare hands.

When I turn my eyes away from the others and focus my gaze on Samis, I almost do a double take. I barely recognize the man lying in the bed. His eyes are closed, and his hair is limp; he seems to have aged twenty years in the last few hours. The vitality that I've always associated with him, that I've almost come to take for granted, is gone. He looks as though a breeze could blow him away.

But before I've made it more than three steps into the room, he opens his eyes, and there's still a spark of life in them.

"Darien," he says, his voice barely audible, even in the silence. "I'm glad you're here."

I walk up to the bed, trying harder than I've ever tried anything before to put on a brave face. "Of course, Samis." My voice trembles almost as badly as my legs. "I'm always here for you."

He smiles weakly and opens his mouth to say something but is interrupted by a fit of coughing. Finally, he manages to choke out, "Ladies, could you please leave us for a moment? I'd like to speak to Darien privately."

Kenessa looks like she doesn't want to leave Samis's side for a moment, but, in the end, she nods. "Alright. But we'll all be right outside if you need us." She gets up and leaves the room without another word. Mother and Emma follow close behind her.

As soon as they've closed the door behind them, Samis turns his attention back to me. "How's Father?"

Tears well up in my eyes. "He's ... well." *Forgive me for lying*. "The healers say he may yet recover."

Samis laughs weakly; for the briefest of moments, he looks like his old self. "You never were a good liar." He moves his hand toward mine—even that little effort seems to tire him—and I grasp it. "Listen to me carefully. I know I don't have much time left."

I shake my head, tears flying away from my cheeks, but he doesn't let go of my hand.

"It's alright, Darien. I know it's not what you wanted, but you'll be a good king. I believe in you."

His words hit me like a tidal wave, ice-cold and overwhelming. I'm powerless to do anything but succumb to it. It feels like a betrayal to be pitying myself when he's the one dying, but I can't help it. "I don't know if I can do this, Samis." My voice is barely above a whisper. "I'm not ready."

"Nobody ever is." His voice is even weaker than it was before. "You have a good heart, and that's all you need. You just have to promise me two things."

I nod, barely able to see through my tears. "Anything."

"Promise me you'll be there for Kenessa when I'm gone. I know she can take care of herself but tell me you'll do whatever you can to help her."

"I promise, Samis." *As though I could ever do otherwise.*

I wait for him to tell me the second thing, but he's silent for so long that I start to wonder if he's fallen asleep. When he does speak, his voice is barely audible: "Promise me you won't let anything come between you and Tag." He sounds winded, like it's an extreme effort just to speak.

"Not Arbois, not the council, not *anyone*. You two are good for each other, and you'll be happy together."

My eyes sting with a sudden flood of tears. "I promise." My voice is only slightly louder than his.

"Good." He smiles again, and, for a moment, he looks so tranquil and untroubled I could almost believe he's not dying. "You'll do well, brother. I know it."

Samis dies almost six hours later, with what remains of our family at his side. One minute he's breathing, and the next minute he's not. When he lets out his last dying rattle, my vision grows dim, as though the light of the world departed along with him, and, for one blessed moment, I feel nothing, like my mind can't quite comprehend how devastating, how crushing, this is.

Then a dam breaks, and all the grief and fear and anguish and desperation that I've been just barely holding in for the last few days breaks free. It's like I'm being torn apart, like my heart is being ripped out of my chest and shredded to pieces before me. The pain of it is so much worse than anything I've ever felt before. Suddenly, I can't be in this room, where my only brother lies dead not feet away from me, anymore, and I lurch out of the bedroom as fast as my feet will take me, barely even noticing that I nearly fall over more than once.

As soon as I get out of the room, that horrible, hateful room, I realize tears are streaming down my cheeks, and I lean against the wall of Samis's antechamber and let myself cry. I don't think I could stop myself even if I wanted to. Someone—I'm not sure who—puts a comforting hand on my shoulder and murmurs something, but I ignore them, and, soon enough, they go away.

It takes an eternity for the pain to recede, but once it does, I almost wish for it to come back, because all that's left behind is pure emptiness, like I'll never care about anything ever again. When the healers come to take Samis to the mortuary, afternoon sunlight making their white robes glow gold, I watch them go into his bedroom with disinterest, as though I'm in some horrible dream instead of real life. All I can do is fight a losing battle against the desolation that's taken over my mind.

When I do finally manage to regain some semblance of sanity, the sky is dark, and I'm standing outside the door to my rooms, with no idea how or when I got here. It hits me that the last time I walked through these doors I was a prince, but now I'm the king, and the emptiness I've been fighting all day rears its hollow head once again. I have to stop and take a few moments to breathe before I have the strength to reach out and turn the handle.

Just like last night, Tag is waiting for me in my bedroom, sitting in a chair next to my bed. Seeing him reminds me of the promise I made to Samis, the one I don't know if I can keep, and stabbing pain blooms in the pit of my stomach.

Tag takes one look at me and then wordlessly wraps me in his arms again. As he holds me, I try to feel *something*, even if it's painful, even if it will make me collapse into a pile on the floor, but all I feel is that all-encompassing emptiness, as though I've been opened up and all my emotions have been scooped out and discarded like the waste they are.

After holding me for a minute or a week, Tag leads me over to the bed. When we get there, I lie down, still fully clothed, and he lies next to me, holding me close to his beating heart. "It's going to be okay," he murmurs. "I know it hurts now, but it'll get better."

I'm not sure what it is, but something—perhaps the gentleness of his touch, or the warmth of his body next to me—finally breaks through the fog in my head. "This is all wrong," I say, my voice shaky and hoarse. My tears start flowing again, like little rivers of despair running down my cheeks. "They *can't* be gone. I need them here. What am I going to do, Tag?"

He starts to stroke my hair, his hand slowly moving back and forth, almost rhythmically. "You'll do the best you can, my dear prince." He says it as though it's an unassailable truth. "You're going to make them proud."

# CHAPTER SEVENTEEN

When I wake the next morning, feeling like something that's been scraped off the sole of my boot, Tag is gone. I don't have the energy to wonder where he went.

Maybe it's a good thing he's not around, because I stumble in a daze, desperately wondering when I'm going to wake from this nightmare. Father and Samis's funerals are even worse, as everything seems to blur together, save for a few moments that seared into my memory: me, Emma, and Kenessa, sitting together, surrounded by courtiers with somber faces dressed in mourning, as Kerion extols Father's virtues. A speech that I don't remember writing and barely remember making. Gripping the pew I sit on so hard my hands hurt, I welcome the pain, because at least I feel *something*. Then doing it all over again the next day for Samis, and somehow it's even worse this time, because he was the only brother I'll ever have, because he was young, because he's the one who should be king now, not me.

It's only once the funerals are over that I fully come back to myself, and I almost wish I hadn't, because I still can't quite make myself believe that this is all real. Sometimes, for a fleeting moment, I forget they're gone. But then reality crashes back a few seconds later, without fail. Each time it happens, the pain gets worse, like a wound that's festering, rotting me from the inside out.

The council schedules my coronation for the day after Samis's funeral, a day that begins with golden light streaming in through my windows, the same golden color as the crown that will soon be placed upon my head. I might think it's a good omen if I hadn't spent the entire night lying wide awake, unable to get anything resembling rest. A servant enters my room shortly after dawn, presumably to wake me. She seems surprised to find that I'm already awake. I don't blame her.

Ten minutes later, my valet comes to help me get dressed. In any other situation, I'd think my outfit looks ridiculous—everything trimmed with royal purple, gold, silver, or some combination of the three, with a metallic sheen that reflects the light coming in through the window, to the point that I almost wonder if I'll accidentally blind someone if I position myself the wrong way. But right now all I can think about is how it should be Samis here, not me. *It should* never *have been me.*

The coronation is held in the Throne Hall, a large room that takes up one wing of the palace and is named for the throne that sits on a grand pedestal towards one end of the room. The throne itself is rather plain—it's made of glazed red oak, with a stylized wolf's head painted in silver on the back. It's been smoothed by the various kings and queens who have sat in it over the centuries, but when sunlight streams through the large soda-lime windows behind the throne, it glitters so much one could almost believe it's actually made of gold.

It's a throne fit for a king or queen. But when I take my seat, with the leading lords and ladies of Soeria, and whatever foreign dignitaries happen to be in Cedelia at the moment—including Arbois—seated before me, it feels *wrong*, like the world turned completely upside down when I wasn't looking. I barely pay attention to Kerion—who, as High Chancellor, is in charge of running ceremonies like this and royal funerals—as he reads the formulaic words that have been passed down from before the time when Soeria was just another part of the Idrian Empire. Instead, I try my best not to break down and cry in front of everyone.

But then Kerion stops speaking and takes a small wooden box from a page, and I snap to attention. He walks toward me, his expression grim, pausing only to bow as he nears. "Your Majesty," he says as he rises. He opens the box, revealing a golden crown within, resting on a blue satin pillow. *Such a plain box for such an important thing.* The crown itself is a golden monstrosity fashioned to look like a vine circlet, with flowers and leaves so detailed they almost look alive and embossed with two wolves howling at a full moon. "Do you, Darien Garros, affirm that you shall serve and protect the people of Soeria until your last breath?"

I swallow, my mouth dry. "I do." It comes out as barely a whisper.

"Then by my authority as High Chancellor, I declare you King of Soeria." He takes the crown out of the box and gently places the crown on my head, and in that moment, it feels like it weighs a hundred pounds.

The instant the crown touches my head, the audience shouts out, as one, "Long live the King!" Kerion signals to the crowd, and they start to come forward so they can kneel before me and swear fealty to Soeria. I stare out into the sea of faces, young and old, but I only have eyes for one, sitting all the way in the back of the hall, and even though Tag is far away I can see that his expression is one of unease and fear.

The time after my coronation is busy, busier than I've ever been in my entire life. Just getting used to being king—a role I never imagined I'd be thrust into, even in my worst nightmares—takes up nearly all my energy. All of the little things that Father, and occasionally Samis, did without even thinking are completely new to me. During my first council meeting as king, the day after my coronation, a wave of unreality strikes me, like I should be literally anywhere other than here. It appears I'm not the only one—everyone in the palace seems to be on tenterhooks, waiting with bated breath for the other shoe to drop. At times, I feel like the tension in the air is so thick that it will suffocate me if I'm not careful.

With so many other things on my mind, it takes me a while to notice that Tag has been avoiding seeing me in private, since the night after Samis died. At first, I can rationalize his absence—it's not like I'd have a ton of time for him anyway, and maybe he thinks I need some space to deal with my feelings. But as the days pass with no sign of him, I start to wonder whether he's giving me space, or if he's given up on me altogether. Either way, I can't help but feel abandoned. Of course, Mother, Emma, and Kenessa are there for me, but they're not exactly in the best of states themselves. Besides, none of them can replace Tag and the way he makes me feel better with just a touch or a smile.

I really do need him, because if there's one thing the last few days have taught me, it's that life is unpredictable. The only way I'm going to stay sane is to have someone I can count on by my side.

Finally, about a week after Samis died, I decide that I can wait no longer. I send a messenger to the Leara rooms before I can stop myself, with a message asking Tag to come to me as soon as he can.

He shows up in my rooms a short time later with a wary look on his face. "You wanted to see me, Darien?"

"I did. I know I've been busy recently, but I've missed you all the same. I just wanted to know if something's wrong." I pause. "Other than the obvious, I mean."

"Darien..." He licks his lips, his gaze darting away from mine briefly before returning. "I didn't want to trouble you while you were mourning. I just thought maybe you wanted some distance."

"I appreciate that. Really, I mean it." I try to sound as non-accusatory as possible. "But it's not necessary anymore. I want to be with you."

He starts to say something but hesitates, and my heart begins to sink.

"What's wrong?" I ask. "Please tell me."

He gives me a look of pure misery. "Can I sit down?" He gestures to the bed. I nod, and he perches on the edge of bed. I sit next to him, close enough that we're almost touching, but still apart. "Nothing's wrong," he says once he's settled. "I mean, everything's wrong, but not between us. I just ... Do you remember that picnic when we first started courting?"

"Of course." I take his hand in mine and squeeze it, but he doesn't reciprocate. "How could I forget it?"

"I know. It was a silly question." He smiles for a moment that's all too brief before it's extinguished like a candle flame. "I told you then that even though I wanted to court you, I was hesitant because you were a prince. I was afraid I wouldn't be able to deal with the pressure, the spotlight being on me all the time."

"I remember. I promised you that I'd do my best to keep that spotlight off you."

He reaches out and cups my face in one hand. "You have," he says softly. "You've done everything I asked of you, and I truly appreciate it. Maybe it wouldn't be a problem if you were still just a prince. But now..."

He trails off, but I finish the sentence myself. "But now I'm the king, and there's nobody else to absorb all the attention."

He nods, and my heart plummets.

"Tag, I'm still the same person I was back then. I didn't magically change into someone else when they put a crown on my head."

"I know that. And *you* know that I really like you." His eyes start to fill with tears, and I realize that mine have filled too. "But I'm just not sure if I can handle it."

His words hit me like sledgehammers to my gut. "What do you mean you can't handle it? What is there to handle? *I'm* the one who has to wear the crown for the rest of my life, not you!"

He jumps from the bed, as if to escape the heat in my voice, and walks a few feet away, his back to me. "I know, Darien! I know it's not easy for you, and you have every right to be upset." He turns to face me; his jaw is set, but the corners of his lips are quivering. "But don't pretend like it's easy to court a member of the royal family! Sure, you can make the council or whoever accept our courtship, but you can't make them accept *me*, and you certainly can't make them—or anyone—treat me with respect. Samis told me that when he and Kenessa started courting half the court was against it, and they seemed determined to make her life a living hell. And he was only the heir, not the *king*."

"Samis told you that?" For a moment I feel something other than grief when I hear Samis's name, but only until I remember that he's gone, that

I'll never get to talk to him again. "I didn't know the two of you ever spoke to each other without me there."

"Of course we did," Tag replies gently. "Not very often, but a few times. He never quite came out and said it, but it was clear he was trying to find out whether I'm good enough for you." A solitary tear rolls down his cheek. "He cared about you, Darien. I guess he wanted to make sure that I do, too."

I don't even try to hold my tears back at that. I doubt I could if I wanted to. *Promise me you won't let anything come between you and Tag. You two are good for each other, and you'll be happy together.* Samis's words take on a new significance. "Trust me, he liked you." My voice is nearly as broken as my heart is. "If he was testing you, then you should know that you passed."

"Thank you. That means a lot to me." Tag's cheeks are glistening. "But it doesn't change the facts, Darien. I can't stand the thought of everyone whispering behind my back, saying that I'm not good enough for you because I don't have a fancy title."

I'm on my feet before I know it, but he doesn't flinch. "I need you," I say softly. "I don't know if I can do this without you."

He looks even more miserable than before; it hurts me to see him this way, but I need to say what comes next, just like I need him.

"Tag, I love you."

He looks at me, his beautiful, brown eyes meeting mine. "You're not just saying that, are you? Do you really mean it?"

I open my mouth to tell him I do mean it, but he silences me with a hand to my chest. "Please," he says. "I want you to be completely certain before you answer."

I search my heart and mind for a shred of doubt and find absolutely none. "I mean it. I love you, and I want to be with you."

He looks up at me for a second, then wraps his arms around me, his head pressed against my neck and chest. "I love you too, Darien. I really do, I promise." He takes a deep, shuddering breath. "But I don't know if I can be with you."

I feel him sobbing, and I silently stroke his hair as he cries, like he did for me not too long ago. Tears stream down my cheeks too. Once his tears have stopped, I gently put a finger under his chin and lift his head, giving us direct eye contact. "Please, tell me what is it that bothers you about courting a king? Even if it won't change anything, I want to know."

He stares at me for a long moment, then sighs. "Alright. I'll tell you. You deserve that much, at least." He motions to the bed. "We should sit down. It's a long story."

We resume our seats, and he takes another deep breath before speaking. "When I was younger, maybe twelve or thirteen, my father's sister and her husband, who was a Zeteyoni baron, died. My parents took in their daughter, my cousin Jena, who's about a year older than me. She and I were close, but she never really got used to living in the country, so when she came of age, she asked my parents if she could go live with her father's family at the Zeteyoni court in Osella. Not long after she got there, she fell for someone—his name was Alpere, and he was the son of a powerful Archduchess. Apparently, it took Alpere a good while to warm up to her, but once he did, they were inseparable. Eventually he proposed to her, and she said yes, so they went to ask his parents for their approval." He shakes his head. "It ... didn't go well, to say the least. Jena never told me what exactly happened, but it's clear that Alpere's mother was vehemently against her son marrying the daughter of an undistinguished baron. She told them she would *never* give them her approval, forbade Jena from ever seeing her son again, and married her son off to some other woman that she found acceptable.

"But that wasn't the worst of it. Alpere's mother apparently decided to teach her a lesson, because Jena became a pariah at the court overnight. One day everyone treated her normally, and the next day they acted like she was the worst criminal to ever walk the earth. All of her friends deserted her without even a word, pretending like they'd never been friends in the first place, and she came back to our estate not long after. The whole thing broke her, Darien. I don't want to say she never got over it, because she did, eventually, but she was never the same again. Even when she married a perfectly decent man from a family that lived nearby a few years later, she was still pining for Alpere.

"I love you, Darien, but I never want to go through what Jena did. I do know that the Zeteyoni court is far more obsessed with rank than this one, and that your mother is nothing like Alpere's mother. Plus, you told me that Samis would be there to soak up all the attention. I'm sorry if that's callous, but it's true, and it's why I was willing to give courting you a shot. But now that you're king, there's nobody to hide behind. We tried our best, and maybe we should just leave it there. I just don't want everyone to think I'm some upstart, power-hungry foreigner who somehow managed to bring you under my spell. Do you really think the council would be happy if you told them that you want to court me instead of a prince or an archduke or something? Especially now—when everything is so uncertain?"

He falls silent, and I give him a moment before I put an arm around him and pull him close to me. "I can't promise that everyone will be thrilled about us courting," I reply quietly. "But I can promise you that as long as I'm king, you will be treated well at this court. If anyone shows you any disrespect, I'll make sure it reflects badly on them, not you. Besides, the council may advise me, but ultimately, I am the king, and when it comes to whom I court, I get to make the final decision, not them."

He lifts his head up, kisses me gently, and says, "Thank you, Darien," before putting his head back where it was, next to my heart. "But what about Arbois? Aren't you still courting him?"

I take a deep breath. I knew the subject would come up, but that doesn't mean I have to like it. "I don't have a reason to anymore. I don't want to throw away what you and I have, and that means Arbois is out." I'm sure Arbois—and maybe even the council—won't be happy with me, but somehow this feels ... right, in a way that nothing else has recently. "I mean, I'm not going to throw him out of the palace or anything, but I don't intend to marry him. Ever."

Tag lifts his head up again, his eyebrows raised. "I suppose I'm not complaining, but what about the whole 'Soeria needs another alliance' thing? Can you really afford to just rebuff him like that?"

"Well ... that's the thing." I swallow. "You're right. I can't just walk up to him and tell him to go home. I don't know what's going to happen with our alliance with Zeteyon now that Father's dead. But if it is ended, I can't just let Arbois walk away without coming to some sort of agreement with him. Either way, I need him to stick around until I find out what my uncle is thinking."

Tag's eyebrows lift even higher. "So ... you're not going to marry him, but you're going to keep him around? And just hope you can convince him to make an alliance without marrying you?"

"It sounds bad when you say it like that, but yes." I gently cup his face in one hand, lightly stroking one cheek with my thumb. "I promise you that I'm not going to spend one second more with him than absolutely necessary. No matter what, my mind and my heart will be with you. Always."

Tag still looks unconvinced, and the desperation I was feeling before starts to come back. "Please, Tag. I know it's not an ideal situation, but I don't think I can do this without you."

He looks at me for a long moment while my heart pounds furiously, the sound of my blood coursing through my veins almost deafening in the uncomfortable silence. "I ... suppose I can put up with that," he finally says.

I breathe a sigh of relief. "You're in, then?"

"I'm in." He kisses me, and I kiss him back just as deeply. "But, Darien, what if you can't convince Arbois to make an agreement that doesn't include him marrying you?"

I take his hand in mine, lacing our fingers together. "Can we wait and see if that happens first? I don't want to have another thing to worry about right now."

"I guess that's fine for now. I assume that if you're going to pretend to court Arbois, our courtship needs to stay secret for the moment?"

"That's right. Hopefully, I can make a deal with him quickly, and then we can make it official. Does that work for you?" I wait for him to nod. "I do have one request for you, though."

He arches one eyebrow. "Oh? What is it?"

I take a second or two to think about how to phrase what I'm thinking. "Can we go back to sleeping in the same bed at night? I know you're worried we'll get caught, but I ..." I'm starting to get choked up again.

"I just feel so alone, especially at night. I know I'd feel better if I have you next to me."

He leans forward, a sober expression on his beautiful face, and kisses me once, twice, three times. "Of course, my love," he says, his voice as soft as eiderdown and gentle as silk. "I miss sleeping next to you."

"Thank you, Tag." I return his kiss, and he smiles sweetly at me. As he does, I feel a sense of deep relief and love for him. But there's something else there, too, buried deep down yet there all the same. *My love.* Somehow, those two little words are the first ray of hope in what feels like a very long time.

# CHAPTER EIGHTEEN

I 'm sure there are parts of a king's job that are enjoyable—there must be *some* reason why people are willing to fight to the death to wear the crown, after all—but attending meetings of Soeria's Council of State is definitely not one of them. They are almost as boring as reading reports, with the added punishment of having to be around other people.

The first session was short, probably because everyone—including myself—was still in shock. In a way though, it was almost tolerable, since my mind was elsewhere pretty much the entire time. The second one, a few days later, was much the same.

This one, however, is closer to the one I went to what feels like decades ago. There's still a heavy pall in the room, but the shock seems to have worn off. The assorted lords and ladies drone on for hours about random topics like everything is normal. The combination of the raw grief I'm feeling and the constant sense that Samis and Father should be here instead of me makes it seem like time has slowed down. It certainly doesn't help that I never expected to be here, sitting at the head of the table, at least not regularly. The only thing that keeps me going is the knowledge that it *will* end sometime, and that I'll get to see Tag when it's done.

Like the first time, I mostly keep quiet during the discussion, letting the councilors guide me rather than the other way around. For the most part, they seem happy to accommodate my lack of experience, although some of them can be a bit condescending at times. It bothers me a little bit that I can't command the same respect Father did, but I suppose I haven't really earned it yet.

Finally, after what feels like days since the meeting has begun, the discussion of the last item on the agenda—a trade agreement with Raktos—wraps up. I don't waste any more time before asking, "Does anyone have any further business to bring before the Council?"

According to Samis, that's what Father would ask at the end of every meeting, and as far as I know it was uncommon for anyone to respond. *I'm sure I'm not the only one who wants to get away from this room as quickly as possible.*

Not this time, apparently. Duke Zoran Arondel, one of the older members of the council, clears his throat. He's been a common fixture at the court for as long as I can remember; he's old enough to be my great-grandfather, and Father once told me that he's been on the council for nearly six decades. As always, his clothes are rumpled, as though he slept in them and forgot to change. He's apparently almost as deaf as Laya at this point, relying on his ability to read lips to participate in council meetings, but otherwise his mind seems sharp enough considering his advanced age.

"Forgive me, Your Majesty," he says ponderously, stroking his long, white beard. "I realize this meeting has gone on long enough, but there is one more thing I believe we need to discuss."

I nod to him, perhaps a bit more deferentially than I would for another councilor. I have no idea what's so urgent that he feels the need to discuss it now, but it must be important. "Go ahead, Arondel."

"I doubt I need to say that these are turbulent times for Soeria." His voice is deep and resonant, his words heavy with gravity. "I'm certain Your Majesty will agree that it is the job of both this council and Your Majesty to reduce that turbulence, to ensure stability for the kingdom as best we can."

His words are eminently reasonable, but something about them puts my guard up. "Of course I agree with you, Arondel. What would you have me do?"

"Why, the same thing that any young man in Your Majesty's position would do, of course: marry and have children so that the line of succession can be secured. Of course, this council understands that producing an heir will be different for Your Majesty than it would be for some, but surely it would still be best to begin considering suitable candidates for marriage sooner rather than later. Since Your Majesty need not be married before adopting a child, the search for an appropriate heir can proceed in parallel. I understand that your late father did not have any siblings, but there are several members of Your Majesty's extended family who have young children. I'm certain any of them would be happy for Your Majesty to adopt their child as your heir."

My hands clench into fists; fortunately, they're under the table, so nobody can see my annoyance. I can't believe he's discussing this so soon after Father and Samis died. "I understand your concerns, Arondel, but there is already an heir," I say through clenched teeth. "My sister may only be nineteen years old, but she is perfectly capable of stepping in should something unfortunate happen to me."

Arondel nods. "I did not mean to imply that Princess Emma is in any way incapable, Your Majesty. However, in light of recent events, surely we can all agree that it is better to prepare for the worst, even as we hope for the best? Should something happen to Your Majesty and Her Royal Highness before either of you has children, the succession would be in doubt, and Soeria would be thrown into chaos."

I can't deny that what he's saying is true, but I'm nowhere near being in the right state of mind to discuss this now. "You're right, Arondel. I agree that this is something to consider, but it sounds like a complex issue, and one that will take quite a bit of thought before any decisions are made. Perhaps we should discuss this in more detail at a later date, when we've all had some time to come up with a solution?"

He nods again. "That sounds reasonable, Your Majesty."

I nod, not exactly happy about it, but knowing it's the best I'm going to get for now. Something tells me this won't be the last I hear about this.

I go to end the meeting again, but it seems Arondel isn't quite done. "If I may, Your Majesty, even if you are not prepared to adopt an heir just yet, there is still the matter of a potential marriage. The king's hand is a valuable bargaining chip, even if there will be no natural heirs. Your Majesty should at least consider the possibility of forming a connection with another royal family through marriage."

I wish I could tell them about Tag, but I can't, not while everyone thinks I'm courting Arbois. I just need to get them off my back so I can have time to work things out myself. "While I understand your concern, I am in no rush to marry, especially so soon after the deaths of my father and brother. As I'm sure you'll agree, choosing a consort is an important decision, and I would rather consider my options carefully and make the right choice than charge blindly ahead and take the first suitor who comes along."

"What about Prince Arbois of Jirena Sadai?" Archduchess Rolsteg prods. Her green eyes are locked onto mine in a gaze that's almost mesmerizing. "He is here to negotiate a marriage treaty with Your Majesty, is he not? There is no doubt that this council would consider him suitable, and an alliance with Jirena Sadai would inure greatly to Soeria's benefit, especially now that the continuation of our pact with Zeteyon is in doubt. From a political perspective, it is unlikely that Your Majesty will find a better match."

As much as I want to, I don't have the heart to fight them right now. "You are correct, Rolsteg. I can see the benefits of a match with Prince Arbois, but as I said, I'm in no rush. Still, I will continue the negotiations that my father started. I can't say for sure what the end result will be, but if all goes well, I suppose I would be amenable to marrying him." A lie if I've ever told one. "Now then, I suggest we end the meeting there. If necessary, we can continue discussion of this topic at the next meeting."

I can tell that Rolsteg and Arondel, and perhaps a few others, aren't happy with my non-answer, but they appear to recognize it's the best they're going to get for now. With that, we disperse, and I go to my study so I can try to make a dent in the pile of reports and petitions that seems to grow larger with every passing minute. But I can't quite escape the sound of a ticking clock that reverberates in my mind, reminding me that the Council won't let me put them off forever. *I just have to figure out a way to get Arbois to agree to an alliance that doesn't include us getting married before the council gets fed up with me.*

# CHAPTER NINETEEN

As I walk through Mother's chambers later that night, I'm struck by how they look exactly the same as they did before. There's no real reason why they should look any different, but I still feel like *something* should have changed to reflect Father's absence.

I haven't exactly been avoiding her since Father and Samis died, but I haven't been seeking her out either. At least, not until tonight. I know that she's hurting, and I want to be there for her, but seeing her drives home just how much I'm missing, just how much my life has changed in the last week or so. At least now enough time has passed that I feel like I can talk to her without breaking down immediately.

Still, I have been avoiding one particular conversation with her for a couple of reasons, even though it has nothing to do with Father and Samis—not directly, at least—although that will change shortly. It will be painful, but Tag and I decided we need her advice.

When I get to the study, Mother is sitting at the piano, but she isn't playing, just staring at the keys. She looks up when I enter and gives me a smile, but her eyes have the same haunted look they've had since Father first got sick. "Darien! To what do I owe the pleasure?"

"I just wanted to see how you're doing." I take a seat near her. "I know we haven't really had a chance to talk recently, and I wanted to make sure you're okay."

Her smile dries up like autumn leaves. "I'm doing as well as I can be, I suppose. I always knew there was a good chance that I'd outlive your father, but Samis..." She looks away for a moment before she turns her gaze back to me, tears welling up in her eyes. "But I still have you and Emma and Kenessa, and I'm grateful for that. This position is stressful enough as it is; doing it without having people you love and trust around you is next to impossible."

I take her hand in mine and give it a gentle squeeze. "You know you can always talk to me about anything, right?"

She squeezes my hand back and gives me a sardonic grin. "I think I'm the one who's supposed to say that to you."

"Actually, now that you mention it..." I try to return her smile, but I'm nervous, and it vanishes quickly. "There is something I wanted to talk to you about."

She raises one eyebrow. "Oh? Do tell."

I'm silent for a few moments, marshaling my courage. When I feel like I'm as ready as I'm ever going to be, I say, "I assume Father told you about me and Tag Leara?"

She nods slowly, her eyes narrowed a bit. "He did. At least, he said the two of you were courting at one point, but you called it off when he told you about Arbois."

"That's ... not entirely true," I reply, biting my lip. "I mean, the part about us courting is. But we never actually ended our courtship. We just ... kept it private, I suppose."

She closes her eyes and sighs, a long, slow exhale that leaves me with little doubt about what she's thinking. "Darien, my son. I know your father could be ... difficult at times, and I know that you and he didn't always see eye to eye. To be fair, you weren't alone—when he told me he was considering arranging a marriage for you without even getting your input on the matter, I told him he was making a mistake, that he was overreacting to my brother's admittedly stupid squabble with the Khorians." She opens her eyes and fixes her steely gaze on me. "But that was *before* everything changed, before the world turned upside down. Now, with things so unsettled ... I'm sure you and Tag must like each other if you're still courting after all that's occurred. But you must understand that there are other things to consider."

Her gaze bores into mine, but I don't flinch. "You're wrong about one thing," I say quietly. "Tag and I don't like each other. We love each other."

Her expression softens a bit. "I understand, my son. Really, I do. If you were anyone else, maybe that would be enough. But you're not just anyone. You're the king now, the beating heart of Soeria. From now on, the decisions you make affect the entire country, and you must consider not only what's best for you, but what's best for the people you rule. It's not fair, and you may hate it, but that's the way it is. Your father knew that all too well, and he never stopped thinking about how he could work toward the greater good. If you want to be a good king, you'll do the same." Her voice gets quieter, but I can hear it crystal clear. "Even if you hate it, you may have to sacrifice your courtship with Tag, if that's what's best for the country."

I don't dare tell her how close she's come to hitting on one of my deepest fears. "I understand that. But what if there was a way I could stay with Tag and ensure Soeria's security?"

Her brows draw down. "I can't imagine how you'd be able to do that, but if you have a suggestion, then I'm all ears."

*Here goes nothing.* "I know Father was worried that our alliance with Zeteyon might not survive him. But your marriage contract doesn't explicitly say that's the case, right?"

"As I recall, the agreement was clear that the alliance would last during our marriage. But you're correct that it doesn't say what happens once it ends."

"There's a chance we can convince Uncle Zeikas to renew it, then?"

"It's certainly possible. But then, my brother has always been one to follow the letter of the law, not the spirit. He may believe that the agreement is now void. If that's the case, Soeria will be vulnerable, and we'd need to find another alliance. Arbois is our best chance at that."

"He is," I agree. "But who says that I need to marry him in order to create an alliance between us and Jirena Sadai?"

"You think Arbois would be willing to sign a treaty that doesn't include a marriage provision? That seems ... unlikely, to say the least. It's not impossible, but I can't think of what he would accept in exchange for an alliance besides your hand. Like it or not, Jirena Sadai is stronger than us, and they can afford to walk away from this palace without concluding an agreement. I'm not sure that we can say the same."

I bite down rising desperation. "If they don't need us, then why did he come here in the first place? He must be interested in *something*."

"Perhaps," she allows. "But I sincerely doubt that he'll be willing to make an alliance without marrying you in the process."

"It's worth a shot, isn't it? We'll never know if we don't try!"

Mother doesn't respond, and I start to feel even more desperate.

"You said it yourself," I say. "This job is hard enough as it is and doing it without people you love is next to impossible. I love Tag, and I don't want to throw away what we have. If there's a chance that I can stay with him and keep Soeria safe, *any* chance, I'm going to take it."

She stares at me with an inscrutable expression while I sit in silence, breathing heavily, as though I've just spent an hour sword-fighting with Ivy. Then she sighs, looks down, and says, "You're right. I suppose it's worth a try. If there's anything the last few weeks have taught me, it's to value the ones you love, and I can't disagree with you fighting for Tag." She reaches out and takes my hand, holding it like her unblinking eyes still hold mine. "You do understand I'm hardly the only one you have to convince, correct? I doubt the council would be happy with you marrying the son of a viscountess, even if he is distantly related to royalty."

"I know. But even if they're not happy about it, they can't stop me from marrying Tag, can they?"

She gives me a small, rueful smile. "Can they *stop* you? I highly doubt it, not if you're that determined to get your way. But they can certainly make your life—and Tag's life, for that matter—very difficult, and you might find yourself regretting your decision before too long. Although, I suppose it would be much easier to persuade them if we can tell them that we have alliances with Zeteyon and Jirena Sadai to fall back on. But you must understand that it's not as simple or easy as you seem to believe. If Zeikas won't agree to renew our alliance, or if Arbois is only interested in your hand, you may have to marry him whether you like it or not. I didn't always see eye to eye with your father either, but he was absolutely right about Soeria being far more important than any one person."

"I know." I may hate the thought of it, but that doesn't mean she's not right. "But that's not going to happen. My plan will work."

She doesn't need to respond; I know exactly what she's thinking. *Who are you trying to convince, me or yourself?* I push that thought away with all my might.

"So," I continue, with forced confidence, "what's the best way to get a message to Uncle Zeikas? Should I invite the Zeteyoni ambassador to lunch or something and have him report back to Osella?"

She scoffs. "Don't waste your time. Talren's a bumbling fool who would rather lounge around and gamble all day than do anything approaching work. Sometimes, I think Zeikas chose him to be the ambassador just to get him out of Osella, and because he knew that he could just communicate to your father through me if he needed to. You'd be better off writing Zeikas a message yourself."

"I can do that. Will you help me with the language?"

"Of course I will. When do you want to write it?"

I give her a light grin. "There's no time like the present, is there?"

As proposed, I draft the message to Zeikas right then and there, with Mother's help. It takes longer than I thought it would; as Mother reminds me, I need to walk a fine line between arrogance and submission. What we finally come up with is this:

King Zeikas,

I hope this message finds you well. As you know, my late father constantly strove to maintain the strong relationship between Soeria and Zeteyon, and now that I am king, I fully intend to do the same. The alliance between our two nations has been beneficial to both sides, and I greatly appreciate the stability and prosperity that has resulted from your friendship. In addition, I am currently courting Tag Leara, son of Viscountess Catherine Leara, who I am told has ties to your own family. Therefore, I see no reason to break our existing alliance, even though my parents' marriage treaty is technically no longer in force.

In the spirit of continued friendship, I propose that we either reaffirm our existing alliance, or create a new agreement that includes a similar provision. If you prefer the latter and wish to negotiate additional terms, I would be happy to send a representative to Osella or receive your representative here in Cedelia.

Your nephew,
King Darien Garros

"It's quite direct," Mother says, her eyes scanning the text. "But with him, that's probably a good thing. He doesn't really care for sentimentality. He'll appreciate your being straight and to the point."

"You approve, then?"

She nods. "I can't guarantee he'll respond in the way we want him to, but it's our best shot."

Not exactly a ringing endorsement, but I suppose it's good enough. I carefully fold up the letter and seal it with wax before giving it to Mother's steward Lana, with express instructions to send it immediately. Lana goes to carry out my orders, and after thanking Mother and bidding her goodnight, I leave too.

Tag is waiting for me in my bedroom when I get back, and I tell him about the message as we get ready for bed. I try to stay optimistic as I did with Mother, and Tag seems to be confident that our plan will work as well.

But after all the candles are dimmed and the two of us are cuddled up in bed, I can't stop my mind from wandering to Zeikas and Zeteyon, to Arbois and alliances. I can't help but worry that something will go wrong, and even though I'm tired down to my bones, sleep doesn't come easily.

The next morning, I send a message to Arbois asking him to meet me in the palace garden at noon. I'm not exactly looking forward to meeting with him. As long as we haven't discussed the subject, I can believe he'll agree. But the longer I make him wait, the less likely he is to go along with my plan, so I know it's better to do it now. If I'm lucky, I can get some idea of what exactly he wants. I just wish I didn't have to go to him like a supplicant so I can be with Tag.

For better or worse, Arbois is waiting for me as I reach the garden. "Your Majesty," he says with a slight bow as I walk up to him. "You have my condolences for your father and brother. Such a shame."

"Thank you, Arbois. I appreciate it." Just thinking about Father and Samis makes me tear up. "But let's not dwell on such terrible things on a wonderful day like this. Will you walk with me?"

He nods, and we begin to walk around the garden. Summer is upon us, and the flowers have bloomed in full force. There are quite a few people outside enjoying the clear weather, and they all bow to me as I pass by. It's annoying, but I suppose I'll get used to it eventually, like a prisoner gets used to waking up in a cell every morning.

"Forgive me for being blunt," I say to him as we walk. "But I have to ask: are you still interested in continuing the marriage negotiations?"

He takes a few moments before responding. My heart wants him to say he's ready to give up and go home so I can be with Tag. At the same time, my head knows that would be bad for the country, even if it might be good for me personally. I wish I could go back to a time when I didn't have to consider the latter.

"I understand that the situation has changed since our last meeting," he finally says. "Still, it seems to me that there's no reason why we can't resume our courtship now that things have settled down." He turns slightly and looks at me, his expression unreadable. "Wouldn't you agree?"

"Perhaps. But as you just said, the situation has changed. I'm not sure that it's proper for me to be courting so soon after such a tragedy. I worry that it might be ... disrespectful, as it were."

"I can understand that. If we were in Jirena Sadai, I would assure you that none at court would disapprove of us courting, even in a time of mourning such as this. But I can respect the fact that Soerian customs are different." He shakes his head. "Having said that, you must understand that I cannot afford to wait forever, Darien. I sympathize with you, but I must think about what is best for my country. As terrible as it is, matters of state must be dealt with, even when tragedy occurs."

I silently thank him for giving me an opening. "I completely agree. In fact, there's no reason why you and I still can't come to an agreement of sorts."

He looks at me while I hold my breath, and for just a moment there's a calculating look in his eyes, similar to the one I saw when we first met. Then, just when I feel like I'm about to burst, he nods and says, "That is an ... intriguing proposition," and the pressure lessens a bit. "What sort of agreement did you have in mind?"

"I was simply thinking that there are ways to form a connection between our two nations without involving marriage. That way, you can do what's best for Jirena Sadai without having to wait until after the mourning period has ended. I'm sure we can find some arrangement that will benefit both of our countries."

His expression is completely inscrutable, and it's starting to drive me insane. "I see," he replies slowly. "Just for the sake of clarity, you are suggesting we negotiate a treaty between our two nations that doesn't include a marriage between the two of us?"

"That's exactly what I'm suggesting." Hopefully he doesn't hear any anxiety in my voice. "As I'm sure you can understand, I'm quite busy at the moment, so I would likely delegate my side of the negotiating to one of my father's advisors, Lord Kerion. But you have the gist of it."

Once again, he doesn't respond immediately; he stops to smell a flower, while my heart beats against my ribs like a woodpecker against a tree. *He'll agree to it. He has to.*

Eventually, after he's presumably gotten his fill of the scent of that particular orchid, he resumes walking. "I suppose I can consider your suggestion." He turns his head and looks me in the eye, his gaze hard as diamond. "However, while I am willing to negotiate in good faith, I cannot guarantee that I will sign a treaty that doesn't include a provision for a wedding between us. If it becomes impossible to find a compromise that doesn't include marriage, then I will insist we resume discussion of the topic."

"I understand." More importantly, I know it's the best I'm going to get and maybe this will give me time to figure out what he actually wants. "Thank you, Arbois. I appreciate your flexibility. I know this probably isn't what you expected, and I'm grateful you didn't head back to Jirena Sadai at the first sign of trouble."

"Of course, Darien. You and I may be royals, but even we are powerless before the vicissitudes of fortune, and I accept that." He gives me what looks like a genuine smile. "Besides, why would I leave when things are just starting to get interesting?"

# CHAPTER TWENTY

Even though I've only been king for a short time, it's already clear that attending council meetings is my least favorite royal duty. One of the contenders jockeying for position as my second-least-favorite duty is the audiences I hold in the Throne Hall. Everyone in the kingdom is allowed to petition the monarch with their grievances, and a few of them are deemed important enough to warrant my personal attention. For those, the petitioner is called to the palace to present their petition to me in person. I have these audiences twice each week, but they can last anywhere from ten minutes to ten hours, based on how many petitions there are to hear and how complex they are. I dislike them because they're boring—to say the least—but also because whoever designed this part of the palace didn't seem to care for things like 'comfort' and 'airflow.' Even though it's barely summer, it doesn't take long for the room to get stuffy and oppressively hot.

For this particular audience—a few days after my discussion with Arbois—there are only four petitions, which are not terrible, but not ideal either. I try my best to pay attention, but it's not exactly riveting stuff, and the midday heat that's already built up, even though it's before noon, makes it even harder to concentrate. Halfway through the third petition, my mind starts to wander, and my eyes scan the assembled crowd, looking for something, *anything*, interesting. But no, it's just the usual pack of well-dressed people who apparently have nothing better to do than stand around and listen to other people talk for hours on end.

Except, just as I'm about to resign myself to the fact that there really is nothing more interesting in this room than Count Maelke's soliloquy about how some of his best horses were supposedly stolen by a pack of marauding bandits, my eyes land on a woman standing against the wall off to one side of the room. I'm not sure what it is about her that draws my attention—she is nondescript, with shoulder-length blond hair, gray breeches, and a matching jacket. I don't recognize her, but that's not entirely unexpected, given the sheer size of the court and my tendency to avoid meeting new people. At first, she's staring at the crowd intently, but she must have noticed me looking at her, because her eyes flick to me and she nods slightly before turning her attention away again.

I stare at her for a few seconds longer, still not sure exactly why she's captured my attention, until Count Maelke apparently notices I'm not listening to him, and politely clears his throat. I turn my attention—or what's left of it by this point—back to him and try to keep it there while he continues to drone on about his stolen horses, "As I was saying, Your Majesty, I would not be surprised if these bandits were actually Raktosi agents. I have been targeted by the Raktosi before, and ..."

Whatever dregs of energy I had left evaporate as he continues to drone on. I tune him out, paying just enough attention to give the appearance of being engaged, and let my mind wander again. *Hopefully the last petition isn't too bad.*

"You're early," Tag says as I approach him. He stands by one of the fountains in the palace garden, a more-than-welcome sight for sore eyes. "That must have been a quick one. I wasn't expecting you for another hour at least."

"It was shorter than usual," I say. "But it still felt like I was there forever."

He smiles; just seeing it makes love for him swell deep in my heart. "I'm sure you have it bad, but it could be worse. You could, say, have your sister drag you to a vineyard before the crack of dawn so you can get tips on how to maximize wine production on your estate."

"Well, that explains why you were up so early this morning."

He nods, still grinning.

"At least you got to get out of the palace," I continue. I've spent so much time indoors recently that I think I've forgotten what sunshine feels like."

He laughs. "In that case, shall we start walking?"

I nod, and we do as he suggested, following one of the paths that leads away from the palace and deeper into the verdant oasis. Walking together in the garden after audiences has quickly become a tradition for the two of us—although we still don't want anyone to know about our courtship just yet, I don't think I could make it through the petitions if I didn't have this to look forward to, and it's not like it's a secret that we're friends.

We walk slowly, chatting about everything and nothing. The flowers are an explosion of color against the forest green of the sculpted hedges, and the marble statues and fountains sparkle and gleam in the sun. Even though we're not really doing anything special, it's difficult for me to explain just how much I enjoy this, especially coming after two hours of sheer boredom. Although, in truth, I'd probably enjoy doing anything, including sitting through a ten-hour-long audience, as long as Tag was there. I look at him and smile, catching his eye, and he winks back at me.

Other people pass by us, each of them nodding or bowing slightly depending on their station. Occasionally, a guard walks by on patrol, but most of the people here are like me and Tag, nobility and commoners alike strolling in the sun and enjoying the weather. I do my best to politely acknowledge them while keeping my attention on Tag. At one point, it strikes me how different this feels from my walk in the garden with Arbois a few days ago. Granted, I had quite a bit on my mind at the time, and it could certainly have been worse. But being here with Tag just feels so much better, so ... *right*. I definitely needed this.

After we've been walking for maybe fifteen minutes, a woman approaches us. At first, I'm not really paying that much attention, and I assume she's just another person enjoying the fine weather. But instead of walking past us, she stops about ten feet away and bows to me deeply, grabbing my attention. "Your Majesty," she says, a touch of professional respect in her tone. When she straightens up, I see that she's the woman who caught my eye at the audience earlier. "May I have a moment of your time?"

I stop walking, intrigued, and Tag stops beside me. "I suppose so, as long as it's quick. What is it?"

She looks around us; there doesn't seem to be anybody within earshot, but she lowers her voice anyway. "I've just arrived from Zeteyon, and I have something for Your Majesty. King Zeikas instructed me to give it to you personally." Her voice has an accent that I can't quite place. "He said to tell you that it has to do with a message you sent him."

Now I'm definitely intrigued, not least because this could be the first step towards making my courtship with Tag official. "Well? What is it?"

She smiles and steps forward, raising her right arm up as if to hand me something. As she does, the sun flashes off something metallic hidden in her hand—a dagger, barely longer than my own middle finger, but presumably no less deadly for it. Time slows to a crawl as she launches herself toward me and Tag, aiming for my heart, eight feet away, then seven, then six, closing the distance at a worm's crawl, slowly but surely coming ever closer. I want to move, to do something, *anything*, but my body won't respond to any of my commands, like I'm stuck in quicksand. All I can do is watch her get closer, her smile now a leering grimace, four feet away, three, two—

Something silver flickers in the corner of my eye, and a knife blossoms in the would-be assassin's right eye like a steel-gray flower. She stumbles and collapses to the ground, her dagger missing Tag's leg by a few inches. Adrenaline courses through my veins, my senses heightened, as though I can hear every single plant in the garden rustling in the wind.

"Darien!" a voice cries out behind me. "Are you alright?"

I turn toward the newcomer, feeling like the world is moving through molasses, almost afraid of who I'll see.

But it's only Ivy, standing on the path behind me, a stricken expression on her face, and I breathe a huge sigh of relief. She runs to us and stops a few feet away, looking deathly pale. "Are you hurt?" she asks. "Did she get you?"

My heart gallops with residual panic. "I'm fine," I assure her. Tag echoes me, almost as pale as Ivy, looking like he's about to either faint or vomit.

Apparently satisfied, some color returns to Ivy's cheeks, and she exhales deeply. "Good. I'm glad you're both okay." She steps forward, looking at the body lying on the path before us with a hard expression. "You're lucky I was here. Another few seconds, and I think it would have been too late."

"I think you're right." The shock of what just happened hits me, almost like a physical blow, and I can barely get the words out. "Thank you, Ivy. You saved my life."

"It was nothing." Her eyes flicker to the paths around us, the corners of her mouth drawing down. "We might want to continue this conversation somewhere else."

For a bare moment, I'm not sure what she's talking about, until I tear my gaze away from the sight before me and notice a crowd of onlookers has gathered around us. Despite the number of people around, the garden is almost completely silent, the only sounds I hear that of birds singing in the trees and water splashing in one of the fountains a few feet away from us.

"That sounds like a good idea," I agree. "Come on, Tag. Let's all go to my study."

Tag just nods, still looking like he's about to be sick, but he lets me guide him back the way we came with little resistance, Ivy pausing only to alert one of the patrolling guards before returning to us. As we hurry away, I can't stop myself from looking back at the dead woman who tried to kill me, a deep sense of dread and foreboding washing over me at the sight of her body on the gravel.

Not five minutes later, I'm sitting in my study with Tag and Ivy when I hear a voice at the entrance.

"Darien! Are you hurt?" Mother rushes up to me, the concern in her eyes tempered by anger. "What happened?"

"I'm fine," I reply, in what I hope is a reassuring tone. "Not even a scratch."

I motion to a couch and Mother takes a seat, perching on the edge of it, ready to jump up at the first sign that I'm lying about my lack of injuries. She's the last to arrive—Ivy, Tag, and I are all seated already, as are Emma and Kenessa. I sent messengers for the three of them as soon as I got here, and they all came as quickly as I could have hoped. No doubt the news that the king was attacked is already spreading like wildfire throughout the court.

I recount what happened, and when I finish, everyone sits silently, with expressions ranging from shock to fear to anger.

Eventually, Mother turns to her right, facing Ivy. "Thank you for saving my son." The warmth in her voice is a contrast to her dark expression. "We're all in your debt. If Darien had been hurt, after what's already happened..."

Ivy shrugs uncomfortably. "Of course, Your Majesty. But I only did what anyone else would do in that situation. I'm sure Darien would have done the same for me."

"For your sake, I hope we don't get the chance to test that," I say dryly. "If I threw a knife, I'd be more likely to hit *you* than whoever I was aiming for."

"Fair enough. I doubt anyone will be trying to kill me anytime soon, though." She leans forward, her expression grim. "But then, I would have said the same thing about you up until half an hour ago. Why would anyone want you dead so badly that they'd try to assassinate you in broad daylight?"

Mother adds, "I suppose it's possible that she was acting alone, but I doubt it. It's far more likely that someone paid her. I mean no offense to you, Ivy, but I think we should be asking a different question—namely, who would want Darien dead so badly that they'd be willing to pay an exorbitant amount of money to assassinate a king?"

Everyone's silent again as we chew on this question. "You know," I say hesitantly, "she did say Uncle Zeikas sent her. I suppose that could have been a lie, but she must have known about the message we sent him. Do you think ...?"

Mother shakes her head vigorously. "I understand your concern, Darien, but I think I can safely assure you that my own brother didn't try to have you killed. She probably just said that so she could get close enough to hurt you without raising your hackles." She frowns. "Although, if she *did* actually know about the message we sent him, that could indicate that there's a spy in our midst, in addition to a would-be assassin. It's far more likely that it was someone here, in Cedelia, perhaps in the palace itself."

I can't help but shudder. *Now there's a scary thought.* If I'm not safe here, in my own home, then where? Or is this going to be the rest of my life, wondering if there's an assassin around every corner, if all the smiling faces I see around me are waiting to plunge a knife in my back? I wonder if Arbois has to deal with this sort of thing too, or if it's just me.

Thinking about him brings back a memory, one from a time that feels long ago but was, in reality, only a few weeks. "Maybe she wasn't paid to kill me," I say, more to myself than to everyone else. "Maybe she really was the one who wanted me dead."

I look up to see just about everyone staring at me with eyebrows raised.

"What makes you think that, exactly?" Mother asks, tapping a finger lightly against the arm of her chair.

I pause to gather my thoughts. "Back before Samis and Father got sick, I overheard Arbois talking to his steward about a woman who would try to stop him if she found out what he's doing. Maybe the woman he was talking about was the assassin, and she decided to stop *me* instead of him. After all, he can't marry me if I'm dead, right?"

Mother's finger tapping intensifies. "Believe me, Darien, there are many, *many* easier ways to stop a marriage than assassinating one of the betrothed, especially when one of them is a king. And while it wouldn't surprise me to find out that Arbois has an ulterior motive in coming here, I can't imagine that it would be so inimical as to warrant murdering you—or him—in broad daylight to prevent it. Although, I suppose it's possible she was Arbois's lover at some point and he spurned her, and she took it badly enough that killing you seemed like a good option. She certainly wouldn't be the first person to take extreme measures to try to win back an ex-lover. In any event, we need to investigate this. But who can we trust?"

She said that last part like it was a rhetorical question, but I answer her anyway. "Why not have Ivy investigate it? She's already saved my life once, so I think we can trust her. If any of the rest of us start asking questions, people will notice. Ivy can do some snooping without raising half the court's hackles. Besides I think she can handle herself in a fight should it come to that." I turn to Ivy. "Assuming you're willing, of course."

She nods slowly. "I can do that. I can't guarantee that I'll find anything, but I can certainly try."

Mother thinks about it for a moment, then nods. "That sounds like a good idea. In the meantime, I'll start a rumor that the woman in the garden held a grudge against you for some reason. Maybe you denied her petition, or she was a supporter of that Verreenese fool who's declared herself the new empress. Whoever really sent her knows the truth, obviously, but perhaps it will stop the rest of the court from asking questions we can't answer." She claps her hands together once. "Now, unless there's anything else?"

To my surprise, Emma clears her throat. "I may have something to add," she says. "I didn't want to bring this up until I was certain, but I suppose I don't have much of a choice now. Back when we first started hearing about wasting fever cases in the area, I wanted to help, so I did quite a bit of research—not just on how to treat it, but how to recognize the symptoms and prevent others from catching it. After Father and Samis died, I did even more research, just in case someone else in this room got sick too. I'm not an expert by any means, but by now I have a pretty good idea of the disease and how it runs its course. The more I learned, the more I came to realize that Father's and Samis's symptoms didn't quite match up with what we would expect." Her eyes flicker to each of us in turn, as though she's making sure we're listening. "What I'm trying to say is that I don't think Father and Samis ever had wasting fever, much less died from it."

When she stops talking, there's silence for a few heartbeats. "So, if it wasn't wasting fever," I ask, "then what was it?"

Emma looks directly at me, her gaze hard, and, somehow, I know what she's going to say before she says it. "I think they were poisoned."

# CHAPTER TWENTY-ONE

mma's words hang heavy in the air. The room is so quiet that my own heartbeat sounds like a pounding drum. Everyone is looking at her with wide-eyed stares, even Ivy and Tag. *Poisoned*? *That can't be true*! But then, I know Emma, and she wouldn't have said it unless she was sure. *Who would want to poison them*? *And why*?

Eventually, Mother breaks the silence. "Emma, I don't mean to insult you," she says, her voice as tight as a bowstring, "but what you're saying is ... improbable, to say the least. Do you have any evidence?"

Emma meets Mother's gaze as directly as she met mine a moment ago; if she's feeling pressured, she's doing a good job of not showing it. "I understand why you might be skeptical. I almost didn't believe it myself at first. But the more I thought about it, the more it didn't make sense. Quite a few people in the area—and in the palace itself, for that matter—have caught wasting fever in the last few months. Most of the patients I've talked to—or their families, if they've passed away—have said the same thing: they got sick for a few days, maybe a week, *but then they got better*. Then, for some of them, maybe one out of every five or six, it came back, and they got seriously ill. But even the ones who had it worst, even the ones who died, had a day or two where their condition improved." She pauses to take a breath. "On the other hand, once Father and Samis got sick, they just went steadily downhill. If they had wasting fever, there would have been some period where they were feeling better."

"Forgive me, Emma," Kenessa says, "but you said most patients, not all of them. Maybe your father and Samis were the odd ones out."

Emma shakes her head. "I suppose it would be possible if it had happened to one of them, but the chances of them both being outliers is very small."

Mother holds up a hand. "Even if you're correct, that still doesn't tell us what did kill them. What poison do you think was used? And why didn't the healers think of this?"

"I don't think the idea that it was poison ever entered the healers' minds, not when they were busy dealing with so many other patients who actually *did* have wasting fever. I don't blame them for getting it wrong—Samis's and Father's symptoms were very similar, and it would be an easy mistake to make. As for your other question," the corners of Emma's mouth twist down—the tell-tale sign that not knowing is bothering her, "there are any number of things it could be, but I haven't found anything that matches their symptoms exactly. I need to do more research."

"Wait a moment," I say. "How is it that the two of them could be poisoned, but not the rest of us? Someone would have slipped something into their food, right? But Samis usually ate with Kenessa, and Father with Mother. Why didn't the two of you get sick too?"

"Usually, yes," Kenessa replies, "but they went to Fort Alesen right before they got sick, remember? Samis told me they dined with the commander of the garrison one night, but otherwise they ate alone. Someone could have slipped something into their meals without anyone noticing. But then, who at Fort Alesen would want them—or Darien—dead?"

We all chew on this for a few moments before Mother shakes her head. "I find it hard to believe that someone in the Soerian military would assassinate two members of the royal family in such a manner. I suppose it's possible that some disgruntled soldier held a grudge against Tolmir, but for what purpose would they take such a drastic action? How would they benefit from Tolmir and Samis's deaths? Why target Darien, too? It just doesn't make sense."

A thought comes to me, one that's so monstrous I can barely comprehend it. "What if..." My mouth is suddenly as dry as a desert. "What if the person who poisoned them wasn't a soldier?" Five pairs of eyes turn to face me as one. "Didn't a few councilors go with them? I know Rolsteg and Belling did, at least. Samis told me that Rolsteg was acting strange before he left for Fort Alesen! I didn't think of it at the time, but maybe...." I trail off.

Mother finishes the thought for me. "Maybe she was the one who poisoned them? That's not an accusation to be taken lightly. Do you remember exactly what Samis said?"

"He said ..." I close my eyes and try to cast my mind back into that memory of a time that feels like centuries ago. "He, Father, and Arbois had dinner with some of the council, and he said she kept asking Arbois questions about Jirena Sadai the whole night. He told me she was more animated than he'd ever seen her before, and that he thought it was strange. That's all. But if she went to Fort Alesen with Father and Samis, she certainly would have had the opportunity to poison them."

"Forgive me for interrupting, Your Majesty," Ivy says, with a nod to Mother. "But, Darien, why would Archduchess Rolsteg want to hurt you or your family? I can't say I know her all that well, but she'd have to have a pretty good reason if she was willing to murder three members of the royal family."

It's a good question; if someone really did poison Samis and Father and try to have me killed, they'd have to know they'd face execution if they were caught. "Her family made money selling weapons, right? Maybe she's trying to start a war between us and Jirena Sadai so she can turn a profit. Or maybe she's the one that Arbois meant when he said someone was trying to stop him. Or maybe—"

"Or maybe she's perfectly innocent," Mother interrupts, drumming her fingers on the arm of her chair again. "Acting strange at one dinner several weeks ago isn't evidence of regicide. That's *if* Emma is correct that Samis and Tolmir were even poisoned in the first place." Mother holds up a hand just as I open my mouth. "Yes, Darien, I know that someone tried to kill you not half an hour ago, and that clearly *someone* was behind that. I just don't think we should spend too much time speculating wildly when we should be gathering information instead."

*Can't really argue with that.* "In that case, should I talk to Arbois about what I overheard? Maybe he can shed some light on the situation."

Mother thinks about it for a moment, then shakes her head. "No. Not yet, at least. The fewer people who know about this, the better. It's not that I don't trust him, but if someone is really trying to kill members of this family, I don't want them to know that we're onto them. Arbois would certainly want to know why we're asking, and I don't know if he can keep a secret. Let Emma and Ivy see what they can find, and then we'll reassess. I'll keep an eye on Rolsteg, just in case."

Ivy clears her throat. "If I may make a suggestion...?" She waits for Mother to nod before turning to me. "Darien, if someone was willing to attack you here in the palace once, they might try again. I highly recommend that you—and the Queen, and Princesses Emma and Kenessa, for that matter—have guards with you whenever you're not in your rooms. I'd be happy to work with Colonel Belling to choose some dependable soldiers and set up a rotation—you know I'm pretty close with the garrison, and I've got a few choices in mind already."

*Guarded at all times*? It sounds horrible, like I need to be babysat in my own home. What if I want to take a walk alone, or have some private time with Tag? I don't want to be followed around the palace whenever I leave my rooms, as though I need to be watched to ensure I don't steal anything.

But then, I can't deny that I was attacked not half an hour ago in my own garden, and that it probably would have been prevented if I had had guards with me. "I suppose I can handle it," I say slowly. "At least until we find out who's behind this and deal with them."

"I agree," Mother says. "We may not enjoy it, but it's far better to be annoyed than dead."

"Alright then, I guess that's settled." I turn back to Ivy. "What about you, though? Shouldn't you have guards too?" I purposefully don't mention Tag—only the two of us and Mother know about our courtship, and I don't want to put a target on his back by making everyone wonder why he needs security. But Ivy, on the other hand... "Whoever sent the assassin after me might try to retaliate against you for stopping their plans."

Ivy shakes her head. "I appreciate the thought, Darien, but I think it would be a bad idea. If I'm to investigate who sent the assassin, having guards around me all the time would bring unwanted attention." She smiles tightly. "Besides, I can handle myself in a fight."

With that, the conversation ends, and everyone begins to leave my study, their expressions ranging from grim to determined. But I remain seated, and before Tag can get more than a step or two away from me, I reach out and stop him with a hand. "Can I talk to you for a moment?"

He nods and resumes his seat on the couch next to me, looking only a little less pale than he did before. Once he's settled, I take his hand in mine. "Are you alright?" I ask quietly, trying not to sound too worried. "You've barely said two sentences since ... since we left the garden."

He shakes himself as though he's trying to wake up from a deep sleep. "I'm fine." But his expression contradicts his words. "I'm just a little rattled, I guess. It's not like this sort of thing happens every day, you know. And..."

I give him a chance to complete the sentence, but he remains silent. "And what?"

He opens his mouth as if to say something, then closes it again.

"It's okay," I say, as gently as I possibly can. "Whatever it is, you can tell me."

He seems to notice that I'm holding his hand and gives mine a light squeeze. "I'm sorry," he says, his voice almost as quiet as a whisper. "It's just that when that woman..." He gulps audibly. "When she attacked you, for just a split second it was like I had this, this *vision* of my life without you in it, and I..." He looks down for a moment; when he looks back up, there are tears running down his cheeks. "When I first came here, I thought I was going to stay here for a year, perhaps two at most. I figured I would meet some of Riella's friends, and maybe make a few of my own, but I always knew that before too long I would go back to my family's estate in Zeteyon. All I wanted to do was live out in the country, away from all the noise and craziness and crowds, and if someone told me that, for the rest of my life, I'd never see a city again, I'd have been okay with that. But then I met you, and that changed everything. I never expected I would fall in love with anyone here, much less a member of the royal family, but I did. Now the thought of not being with you is..." He takes a deep breath; it seems to calm him a bit. "When she attacked you, I thought that if you died, I wouldn't know what I'd do. I love you so much, and I don't want anything to happen to you. What if whoever sent her sends another once they find out you're still alive? How do you know the next one won't succeed where she failed?"

I wrap my arms around him and pull him close to me. "Nothing's going to happen to me," I say soothingly. "You heard Mother. I'll have guards around me all the time from now on. Until we catch whoever did this, at least. But in the meantime, nobody's going to hurt me."

"I want to believe that." he says, his voice muffled. He pulls away from me, just enough so he can look directly into my eyes. "But even if you're right, I still might lose you. I know you sent that message to your uncle, but what if he says no, or doesn't respond at all? How long would it be until the council insists that you marry Arbois or some other prince instead?"

I take his face gently in my hands and kiss him deeply on the lips. "That will *never* happen, my love," I say, my voice quiet, yet firm. "I won't let it. I promise you."

Tag gives me a hesitant smile, seemingly reassured by my answer. But, for a moment, I feel like the assassin's dagger did manage to strike me in the heart, because deep down, I know that no matter how much I want to, I might not be able to keep that promise in the end.

# CHAPTER TWENTY-TWO

The days after the assassination attempt are ... tense, to say the least. As Mother suggested, I now have guards around me pretty much all the time, except when I'm in my own chambers. Even then, they stand outside, presumably ready to stop any assassins who are stupid enough to try to walk through my main door. At first, it's disconcerting to have them around all the time, but, after a while, I get used to their presence, to the point where I can almost forget that they're there sometimes. What's more disconcerting is that I need them in the first place. The palace is my home—and always has been, no matter how much I dislike it at times—and it feels like it's the one place where I should be safe. Now, I wonder whether I'm safe anywhere, if there are going to be people trying to murder me no matter where I go.

Beyond that, most of the court seems to be on edge. It doesn't take long before just about everyone knows I was attacked, even if the details twist and turn with repeated telling and rumors about who might have done it abound, each one wilder than the next. I don't like the constant whispering, but in truth it would have been nearly impossible to prevent the people from finding out about the attack considering it was in the middle of the garden, in broad daylight, and in full view of the public.

The fact that Samis and Father may have been poisoned, however, is a completely different matter. Unless one of the healers happens to come to the same revelation that Emma did, there's no reason for anyone to think their deaths were anything but natural. The six of us who know are still keeping it under wraps, at least until we know more.

Part of me wants to tell the council—well, some of them, at least—about our suspicions, in the hopes they can help us find the perpetrator. If Rolsteg really *is* behind this, it would be a good idea to have as much help as we can. I'd have to choose who I told very carefully, and I'd have to swear them to secrecy, yet if there's any chance they can help uncover the truth, it might be worth it.

But when I run this idea by Mother, she shuts it down immediately. "Just for the record, I think you're wrong about Rolsteg," she says. "Even if you are right, though, it will look extremely bad for you to be accusing a member of the council without much in the way of proof. I mean it, Darien—if there's one thing you don't need right now, it's a power struggle with the council. Those almost never end well for the monarch. If it turns out that it wasn't her, you'd have gained nothing and lost quite a bit."

"What if I just tell them that we suspect Father and Samis were poisoned, without telling them who we think did it? Would that work?"

She thinks about it for a moment. "That's a better idea, but now is not the right time. For the moment, we don't know if it's true, and we don't want to stir the pot when we're not sure whether doing so is a good idea. To be honest, even if Emma were to walk into this room right now with clear proof that their deaths weren't natural, I might still advise you not to tell the council. I'm sure Belling or Voeli or whoever could be helpful, but I doubt they could keep it a secret for very long. Someone would inevitably let it slip, and if the poisoner gets wind that we're onto them, they might be able to get away before we can catch them."

It's not what I wanted to hear, but I know she's right. Still, I can't stop myself from surreptitiously paying closer attention to Rolsteg's actions during the council meetings in the days after the assassination attempt, but she gives nothing away. Sure, she seems a bit rattled—*maybe she's upset that I'm still here?*—but then, so does everyone, and I don't really blame them after all that's happened recently. Either Rolsteg is very good at hiding her guilty conscience, or she's actually innocent.

All in all, it's a very stressful few days, to say the least. So, when Ivy comes to my study four days after the attempt on my life, nodding to the guards standing outside my door as she walks in, I'm starting to feel desperate.

"Please tell me you have something for me," I say.

To my great relief, she nods. "You might not like it, though," she says. "May I sit?"

I nod, and she takes a seat near mine.

"I know you're anxious for news," she continues, "so I'll get straight to the point. I figured a good place to start would be discreetly asking around at some of the city's inns to see if any of them had a visitor who matched the assassin's description. It turns out someone matching her description was staying at one called the Weary Traveler, under the name Moira—who knows whether that was her real name or just a pseudonym, but either way I'm pretty sure she was the same woman who tried to kill you. The innkeeper remembered her surprisingly well, as apparently on the day of the assassination attempt, the room where she was staying was completely cleaned out by two men claiming to be friends of hers, and that made an impression on him." She leans forward, grimacing a bit. "That means that whoever sent her is in Cedelia. Or, they at least have accomplices here since they were able to clear out her room so quickly. Whoever it was probably sent those men as soon as they heard that she failed, so they could get rid of anything that could identify her."

*Someone in the city itself? That's much closer than I'd like.* "That's not good, although I suppose I should have expected it. They really didn't leave anything behind?"

Ivy gives me a faint grin. "Actually, I did find one thing," she says, reaching into her back pocket. "It was hidden behind a dresser, hard to reach even for me. The men who cleaned out the room probably just missed it."

She holds out her hand and drops a small, cold object into my hand. A golden coin. *And is that?* I hold it up to get a better look. The sunlight streaming in from a nearby window shines on an engraving of a young woman with an austere face, who looks quite a bit like Arbois. "It's Jirenian," I say softly, more to myself than Ivy. "Does that mean whoever hired her is from Jirena Sadai?"

"No idea," Ivy replies, shrugging. "I don't know if that coin has anything to do with Moira—if that is her name—or even with the person who sent her. For all I know, it could have been there for years."

"That's true. But it's the only evidence we have so far." I stare at it for a moment longer, then shake myself a bit. "Thank you, Ivy. Keep investigating and see what you can come up with."

She nods but doesn't leave immediately. "Darien, I know you're trying to keep this quiet, but do you think it might be a good idea to get the city garrison involved? I'm happy to keep investigating, but I'm only one person. I could pick out a few trustworthy soldiers to help. We don't even need to tell them the whole story—just enough so they know what to look for."

I think silently for a few moments before shaking my head. "It's not that I don't trust you—or the army, for that matter—but I think it would be best to keep this on a need-to-know basis, at least for now. If things escalate, then maybe I'll change for mind. But for now, let's keep the army out of it."

"Fair enough. I'll let you know if I find anything." With that, she goes, leaving me to consider the mystery that's now on my hands.

I know Ivy was right that this coin might mean nothing, but, for the moment, I have to assume it's connected to Moira somehow. Yet, making that assumption raises a slew of new questions that I'm not sure I can answer. Of course, it's possible that whoever's really behind all this—whether it's Rolsteg or someone else—isn't actually Jirenian, but that they paid Moira in Jirenian coins because they wanted to throw me off their trail, or because it's just what they happened to have on hand. Besides, the only Jirenians I know in Cedelia—excepting the ambassador and her staff—are Arbois and his steward, and I can't imagine why either of them would want to kill me. Maybe if Arbois had come here for some other reason, I could believe it, but he can't marry me if I'm dead. Even if we were already married, it's not like he'd gain anything from my death. Maybe Rolsteg or the Jirenian government don't want us to get married for some reason? I would think there would be much easier ways to derail the negotiations than to assassinate a king. Still, I suppose it's possible...

To make things more complicated, there was that time I heard Arbois telling someone that if he wasted too much time here, "she" would find out what he's doing, and try to stop him. It's possible that was unrelated to what's happening now, but it's not like I have anything else to go on. At the time, I thought he might have been referring to his sister, the Queen of Jirena Sadai, or perhaps a spurned lover. Thinking about it now, the former wouldn't really make sense—even if Arbois did come here without his sister's knowledge, I'm pretty sure she could figure out a way to stop him that doesn't involve killing me.

On the other hand, if Arbois really does have a jealous ex-lover, depending on who she is, she might see me as an obstacle to them getting back together. If she's rich or powerful enough, this mystery woman might have decided to pay Moira to kill me in the hopes that Arbois would end up with her instead.

Now that I think about it, there's a third option—what if he was referring to Rolsteg herself? But then, she obviously knows he's here to marry me, so what exactly would he be trying to keep from her? *If only I had more information.* I distantly realize that I'm pacing, my hands clenched into fists. *Then I could stop wondering if tomorrow's going to be the day someone tries to kill me again.* I run a hand through my hair, barely noticing the slight pain where my fingernails have bitten into my palm. *But how to get it?*

Just like that, it comes to me, and my mind is made up. I get up and walk out of my study so fast I'm almost running, afraid that if I slow down, I'll realize how idiotic my idea is and stop myself from carrying it out. I can't let that happen, because now is not the time for caution.

The man who answers my knock on Arbois's door a few minutes later is quite tall—at least half a foot taller than me—burly, and completely bald except for a thick, red mustache. I ask if Arbois is available, and he bows to me, his eyes never leaving mine.

"Unfortunately, His Grace is not present at the moment," he says, his voice deep and low. Hearing it, I realize that he must have been the person I overheard Arbois talking with so long ago. "However, I believe he will return shortly. If Your Majesty would like, you can wait for him in his study." He gestures me forward when I nod. "Please follow me, then."

He silently guides me to Arbois's study, bows to me again, and leaves me alone. *Just as I hoped.* I wait for a full minute, just to be sure he's not going to come back anytime soon, before I hesitantly walk over to Arbois's desk, not entirely sure what I'm looking for, or that I should even be looking for anything in the first place.

Pushing down my moral qualms, I look through the stack of papers on the desk. Fortunately, it's already rather cluttered, so I don't think I have to worry that Arbois will notice that I went through his things.

At first, all I find seems innocuous—history books, notes from the marriage negotiations, that sort of thing. I scan through these quickly, hoping to find even a drop of useful information, but nothing jumps out at me. *There has to be something here.*

Five minutes pass, then ten, and the courage I mustered slowly trickles away like sand in an hourglass. I'm starting to debate whether I should just give up on this ridiculous scheme when I shift a couple papers, uncovering a letter. At first glance, it looks no different from any of the other papers from his desk, but a familiar name pops out at me, and I pick the paper up and read it without giving myself time to change my mind.

Your Grace,

As per your suggestion, I spoke with King Zeikas again today; to my great surprise, he was much more amenable to our proposal than he was just two days ago. I don't know how Your Grace knew the situation would change so quickly, but I suppose it is of little importance in the end. I would caution Your Grace that there are still substantial hurdles that must be overcome, especially given Zeikas's current preoccupation with the Khorians. Perhaps this is a good thing, however—the faster we move, the more likely it is that she will find out what we are doing and attempt to stop us. In any event, I will keep Your Grace updated should any further developments occur.

Sincerely,
Lord Bargadon
Ambassador to Zeteyon

I read it once, then a second time, before I put the letter back where it was on the desk, my scalp prickling. What could Arbois be proposing to Zeikas? And what made Zeikas change his mind about whatever it is? It could be anything—Zeikas and Arbois are both representatives of their nations, and nations make agreements with each other all the time.

Then there's another reference to the mysterious 'she,' who might try to stop him. I thought it might have been a lover, but that doesn't fit with what I just read—why would she want to stop a hypothetical agreement between Zeteyon and Jirena Sadai? It could be referring to Arbois's sister, the queen. But why would he need to conduct diplomacy behind her back? *What am I missing?*

I'm so deep in thought I nearly jump out of my skin when I hear a voice behind me. "Hello, Darien," Arbois says. "I certainly didn't expect to see *you* in my study."

My heart now racing almost as fast as my mind, I turn to see Arbois standing by the door, his eyes narrowed in suspicion. "I just came to ask you if you wanted to go tour the palace art collection," I tell him, somehow managing to keep my voice even. "I would have sent a message, but I was walking by your rooms, and I figured it would save time to just ask you in person. Your steward said I could wait for you here."

His cryptic expression lasts for another second before he breaks into a smile that doesn't quite reach his eyes. "Ah, you met Tholin, then? He told me that you came by here, but I didn't quite believe him. In any event, I'd love to look at some art with you, but I'm busy at the moment. Are you available later this afternoon, perhaps?"

I nod, my heart still galloping. He's still smiling at me, but his eyes search mine as though he's trying to read my mind. "That sounds wonderful. Just let me know when you're free."

Maybe I'm imagining it, but for just a second, his smile reminds me of a hungry wolf staring at its prey. "That sounds like an excellent idea. I'll have a message sent to your rooms."

"Perfect." I try my hardest to fake an easy grin. "In that case, I'll take my leave."

He nods and steps out of the doorway. I walk past him out of the study, not sure whether to be grateful or annoyed at my near miss. Either way, an uneasy feeling lingers in the pit of my stomach, and I can still feel his eyes on my back for a long time afterwards.

# CHAPTER TWENTY-THREE

"D
arien, do you have a moment?"

I look up from the report I'm reading, my eyes bleary and my mind half-asleep, to see Emma. She's holding a rather large book and is clearly wide awake despite the late hour. I'm sure she's come to deliver bad news—that seems to be the only kind of news people deliver to me these days—but at least whatever it is will occupy my attention for a little while. It's been about ten hours since I almost got caught snooping through Arbois's desk, and that sense of malaise still hasn't gone away completely. "I suppose I do. What is it?"

She comes over to my desk, her steps almost bouncing with energy. Now that she's closer, I can see the complex mixture of emotions in her expression: excitement and fear and relief and anxiety among others; just seeing her this way makes me feel more alert.

"Sorry for bothering you so late," she says, "but I'm pretty sure I just found what I've been looking for."

Some of my fatigue drops away, and I blink a few times. "You mean..."

She nods. "Yes. I think I know which poison was used to kill Father and Samis."

As soon as the words are out of her mouth, I feel like I'm falling, like I'm tumbling untethered through the night air. "Well? What did you find?"

She plonks the book down on my desk in front of me and opens it to a page marked with a small piece of cloth. "Here. Take a look for yourself."

I do. The page is mostly covered with dense, tiny text, although there are a few spaces where the text is interrupted by drawings of what appears to be a rather ordinary-looking mushroom. The words are so small and close to each other that I can barely read it even if I squint, and it doesn't take long before I give up on trying to read it and turn back to Emma. "I think you're just going to have to tell me what it says."

She sighs and points to one of the drawings. "It's called a death cap," she says, her tone as serious as I've ever heard it. "As you can probably guess from the name, it's extremely deadly—maybe as little as half of one could kill a person, and the antidote is extremely rare. Plus, it tastes perfectly fine—if it were mixed into a soup or something and you ate it, you wouldn't even notice that something was wrong. Plus, it takes a few days for the poison to do its work, so most people who eat it don't even make the connection between the innocuous mushroom they ate with dinner last week and their symptoms." She runs a hand through her hair. "Speaking of which, assuming that book is right, then the symptoms of death cap poisoning match up *exactly* with what Father and Samis had—the jaundice, the fever, the vomiting, all of it. I thought it would be obvious once I found it, but this..." She taps the page lightly with a knuckle. "It's like it was staring me in the face. I'm almost angry at myself for not figuring it out earlier."

"You would have said that even if you found it ten minutes after you started your research," I tell her. "Is it rare? If it is, and we know where it grows, that could be a clue as to who might have done it."

She shakes her head. "They're not exactly common, but I wouldn't say they're rare either. I think there might even be a few growing in the palace garden, but I'm not sure. I certainly wouldn't be surprised if there were."

Well, that doesn't narrow it down much. *In fact...* "Wait a moment. If they grow around here, could it just have been an accident?"

"I suppose it's possible, but it seems unlikely given both of their deaths. I assume most of the farmers who supply the palace kitchens know enough to avoid them. If for whatever reason they did make a mistake, I can't see how only Father and Samis would have gotten sick, and no one else. No, it has to have been intentional."

"Alright, I'll take your word for it." I lean back. "What's the next step, then?"

"I'm ... not sure." Emma frowns deeply; I know her well enough to tell that she's not upset with me so much as the situation. "Has Ivy found anything?"

"Not really." I briefly summarize Ivy's investigation so far, and, after a moment's hesitation, add in the letter I found on Arbois's desk. Maybe she'll see something that I didn't. "I'm not sure whether any of it's connected," I conclude. "If it is, I can't see how."

She ponders it for a moment, her analytical mind presumably working through all the evidence we've gathered. "Have you considered that Rolsteg or whoever might be trying to frame Arbois?" she finally asks. "The letter could have been about anything. Plus, it's not like it's that difficult to get Jirenian coins, especially since the one Ivy found might have been planted. Maybe Rolsteg, or even Raktos or Verreene, wants to prevent an alliance between us and Jirena Sadai for some reason."

"Do you really think they'd want to stop us so much that they'd be willing to assassinate three members of the royal family? There have to be less extreme ways to stop a marriage and why would they kill Father and Samis too, not just me?"

She shrugs. "I don't know, Darien. It's not very much to go on, but I promise you I'll keep thinking about it."

I close my eyes and let out a breath. "I know you will," I say, my voice quiet. I open my eyes again. "You did a good job figuring out what the poison was, and I know that if anyone can make sense of this whole mess, it's you."

"Thank you," she says, a faint smile creasing her face for a brief moment. "We'll figure it out together." She takes the book from my desk, carefully marking the page with the piece of cloth that was there before. "Now, if you'll excuse me, I'm going to tell Mother what I found."

She leaves me sitting alone in my study, more than exhausted, even though I know I won't be sleeping anytime soon.

The following days pass slowly, each one seeming to last a week, as I wait for a response from Zeikas. In the meantime, negotiations with Arbois continue. Just as I told Arbois, I don't attend them personally—instead, Lord Kerion acts as my representative. He gives me updates every so often and continues to perform much the same role he did for Father.

His experience is a great help, and I trust him completely when it comes to handling matters of state.

Although in truth, when it comes to the negotiations with Arbois, he hasn't had much to update me on recently. From what he tells me, Arbois doesn't seem *too* keen on making a deal that doesn't include a marriage. Which isn't entirely surprising, considering he came here specifically to marry me. Still, it seems he's still at least willing to entertain the idea, so that's something.

The problem is that as the days pass, the fact that Arbois is still willing to humor me feels like the only thing that's even remotely going my way. Despite their best efforts, Ivy and Emma don't make any further progress on their respective investigations, and the guards that surround me for nearly all my waking hours are a constant reminder that I'm no longer safe in my own home.

The stress builds and builds until finally, one morning a few days after Emma's discovery, as I'm reviewing an extremely dry routine report from Colonel Belling on the state of the city's garrison, something in me snaps, and I decide that I need to take a break if I want to stop myself from going insane, even if it's just for a few hours. I lean back in my chair and rub my eyes as I try to think of something that will take my mind off my work.

As I'm idly thinking, I look out one of the study windows, with a view of the city and the fields beyond. My gaze falls on a cliff not far outside the city walls, covered in green, and in a flash I realize that I know exactly what I want to do. I get up without a second thought and walk out of my study, more than ready to leave my worries behind for a few hours.

I head toward the suite the Learas are occupying, my steps already feeling lighter than they were before. Two guards follow me, close enough to intervene should anything happen but far enough away to be unobtrusive. Well, mostly unobtrusive. It occurs to me that I'm going to have to convince them to stay back once Tag and I have reached our destination; I'm very glad that they're taking their jobs seriously, but if I'm going to take a break from everything, I want it to be just me and Tag, without anyone else intruding. Fortunately, the place where we're going isn't exactly dangerous, and I expect we'll be the only people there, so hopefully the guards will relax a bit and leave us alone.

I'm so caught up in my thoughts that I almost walk past the Learas' rooms. Shaking my head a bit, I go to knock on the wide wooden door.

But before I can touch the wood, I hear a familiar voice coming from farther down the hall. *What is Arbois doing around here?* I can't see him, and he's far enough away that I can't make out what he's saying, but I'm sure it's him. I lower my hand and walk toward his voice, letting my feet guide me rather than my mind. As I get closer, I hear someone else talking—whoever it is, their voice sounds familiar, but I don't recognize it off the top of my head. Neither voice sounds particularly angry, although it's hard to tell from this far away.

The voices get louder as I walk down the hallway, away from the Learas' rooms, but I still can't make out what they're saying. At first, I'm not quite sure where the voices are coming from, but as I approach an intersection, they get louder, so I stop walking and peek around the corner. There, about fifteen feet down the corridor, is Arbois, his back turned to me; facing him is Rolsteg. They're speaking quietly enough that I still can't quite make out what they're saying, but seeing Rolsteg only increases my curiosity. What in the world could they be talking about?

I pull my head back for the moment so they can't see me snooping, debating whether I want to try to get closer and find out. There's a chance that it's innocuous—as far as I know, Rolsteg's family does quite a bit of business in Jirena Sadai—but no matter what Mother says, I still don't trust her. *She can't be the woman who's trying to stop him, can she? Or is she trying to draw him into her plot?* Either way, I have to know what they're saying. It seems like it would be difficult to get much closer to them without being seen, but maybe I could circle around and try to listen from the other end of the corridor they're standing. Or maybe I could have one of the guards walk by and hope they ignore her. Or I could—

Someone touches my arm, interrupting my train of thought, and I almost jump out of my skin. I turn to see Riella standing there with a concerned expression.

"Are you alright?" she asks. "You looked like you were a thousand miles away. Is something wrong?"

Presumably the others heard her, because Arbois's voice cuts off as soon as Riella speaks. "I'm fine," I tell Riella. "I heard someone talking and I thought I recognized the voice. I just wanted to see who it was." Almost involuntarily, I peek around the corner again, only to see Arbois and Rolsteg both walking down the corridor, away from me and Riella.

I turn back to Riella, feeling absurdly disappointed. *I'll have to figure out what she's up to some other way.* "Actually, I was coming to see if Tag is available. Do you know if he's around?"

"He is, in fact. He's in the drawing room reading some enormously book. Or at least, that's what he was doing when I left a minute ago. Why, did you want to ask him something?" She points back down the hallway, in the direction that I came from. "Also, you do know our rooms are *that* way, right?"

"Yes, I am aware of that," I reply, rolling my eyes at her, while at the same time hoping she doesn't notice that something's off. "And to answer your question, I was planning on asking him if he wants to go riding with me. I need to take a break from the paperwork that's piling up on my desk, and I figured it would be nice to have someone to talk to."

Her eyes light up. "Oh, how nice of you!" she exclaims. "I'm glad you thought of him. Although, I guess you two have been spending a lot of time together lately, haven't you? See, I knew you two would be good friends."

I honestly can't tell if she's implying that she knows about us, or if I should just take her words at face value, so I err on the side of caution. "We have been. It's nice to have someone to talk to about things other than work. Besides you and Ivy, I mean."

She nods. I think her smile might be a bit wider than it was before, but I can't be certain. "That's understandable. Well, I hope you two have fun. You're going riding, huh? Give Laya a treat for me. I assume she's still your favorite?"

"Yes, she is," I say, a bit defensively. "Just because she's deaf doesn't mean she's not a good horse, or whatever it is people think. You know I love her anyway."

She pats me on the arm. "I'm sure you do. It's just nice to know that *some* things haven't changed. Now, come on. Let's go find my brother and see if he's available."

Although Tag seems a bit surprised to see me in the middle of the day, he readily accepts my offer to go riding. After bidding Riella goodbye, we head to the stables. While the grooms are saddling Kemi and Laya, as well as two horses for my guards, a servant arrives from the kitchen with a basket of food. Once the horses are ready to go, we're off. Tag doesn't ask where we're going, but I think he can probably guess.

When we reach our destination half an hour or so later, a pang of nostalgia hits me, even though it hasn't been very long since last we were here. The sea of flowers looks much the same as it did back then, which feels strange, considering everything else about my life has changed. After we dismount, I ask the guards to give us some privacy. It only requires a little bit of convincing; the four of us are the only ones in sight, and nobody other than me knew we were coming here.

Tag and I take a blanket and the food to the rock where we sat last time, atop the cliff overlooking the city. The weather is beautiful, as is the company, and I can already feel some of my stress melting away. We talk as we eat, about upcoming balls, our favorite books, his home in Zeteyon—nothing of consequence, but it doesn't need to be. All I want right now is to spend some time with him and forget the burden of being king.

To my surprise, it works. Not completely—I don't think that burden, that weight on my shoulders, will ever be fully gone—but somewhat. *I needed this.*

But as I look at Tag, his face alight with laughter as I tell him just how many times Ivy has beaten me at knife throwing, I realize that I need him, too. Not too long ago, he told me that he didn't know what he'd do without me, and I know that the reverse is true too. If I can't convince Arbois to make a deal, if I can't convince the council that Tag is acceptable, then I'll—

I shake my head. *Not now*, I think to myself. *Worry about all that later. For now, just enjoy being with the man you love.*

If only it were that easy.

By the time Tag and I return to the palace a couple hours later, I feel surprisingly refreshed. When we part ways, I don't kiss him or anything—not in the palace, where someone might see us—but as he turns to go, for a moment all I can think about is how much I love him, and how lucky I am to have found him. Even the possibility of an arranged marriage seems more distant, less scary. I doubt this feeling will last very long, but I'm going to enjoy it while it does.

I walk back into my rooms feeling much better than I did when I left, my guards taking their usual post outside the door. I head to my study, ready to make some headway on the mountain of papers on my desk.

I've only been here for a couple minutes when Joram enters and bows to me. "Forgive me for interrupting, Your Majesty," he says. "A messenger arrived shortly after Your Majesty left and dropped off a message." He holds a bone-white scroll, sealed in red wax with an imprint of a fox, shorter than my forearm.

I take it from him, my heart already pounding in my chest. *That's the royal seal of Zeteyon—it must be a response from Zeikas!* "Thank you, Joram," I say, my voice shaking a bit as I break open the seal. I have to marvel at the perfect timing—if this message says what I hope it says, it'll be the icing on the cake. *Please, let it say he'll renew the alliance.*

It takes a while to open the scroll since my hands shaking in anticipation, but once it's open, I immediately start reading.

It's a short message, but I read it once, then reread it twice more, just to make sure I didn't completely misread it the first time. My heart sinks further and further each time I do. "Joram, please go find my mother and tell her I need to see her." Unlike before, my voice is perfectly flat, without even a hint of a tremor. "*Now.*"

# CHAPTER TWENTY-FOUR

Mother's eyebrows rise higher and higher as she reads the message once, then a second time. *Glad to know I wasn't the only one who did a double take.* Some small part of me was hoping she'd tell me I'm overreacting, or that there's some important factor that I missed, but based on her reaction I'm guessing that's not the case.

After finishing, she wordlessly hands it back to me. I don't need to read the message again, but I do anyway.

King Darien,

Please allow me to offer my condolences on the unfortunate deaths of your father and brother. They were both taken before their time, and all Zeteyon mourns with you.

Still, just because we share your grief, it does not mean that we will blindly act against our own interests. To that end, I regret to inform you that I find your proposal to renew the alliance between our two nations to be most objectionable and, to be frank, mildly insulting. What you suggest would be highly detrimental to Zeteyon, and I cannot in good conscience agree to it. Therefore, I consider the alliance between our two nations to be ended.

Zeikas, King of Zeteyon

Mother and I continue to sit in silence for a little while longer, until she finally says, "Are you certain this is real? Zeikas can be standoffish at times, but this is completely unlike him."

I'd be lying if I said I hadn't had similar thoughts. "Joram said the messenger who delivered it bore papers with proper identification. Besides, the seal is correct, and that would be hard to fake. I suppose we have to accept that it's real. Unless you think differently?"

She shakes her head, and any tiny hope I had clung to that this is a fake vanishes.

"I knew there was a chance Uncle Zeikas wouldn't want to renew the alliance, but how was my letter insulting? I didn't think there was anything objectionable in it, and neither did you."

"Of course I didn't. That's because it was a perfectly reasonable request. I can't imagine how he would find anything in it even remotely insulting." She grimaces. "This just doesn't seem like him. Perhaps I just don't know my brother as well as I think I do."

"You don't really think that's true, do you?"

Her eyes meet mine for a second before she looks down and sighs. "No, probably not. I suppose it's possible that he's gone a bit mad. Or maybe his response doesn't reflect his true feelings—perhaps it was written by someone else, or perhaps he has some political reason for rejecting an alliance that we can't even guess at. But in any event, it's not good."

*Don't I know it.* "Should we write him another letter? Or maybe have our ambassador in Osella go see if they can placate him?"

"I doubt it would do any good. Once he's made up his mind on something, he can be very difficult to sway. I may not know him as well as I used to, but I doubt that much, at least, has changed." She pauses thoughtfully. "Although..."

I wait for her to continue, but when she doesn't, I prod. "Yes?"

She thinks for a few seconds more before snapping back to reality. "Nothing. Just a silly idea." She reaches out and puts her hand on my knee while her gaze meets mine. "Darien, you know what this means. If we don't have the alliance with Zeteyon to fall back on, we'll have to create another. And right now, the best option for that is..."

I taste ashes in my mouth. "I know. Jirena Sadai."

"You don't have to do anything just yet. There's no reason to act rashly as long as Arbois is still interested. Besides, there's still a chance, even if it's a small one, that we'll find out this letter is a hoax." Her gaze, as cold as ice, holds mine fast. "But if it eventually comes to a point where you must choose between marrying Arbois or leaving Soeria vulnerable to attack, there is only one choice you can make. You cannot throw away the country's security just so you can marry someone you love."

"I understand." *This is why I never wanted to be king.* "I just hope it never gets to that point."

"I hope so as well, and I'm going to work my hardest to make sure it doesn't. In the meantime, we'll need to keep this between the two of us. We don't want anyone to hear about this just yet, including the council. But I promise you I'll do what I can to fix this situation."

A few tears start to form in my eyes; I'm not sure whether they're from gratitude for Mother's words or sadness at the thought that I might actually have to marry Arbois. "Thank you, Mother," I reply. "If we're lucky, nobody will find out for a while, and we can keep delaying while we figure out what to do."

I should have known better than to count on luck being on my side.

It starts, unsurprisingly, at a council meeting. By this point, I've accepted the fact that they're boring, and made peace with it. Sometimes, I even appreciate it. When things get interesting, that usually means something bad has happened, and I do not need more bad things in my life right now.

This particular meeting, held three days after I received the disappointing response from Uncle Zeikas, starts off just as boring as the rest of them. Lord Boyhont gives the council an update on the ongoing repairs of the city walls. Count Haeron tells a rambling story that doesn't seem to have a point. Or an ending, for that matter. Duchess Badami requests funds for a school to be built in her hometown of Elikot. That sort of thing.

But just as I'm starting to think I might get away with only a minor headache, Archduchess Rolsteg clears her throat. I can feel hair starting to rise on the back of my neck as she looks at me with a gleam in her eyes.

"Excuse me, Your Majesty," she says, idly playing with her long, brown hair. "I recently heard news that I found very concerning, and I would like to present it to the rest of the council. Hopefully Your Majesty or another councilor can confirm that it is false."

*Does this have something to do with her and Arbois's little chat?* I have no idea what she's up to, but I'm sure it won't be good. "Go ahead, Rolsteg. What is this news?"

She pauses for a bare second, and my heart starts to drop in anticipation. "What I heard, Your Majesty, is that our alliance with Zeteyon no longer exists."

The reaction to her words is as if a bomb went off in the room. Everyone except Rolsteg and myself starts talking loudly, their voices clamoring to be heard immediately. I can't make out what any one person is saying, and they all look either confused, frightened, or disbelieving. Meanwhile, Rolsteg herself does her best to adopt an innocent expression, but I know it's fake. Even if she didn't have anything to do with Father and Samis dying—which I seriously doubt by this point—she must have read the message I received from Zeikas. *But how?*

Then it comes to me. *I wonder if she's been spying on our mail?* That would explain how she found out so quickly. The thought makes me even more furious than I already am, but I try my best to keep it contained. It won't help if I accuse her of being up to no good here and now, without any definitive proof. Besides, I need to figure out how I'm going to respond to this.

It doesn't take me long to realize that I can't lie to the council—they're going to find out the truth sooner or later, and if I lie or evade their questions, they won't trust me later on. In the meantime, I just have to wait for them to calm down enough that I can regain control of this meeting.

It appears Countess Voeli is having similar thoughts, because once the room has quieted somewhat, she says, "Everyone, settle down!" Surprisingly, they actually do get quiet; I silently thank her for her intervention. "That would certainly be concerning," she continues, "*if* it's true. It could just be a rumor, however. There's no point in arguing until we have more information. Rolsteg, where did you hear of this?"

To her credit, Rolsteg doesn't wither under Voeli's unyielding stare. "I met with the Zeteyoni ambassador yesterday. He seemed surprised that I didn't already know about it."

Voeli nods, apparently satisfied, but I know that's a blatant lie. Mother said Zeikas keeps him out of the loop, so he may not even know about the alliance being broken just yet. Besides, from what she told me, I doubt that an indolent fool like Tolren would deign to meet with Rolsteg even if he did know—it would be too much like work for him. I need to find out the truth and stop her before she manages to completely destroy my position.

All this goes through my head in a couple seconds while the rest of the council digests the new information. Then Rolsteg turns to me. "Perhaps Your Majesty could clear up the matter for the council?"

I take a moment before I answer, trying and failing to calm myself down a bit. *This is very bad.* "Unfortunately, what you heard is true," I say through clenched teeth. "I recently received a message from my uncle, King Zeikas, informing me that the alliance between Soeria and Zeteyon is ended. I had hoped to convince him to reinstate it, but it doesn't look likely."

My words set off an even bigger bomb than Rolsteg's did. Almost everyone in the room speaks, their voices mixing so their words are unintelligible, even as the fear and urgency in their tones remain.

I don't say anything immediately, giving them a chance to get it all out. A headache born of anger and fear begins to pound in the back of my head as I listen to the councilors quibble. I wait for them to calm themselves, hoping to restore some semblance of order to this meeting before my head explodes.

But they show no signs of slowing down, and eventually I give in to my emotions. "Everyone, please!" I shout. "There *will* be order!"

I'm almost surprised when they heed my words, although it takes a bit for them to become fully silent; only once they do, I continue. "I know this is not ideal, but it is not the end of the world. Soeria is not at war. We will find new allies in due course."

"We may not be at war now, Your Majesty, but we are certainly vulnerable." Duke Arondel's voice is as ponderous as ever, even as the corners of his mouth turn down in dismay. "Without the Zeteyoni supporting us, other nations may seek to take advantage of our vulnerability."

*Breathe, Darien.* "I am aware of the consequences. I assure you that I am doing my best to ensure that Soeria continues to be protected from outside threats."

Arondel opens his mouth to respond, but Duchess Badami breaks in before he can. "Your Majesty, it seems to me that we are overlooking an obvious solution to this problem," she says. "Aren't marriage negotiations still ongoing between yourself and Prince Arbois? Perhaps we can form an alliance with Jirena Sadai? They would be a far more formidable ally than Zeteyon, and we would be eliminating a threat on our northern border."

To my horror, the confusion and dismay on the faces of the rest of the councilors is largely replaced by relief almost as soon as Badami finishes speaking.

"That sounds like an excellent solution," Voeli says. "It's lucky Prince Arbois is still in the palace. We should accelerate the negotiations immediately."

Councilors are nodding, and my heart starts to race as I realize they might actually go along with this. "I'm afraid that a marriage between Arbois and myself is not an option," I blurt out. "We'll have to figure out some other way to find a new ally."

I look at the rest of the council and see incredulous eyes staring back at me.

"Your Majesty, if I may ask," Badami says carefully, "why do you say that marrying Arbois is not an option? He is here for the express purpose of forming a marriage contract with Your Majesty, is he not?"

"That's ... not exactly true. I mean, yes, that's why he came in the first place. But recently I asked him if he would be willing to form an alliance that doesn't involve a marriage between the two of us, and he agreed to consider the idea."

Some of the councilors share charged looks with each other before turning back to me. "Your Majesty, please forgive me for being blunt," Voeli says, a touch of steel in her tone. "But as I'm sure Your Majesty is aware, the truth is that Jirena Sadai is far more powerful than Soeria. Should there ever be open conflict between the two nations—which I most ardently hope does not occur in my lifetime—I am certain that we would put up a good fight, but I have no illusions that we would win. At least, not without heavy luck, and even heavier bloodshed." She pauses and sighs, her eyes briefly darting to the ceiling before returning to mine. "What I'm trying to say, Your Majesty, is that it would be far better to have Jirena Sadai as our ally than our enemy, or even a potential enemy. We have little else to offer that is as valuable as Your Majesty's hand."

I take a deep breath before I respond; it's not her fault everything is falling apart, after all. "I realize that. Perhaps I spoke rashly when I said that marrying him is not an option." I didn't, but I want to get them off my back. "I haven't completely taken marriage off the table. If, for whatever reason, he decides that my terms are unreasonable, then we will resume our discussion of the topic." They look slightly mollified, but still concerned. Fortunately, I have one more card I can play. Plus, maybe I can get a sense of how they'd react to me and Tag. "We can even kill two birds with one stone. If we can come to some agreement with Jirena Sadai as I've suggested, I would still be able to form another alliance by marrying a noble from some other nation. I'm sure I could find someone that would be acceptable to this Council. Someone like Tag Leara, perhaps. I know his family has connections to the royal family of Zeteyon."

"You mean the son of the Viscountess Leara?" Arondel asks, grimacing. He waves a hand dismissively. "I think I speak for the council when I say that he is far too low-ranking to be an acceptable consort for Your Majesty. Surely, we can all agree that Your Majesty must marry someone of equal station—if not Arbois, then another prince, or perhaps an archduke?" His grimace fades, leaving behind a thoughtful expression. "However, I suppose Your Majesty's proposal regarding Prince Arbois is a good one, assuming he is willing to go along with it. Of course, we must be careful not to try his patience too much, lest he get frustrated and leave before an agreement can be made, but I see no harm in giving Your Majesty a chance to form an alliance under the suggested terms, at least for the moment."

Heads around the table nod at Arondel's words. I should be happy that they're not pressuring me to marry Arbois immediately, yet what I feel most is disappointment. "Thank you, Arondel," I say, trying to keep my true emotions out of my voice. It was worth a shot. "Does anyone else have anything more to add?"

Nobody volunteers anything, so I stand, barely noticing when the rest of the Council rises too. I walk out of the room without a glance back, my mind whirling with thoughts of Arbois and Tag and alliances, with one thought predominating above all the others. *I have to find a way to get them to accept Tag before it's too late.*

# CHAPTER TWENTY-FIVE

By the time I knock on the doors to Mother's chambers the next morning, I'm feeling a little better. I didn't get much sleep last night—I spent a good amount of time lying awake, thinking about how to solve my problems with Arbois and the council—and it wasn't until breakfast that I realized I didn't need to come up with a solution by myself. After all, there's someone in the palace who's gone through an arranged marriage, and has years of dealing with the council, even if only indirectly. *If anyone knows how to help me, it's Mother.* I don't even have to worry about waking her up, since she—like everyone in my family besides me—actually enjoys getting up at the crack of dawn. I've never understood it, and I doubt I ever will.

Mother's steward Lana answers the door, interrupting my train of thought and bows to me deeply. "How may I serve you, Your Majesty?"

I feel like it should be obvious why I'm here, but I suppose she has to ask. "Is Mother here? I'd like to talk to her if she is."

Lana's eyebrows draw down just the tiniest bit, and her mouth tightens slightly at the corners. "Unfortunately, Her Majesty is not here at the moment, Your Majesty," she says guardedly, before she reaches into a pocket and takes out a small envelope, holding it out to me. "However, she left instructions for me in the event that you wished to speak with her."

Now more confused than annoyed, I take the envelope from her. *Mother left instructions?* Written on the front of the envelope in Mother's precise handwriting is my name, and nothing else. Still nonplussed, I open it and remove a small sheet of paper with that same elegant handwriting on it.

Darien,

As soon as I finish writing this letter, I am leaving the palace. By the time you read this, hopefully I will be long gone. I can't tell you where I'm going or why—I won't take the chance that the wrong people will find out and try to stop me—but know that it is important, and that I am acting of my own volition. I will be taking some of the palace guards with me, so there is no reason for you to be concerned about my safety. I can't be certain when I will return, but I expect it will be at least a few weeks, or possibly a month.

I wish I could tell you more, but I cannot. All I can say is that if I am successful—and I have every reason to believe I will be—it will benefit not just Soeria, but you personally as well.

I know you will worry about me, but please trust that I know what I'm doing. More importantly, trust yourself—I know things seem bleak now, but there is not the slightest doubt in my mind that we will make everything right together.

Your Mother

I finish reading the note and stand silently for a few moments, trying to process the letter. She just left without telling me where or why, or even when she'll be back? And who are 'the wrong people'? "Is this a joke?" I ask Lana, my hands and voice both shaking. "Because if it is, it isn't very funny."

When I glance up, Lana's expression looks to be about as far from joking as it can possibly be. "Assuming that letter says what I think it does, I can assure Your Majesty that it is not a joke. Her Majesty left the palace two days ago, and I have not seen her since. As far as I know, nobody forced Her Majesty to leave, and she assured me that she would be safe."

"She left *two days* ago?" I know I shouldn't be angry at Lana—I presume it's not her fault that Mother is gone—but I can't really help it right now. "And you didn't think to tell me about this before now?"

Lana bows deeply again. "I apologize, Your Majesty, but Her Majesty left me strict instructions not to inform you until you came looking for her. She may not have been clear about much else, but she was certainly clear about that."

I stare at her for a moment longer before I look away and sigh. "I see. Thank you, Lana. On the off-chance Mother returns soon, please inform me immediately."

She bows a third time, and I turn to go, wondering why the world is falling apart on me, and whether there's anything I can do to stop it.

As soon as I leave Mother's chambers, I go to find Lord Kerion, and let him know Mother will be away from the palace for a while, a fact that he seems to take in stride. He suggests we come up with a cover story to explain Mother's absence, if only to prevent the rest of the court from becoming suspicious, and after a couple minutes of brainstorming, we decide to quietly let it be known that she has gone to a small castle owned by our family near the border with Verreene, so she can work through the grief she's feeling from the deaths of Father and Samis. The area we picked is a pretty remote, a mountainous region that's sparsely populated, which hopefully explains why no one will get a glimpse of her.

Once that's decided, I ask how the negotiations with Arbois are going, hoping to hear some good news for once.

But Kerion's answer isn't what I'd hoped. "Unfortunately, we haven't made much progress recently, Your Majesty," he says, shifting slightly in his seat. "Prince Arbois seems amenable enough, but he hasn't exactly been clear on what his goals are beyond marrying Your Majesty. Every time I think we're on the right track, he changes the topic to something else. If I didn't know any better, I'd say he's stalling. I can't imagine why that would be the case, though."

I groan. "Is there any way you can speed up the process? I don't want to bargain away the entire country, but I am willing to give way on some points if necessary."

He thinks for a moment. "If Your Majesty is not concerned with getting the best deal possible, I suppose Your Majesty could go to Arbois and make a personal appeal," he says slowly. "Normally, I would advise against Your Majesty—or anyone else, for that matter—getting involved at this point, given the complexity of the negotiation. But it may facilitate the process, especially if Your Majesty can figure out exactly what it is that Arbois wants."

This again. I've been trying to figure out what he wants for months; I don't see why he'd be forthcoming now. Still, I suppose it can't hurt to talk to Arbois myself; presumably, the worst that could happen is that I'll accomplish nothing, and we'll still be in the same position we're in right now. "I understand. Thank you, Kerion."

He nods, and I go to find Arbois, determined to make some headway with him, and hopefully solve one of my many problems while I'm at it.

I find Arbois in his study, sitting on a couch and reading a book. When he sees it's me, he smiles. I'm not sure why, but the sight unnerves me, just a bit—for some reason I can't quite put my finger on, it looks fake, like he's putting on a show. "Darien!" he exclaims, setting his book down. "To what do I owe the pleasure?"

"I just got an update from Kerion regarding the negotiations. I was hoping we could discuss them, just the two of us."

He nods and gestures to a couch across from his own. "Of course. Please take a seat." I do as he suggested. "Well then, what did you want to discuss?"

I take a deep breath before responding. *Here goes nothing.* "I wanted to see if there was any way I could help the process along. If there are any sticking points or obstacles you're facing, perhaps we could work them out together, here and now? Whatever it takes to get a deal done that benefits the both of us."

"Now, that's an interesting idea. To tell you the truth, if you hadn't come to see me just now, I probably would have sought you out within the next day or two. You see, you and I have much to discuss, starting with the recent change in your circumstances."

That sounds like a good sign, but the last part puts me on edge. "Change in my circumstances? I'm not quite sure what you mean."

Arbois cocks his head to the left slightly. "Surely you remember getting a letter from a certain uncle of yours, don't you? It was only a few days ago, if I recall correctly."

His words slam into me, shattering any confidence I had left; it's only with great difficulty that I manage to maintain some semblance of composure. "I'm not sure what you're talking about, Arbois. Or what any of this has to do with our negotiations, for that matter."

His smile turns into a sneer, one that's full of naked contempt. "Don't play coy with me. I know that your alliance with Zeteyon is no more."

"Is that what Rolsteg told you?" It's only with concerted effort that I keep my voice from shaking. "I saw the two of you talking together a few days ago. But you should be aware that she doesn't know nearly as much as she thinks she does."

Apparently he sees through my bluff, because he laughs. "No, Darien. *I* told *her*. She was quite upset at being left out of the loop, and I bet the rest of the council felt much the same, didn't they?" He shrugs. "Who can blame them? They know—as you should—that this changes everything, Darien. Now you need an alliance with Jirena Sadai, or you'll be left to face the rest of the world alone. How long do you think Soeria would last if Verreene or Raktos—or both, perhaps—decided to invade?"

This is very, very bad. All I can do is desperately claw for a way to regain some of the footing I've lost. "Even if what you're saying is true, that's all the more reason to make a deal sooner rather than later. That is why you came here in the first place, isn't it?"

"I suppose that's true, in a certain sense. But as I said, the circumstances have changed, and I'm afraid that means my position has changed as well."

Hearing that, I relax just a tiny bit. He's just trying to play hardball with me, scare me so I'll give him a better deal. "I understand. What is your position now?"

"I'm sure you recall our discussion some time ago where I agreed to consider a pact that does not include a marriage between the two of us, yes? I said I would only consider such an arrangement until my patience ran out." He sighs theatrically. "Well, Darien, my patience has run out. I must now insist that you agree to marry me, or there will be no agreement at all."

My heart drops to my toes, then further, into the cold stone beneath my feet. "That seems a bit hasty," I say, my throat feeling parched. "I realize that what I suggested was unorthodox, but—"

"I don't think you quite understand what I'm saying, Darien." His eyes, sparkling with some emotion I can't quite place, hold my gaze fast. "You have two options, and *only* two options, right now: marry me or face the consequences."

I must have sunk into the ground too at some point, because my heartbeat once again thunders in my ears, almost drowning out everything else. "What do you mean, face the consequences?" My voice comes out barely louder than a whisper. "What exactly do you think you can do to me?"

"I can see you're not quite understanding the situation, so let me be blunt." He leans even further forward, his face filling my vision. "If you don't agree to marry me this very day, Jirena Sadai will declare war on Soeria."

# CHAPTER TWENTY-SIX

His words hang in the air like static after lightning while I struggle to comprehend them.

"You'll declare war on us?" Too late, far too late, it dawns on me that I was wrong, that he's not trying to get the upper hand; this is something else entirely, beyond simple negotiations over a marriage treaty. I'm out of my depth, well and truly trapped in this sudden nightmare, like a boat caught at sea in a hurricane. "But ... why?"

"That's right. How long do you think Soeria will last when Jirena Sadai invades? A week? Two, perhaps?" He looks at me with that hateful grin of his; now, it has a hint of insanity in it. "Either way, the result will be the same. Your head on a pike—and your mother's and sister's heads too, for that matter. But not before thousands of your countrymen die in agony, fighting a battle they can't win."

A wave of disgust cuts through the sense of unreality, so strong I almost want to vomit. "Why? Why would you ever do such a thing? What is *wrong* with you?"

"Wrong? Absolutely nothing." He sounds so sincere I could almost believe he thinks he's telling the truth. "You see, Darien, you and I may have similar titles, but there's one crucial difference between us: I'm willing to do what must be done, and you're not. It's as simple as that."

I don't think I've ever been more confused in my life. "What must be done? For what? What in the world are you talking about?"

"Come on, Darien! Don't play dumb with me." He pauses, and when he speaks again, his voice has an exaggerated lecturing tone. "It's been less than a century since the War of Dissolution, yet the whole world seems to have forgotten that once, not too long ago, they were part of something greater than themselves. They've convinced themselves that the Empire's gone, that it's never coming back." The corners of his lips quirk up into a tiny smile. "Well, they may be right about the former, but they're wrong about the latter. After all, the pieces are still there, just waiting to be picked up. All it would take is someone with the vision, with the *will*, to bring it back."

What he said makes so little sense that I'm starting to wonder whether he's lost his mind, or if I've lost mine. "You think you can, what, just declare yourself the Emperor? Then somehow force Raktos and Verreene and Zeteyon and the rest to acknowledge you as their ruler?"

He nods once, his expression unchanged.

I laugh; it sounds jagged, even to my ears. "Why would anyone in their right mind follow you? You're just some prince, not a king! You have no lands, no army, nothing!"

"Darien, Darien, Darien. Don't you think I've considered that already? I've been planning this for years." A fire burns in his eyes, an inferno of madness and ambition and monstrosity. "I may be just a prince for now, but let's just say that my sister won't be on the throne for much longer. But even once I've taken her place, I'll need at least one more crown. That's where *you* come in." His smile widens. "You see, once we're married, you're going to give me control of the Soerian military—assuming you want your mother and sister to continue to be among the living, that is. Once I have the might of the Jirenian army and the Soerian army behind me ... Well, I'm sure there will be fools stupid enough to try to stand in my way, but I'll just swat them aside like the flies that they are."

"You and Rolsteg cooked up this plot together, then? Or is she just stringing you along for the ride and making you do all the dirty work for her?"

Arbois looks at me like I'm the one who's spouting nonsense. "What in the world are you talking about, Darien? She has nothing to do with this. I only told her about Zeteyon because I had to get someone on the council to burst your little bubble, and she was the first one I happened to come across."

I gape at him for a few moments, not quite sure what to say. "But... But then...." My mind feels like it's floating, as though it's been disconnected from my body. "I don't understand. You planned for years to marry me and take over the Soerian military? I was just a prince when you got here. How could you know..."

In a flash, a moment of pure horror, the implication of what I'm saying bursts through my mind, and when I speak again, my voice comes out as a whisper. "It was you. You dined with Father and Samis a few days before they died. You poisoned them to make sure I'd become king."

He claps his hands together, almost gleefully. "You finally figured it out! Yes, I killed them. It was far easier than I expected." He leans forward slightly and lowers his voice again. "Just between you and me, I had nothing against either of them—not on a personal level, at least. But they were in my way, so they had to go."

Everything shifts around me, and it takes me a moment to realize that's because I've shot to my feet, rage clouding my mind like a feverish red fog. "You disgusting excuse for a human being," I growl, stepping toward the object of my fury. "I should—"

He holds up a hand. "Careful, Darien. I wouldn't do anything rash if I were you."

I barely manage to restrain myself from reaching out and grabbing his throat. "Give me one good reason not to throttle you here and now."

Arbois seems remarkably composed for someone who's just admitted to regicide twice over. "Think about it," he says, his voice even. "Sure, you might be able to kill me, although I'd certainly put up a fight. But let's say you succeed. How do you think it will look if you kill a foreign prince in your own palace? Do you think my sister would just sit on her hands and do nothing? You'd probably just end up starting a war anyway. Is that what you want, Darien?"

"You *killed my father and brother*." My voice is strained, like I'm holding it back as much as I'm restraining myself from attacking Arbois. "Nobody in their right mind would blame me for doing the same to you."

He snorts. "Perhaps. But that's only if they believe you. After all, the only evidence you have is my confession, and I can't exactly repeat that if I'm dead, can I? Besides, my sister may be many things, but conciliatory isn't one of them. She wouldn't wait to hear your side of the story before she decided to punish you for your crime."

"Oh, but you're wrong about one thing. I do have evidence."

He tilts his head, looking genuinely confused.

"I found a Jirenian coin in the room where that assassin you sent after me was staying. Who else..." I trail off. "Wait a minute. You did send her, didn't you? But if you need me to marry you, why did you try to have me killed?"

"I assume you mean the woman in the garden?" A faint smile crosses his lips. "Yes, I sent her. But who ever said she was trying to kill *you*?"

For a second, I just stare at him, deeply confused. "But then who...?" My eyes widen. "You were trying to kill *Tag*, weren't you? But how did you know—"

"That the two of you were courting each other behind my back?" He laughs, as though this is all some big joke—maybe it is, to him. "It was obvious. You had a chance to make a match with someone far superior to you in terms of power and prestige, and yet you delayed as long as you could, even as your situation became more and more dire. Once I knew what I was looking for, it wasn't exactly hard to see that you were fixated on the Leara boy." He leans back on the couch, the perfect picture of a relaxed prince lounging away, everything under control. "But I digress. Right now, all you need to know is that I have made you an offer, and this is your only chance to take it. What will it be, Darien? Will you bring the might of Jirena Sadai down on yourself and your countrymen? Or will you do the smart thing, and save thousands of lives in the process?"

When he stops talking, my legs feel weak, and I collapse onto the couch, as though all the energy in my body has drained away. As much as I desperately wish I could believe he's bluffing, I'm terrified he might not be. *And if he isn't bluffing...*

I hate myself for admitting it, but he's right. I can't be the king who leads his people to a slaughter when he could save them. He may be a monster—he is a monster—but I'm not. If the price I need to pay is marrying the man who killed my father and brother ... *I don't have a choice, do I?*

"Fine," I finally say, my voice dull and lifeless. "I'll marry you, even though I hate you." I rouse myself a bit, trying to put some fire into my voice. "But if you hurt anyone else I love, I promise I'll kill you with my own bare hands."

"I don't really think you're in a position to make threats, Darien." He reaches out and pats my knee like I'm a favorite pet; it takes almost everything I have not to grab his hand and break his wrist. "I suppose I can be magnanimous for the moment, so long as you continue to be compliant. We are to be wedded soon, after all." His eyes freeze on mine, and a hint of menace enters his voice. "Mark my words, though: if you do the slightest thing against my wishes, I will not be so kind. If that happens, you—and your family—will be punished. Do you understand?"

I nod, my jaw set to keep it from quivering.

He smiles. "Good. I'm done with you for now. You may go."

I do as he ordered, fighting to look as dignified as I can right now. Through some inner source of strength I didn't know I had, I manage to hold everything in until I've gotten out of his rooms and back to the hallway. Only then do I slump against the wall, unmoving, beaten and broken.

# CHAPTER TWENTY-SEVEN

For better or worse, when I open the door to my bedroom, Tag is sitting at my desk, writing. Seeing him sends a bolt of mental anguish so strong it almost physically hurts, but I don't let myself falter. I know what I have to do, even if it's going to hurt like nothing else ever has before.

Oblivious to my distress, Tag continues to write. "Hello Darien," he says, still looking down. "I didn't expect you this—"

He looks up at me, his expression morphing into one of instant concern. He stands from the desk, walks over to me, and gently cups my face in one hand. "What's wrong, my love? You look like you've seen a ghost."

I open my mouth to tell him that he has to go, that it's not safe for him here, but something shatters deep within my heart, and nothing comes out. The floor flies up toward me, and before I know it, I'm sitting on the edge of my bed, crying, with my head in my hands and Tag's arms wrapped around me.

"It's alright," he murmurs gently, stroking my back with one hand. "I don't know what's going on, but I promise it'll be alright."

I look up at him, his beautiful face blurry through my tears, and try, once again, to tell him that everything is not alright, that it's as far from alright as it could possibly be. But once again, I can't make myself form the words, so I put my head down again and let Tag hold me for what may be the last time ever.

It takes a good five minutes for my tears to subside. When they do, Tag keeps holding me close, and I let myself take bittersweet comfort in his warmth, enjoying it while I still can.

Finally, after a few more minutes of silence, Tag whispers, "Now will you tell me what's wrong, my love? Did someone else get sick?"

I shake my head. "No, that's not it." Even though I'm not crying anymore, my voice still trembles when I speak. "Tag, you know that I'll always love you, right?"

He kisses me on the cheek. "Of course I do. Please, just tell me what's wrong. Start at the beginning."

*The beginning.* It feels like it was ages ago that I went to find Mother, even though it's only been a couple of hours. I take a deep breath, trying to steel myself. "The council found out that my uncle broke the alliance. I went to see if Mother had any idea how to handle them. But she..."

I tell him about Mother being gone and my conversation with Arbois. At first, the words spill out of me like a waterfall. But when I get to Arbois's threat and his revelation that he's responsible for the deaths of Father and Samis, a surge of grief rushes through my mind, and I have to pause until it dies away before I can continue. When I tell Tag that the only way I can keep Soeria safe is to marry Arbois, the pain is so great that it's like my heart has been ripped out of my chest and torn to pieces in front of me.

When I finally finish speaking, there's a deafening silence, neither of us apparently willing to say what must be said. Some part of me wants to look at him, but I think if I do, I might just break down again. And I need to be strong for what comes next.

Tag is the first one to speak. "I'm so sorry," he says, his voice thick with love and sorrow. "We can get through this together. I know it seems bad now, but we'll figure out a way. I'm here for you, and I always will be."

"Thank you, my love. But there's only one thing I need from you right now." I force myself to look him in the eye. "You have to leave the palace, *now*. Take Riella and your parents with you." I let my voice drop to a whisper. "And you can never, *ever* come back."

His face is ashen, and he almost seems to shrink in on himself. "Leave? What do you mean?" His voice is small and uncertain. "But I love you—"

I can't let him finish that sentence, so I pull him into a deep kiss before he can get the words out. "I love you more than anything in the world," I tell him. Tears run down my cheeks, and a dull ache pounds in my chest. "But that doesn't matter. You can't stay, not as long as Arbois is here."

The look of shock and pain on his face nearly breaks me in two. "Darien, you're not *actually* going to marry him, are you? You can't just give in without putting up a fight!"

"I have to give in, whether I like it or not. I hate him, and I would a million times rather be with you." The ache in my chest swells into a throbbing pain, like I've been stabbed in the heart. "But I have to do what's right for Soeria, and that means I have to do what Arbois says."

I reach out to cup his face, intending to reassure him—if I even can right now—but he jumps up from the bed and walks a few feet away from me. "I can't believe I'm hearing this!" he exclaims. "How can you even consider letting that ... that murderous snake get what he wants?"

I get up, walk over to him, and gently wrap my arms around him, trying my hardest to stay strong, to not collapse in a pile onto the floor. "Trust me, I don't want to," I say quietly. "You know better than anyone that I never wanted to marry someone who only cared about my title. But I don't have a choice."

"You *do* have a choice," he says. He turns around to face me, tears running down his cheeks. "You don't have to marry someone who doesn't love or respect you." His voice drops until it's barely above a whisper. "You can marry *me*."

I want so badly to say yes, to throw away this burden of kingship that's been crushing me under its weight ever since it was placed on my shoulders, and just do what makes me happy. I want to tell Tag that I'm his, and he's mine, and that we'll be together for the rest of our lives. I want that more than anything in the world.

Which is why saying no to him is the hardest thing I've ever done in my life. "I can't," I whisper. "If it was up to me, I'd marry you this second. I love you, and I would gladly spend the rest of my life with you." A sensation of cold darkness flows through me, as though I've just been locked in the deepest prison cell, as though the door to a happy future has been slammed shut and the key thrown away. "But I can't have innocent blood on my hands because I wasn't willing to do what needed to be done. If he really *is* willing to start a war, to put thousands of Soerians in danger..." The very thought makes my stomach turn. "I won't let my people die because I chose the easy way out."

Tag lets out a strangled sob and sways slightly on his feet. "But... But... Even if you do marry him, that doesn't mean you and I can't still be together! If all he wants is to control the army, why should he care if you and I are still together unofficially? You wouldn't be the first monarch to take a lover." His voice lowers until I can barely hear it, even though we're separated by mere inches. "You don't have to do this, Darien. Please, don't do this to me. We can figure out a way. I know we can." He says it like it's the most reasonable thing in the world.

When I respond, it feels like the words are being ripped out of me, leaving little holes in my chest. "Don't you get it, Tag? As long as you're in the palace, *your life is in danger*. He's already tried to have you killed once, and I don't think he'd hesitate to try again! If anything happened to you because of me..." The prospect is too horrific to voice aloud. "I can't let that happen to you, Tag. I just *can't*."

He leans forward, his forehead touching mine. "Please don't do this to me, Darien," he whispers. "There has to be a way we can be together. There has to be!" His cheeks are wet, and I can feel tears still running down his face. "Please, Darien. I love you."

"I love you, too, Tag. Never forget that." It takes everything I have and more to make myself say the next words. "But you have to leave. As long as Arbois is here, you're in danger."

He stares at me for a few seconds, like he can't quite comprehend what just happened. Then he says, "I understand," his voice leaden. He kisses me one last time, his warm lips pressing against mine for an instant that's far too short. "Goodbye, Darien."

He turns to go without waiting for a response, his head down and his shoulders slumped, the very picture of defeat, and exits without looking back. The sound of the door latch clicking shut drives it home to me that I'll never see him again, and without warning my legs turn to jelly. I stumble to my bed and collapse on it, my head in my hands, letting my tears flow freely once again.

# CHAPTER TWENTY-EIGHT

I lay there, curled up in a ball in my bed, for quite some time, unable to summon the energy to get up, or even to care. At some point, someone knocks on the bedroom door—probably a servant trying to bring me dinner—but I don't answer, and they go away after a while. I know I probably should get up and do whatever it is that I'm supposed to be doing, but right now even thinking of going out there and pretending like everything's okay hurts too much. If only everything else I'm thinking about didn't hurt too.

Day passes into night, and I watch as my room slowly darkens, not even bothering to light a glowbulb so I can see. The dark feels like a kindness, as though I can forget that Tag is gone if I can't see that his side of the bed is empty. Some part of me wishes he would walk in through my bedroom door and tell me that he's not leaving, that he'll *never* leave me. But having him back would be a cold comfort as long as Arbois is here.

At some point, I must have drifted off, because I wake with a start. It must be morning, because golden sunlight is streaming in through the windows, and I can see a cloudless sky, mocking me with its brilliance. For a bare moment I wonder why I woke, until I realize someone is pounding on my bedroom door. I assume it's another servant, with breakfast this time, but I'm still not hungry, so I roll over and wait for whoever it is to give up and leave me alone.

Apparently I was wrong, because instead of going away, the mystery knocker opens the door. I roll back over, ready to tell them to go away, but the words die in my throat when I see it's Emma. *I should have known she'd come find me.*

She closes the door behind her and steps into the room, looking at me with a steady gaze. "Good, you're awake," she says, her tone brisk. "We need to talk."

I almost tell her to go away and leave me in my misery. But I know that she's not going to give in easily, and I don't have the energy to fight with her right now, so I just sit up.

"I suppose we do," I say, my voice raspy. Hearing myself makes me realize that I haven't had anything to drink since yesterday afternoon, and I gesture to a pitcher of water on a table near my window. "Would you mind..."

She nods, pours a glass of water, and hands it to me. It's warm, but it still tastes sweet. When the glass is empty, I hand it back to Emma, who puts it back on the table.

"Much better," I tell her. "Thank you."

"You're welcome." She perches on the edge of my bed. "Now tell me: what happened between you and Tag yesterday? The Learas left the palace this morning, and it didn't look like they were planning on coming back anytime soon. When I asked why they were going, they all seemed just as confused as I am. All of them except for Tag, that is, and all he would tell me is that I should talk to you." She squints at me. "I thought you two are in love? Did you fight?"

Thinking about him makes the pain I'm feeling surge, but this time there's more than a little relief mixed in. *Good. He heeded my advice.* "I did love him. I *do* love him. But..." I trail off as I realize what she just said. "You... You know about me and Tag?"

She gives me a flat look, and somehow I can tell she's struggling not to roll her eyes. "I figured it out ages ago. You may have been able to fool most of the court, but I'm your sister." She sighs and settles back a bit. "Now, will you please tell me what happened?"

It hits me now that I have to tell her the truth about what happened to Father and Samis. "Listen, Emma, I'll tell you everything. But you have to promise you'll hear me out. You're going to be angry, but I need you to promise me you won't run off until I've had a chance to finish."

Her brow furrows, and she tilts her head slightly. "Why would I be angry? You didn't cheat on Tag, did you?" She sighs. "Alright, fine. I promise. Now will you please tell me what's going on?"

I begin recounting yesterday's events, and when I tell her about Arbois threatening me, her lips tighten and a spark lights in her eyes. That spark grows stronger when I tell her about Arbois poisoning Father and Samis, and it stays there while I recount my argument with Tag. Just remembering all of it brings back the fierce ache in my chest, but in a way, it feels good to be able to share all of this with someone. Besides, I think she might have killed me if I tried to keep it a secret from her.

When I finish speaking, she sits silently for a few moments. Then she stands and walks toward the door without saying a word.

"Where are you going?" I ask, afraid I already know the answer.

She stops and turns to look at me; her expression is carefully neutral, but the spark in her eyes has blossomed into a full-fledged flame of fury. "Where do you think I'm going?" she replies, her voice tightly controlled. "I'm going to have the guards arrest Arbois. Or better yet, strangle him myself. Now if you'll excuse me..."

She turns to go again, and a spike of fear that hits me gives me energy enough to finally get out of my bed.

"Wait! Please, just hang on a second. Can we talk about this first?"

I'm afraid she's not going to listen to me, but fortunately she stops and turns again before she reaches the door. "Talk about it? What is there to talk about? He murdered our father and our brother, and he threatened our entire country! What am I supposed to do, ignore that and just pretend like everything's okay?"

I take a small step toward her. "Think about it," I say, keeping my voice low, as though I'm calming a spooked horse. "I understand how you feel. Trust me, I do. But if we do *anything* to him without any evidence besides his own word, we'll just be signing our own death warrants, and probably Mother's too. He may be a lying snake, but I believe him when he says that Jirena Sadai will invade if we arrest him or try to kill him." Another step forward. "I know you want revenge. I do too. But not if it means starting a war that could leave thousands of Soerians dead."

She stares at me, unblinking, clearly considering my words. I stand completely still, yet I'm ready to move at the slightest notice. I'm not exactly sure what I could do to stop her if she decides to go after him—it's not like I can have her confined to her room until she calms down—but at the same time, I can't let her start a war. *Come on, Emma*, I silently urge her. *Don't make me have to choose.*

After a few more moments of unbearable tension, she sighs and nods. "I suppose you're right," she says.

I breathe a sigh of deep relief, but her eyes, still burning with those red-hot flames, meet mine. "But don't expect me to be civil to that...that butcher, even if you marry him. I don't care if it causes an international incident. I'm not going to act like this is a normal situation."

"That's fine." Far easier to make up a reason why my sister doesn't like my husband than why she strangled him to death with her own bare hands. "Just so you know, I'm not happy either. Far from it. But I *have* to marry him, even if I hate it."

The flames in her eyes recede, and she walks over to me and gently pats my shoulder. "I understand," she says, her voice not exactly gentle, but softer than it was before. "You had a difficult decision to make, and you did what you felt was right, instead of what was easy. Not everyone could have done the same."

She turns towards the door for a third time, her step no less certain than before, but this time I let her go. I stand there for a good long while after she goes, chewing on her words. *Something tells me this isn't the last time I'll have to make a tough decision.*

# CHAPTER TWENTY-NINE

The next few days are some of the worst of my life—maybe even worse than the days after Samis and Father died. At least then, I still had some hope that things would turn out okay, if only I could just make it through to the other side.

But now ... not only are Samis and Father gone, but Tag is too, and I'm never going to get him back. Plus, I don't even know where Mother is, and I could use her love and support now more than ever. The only silver lining is that wherever she is, it has to be less dangerous than here. Maybe, in a twisted way, it's good that she's not here—I don't doubt that Arbois would threaten her in order to keep me in line. I just hope that wherever she is, she's okay.

True to her word, Emma does her best to ignore Arbois, at least from what I can tell. It wouldn't surprise me in the slightest to find out that she's silently fantasizing about ways to get rid of him, but as long as she doesn't act on any of them, I'm okay with it. Not that I could do much to stop her if she really decided to follow through with it, though. There's not much I can do to stop anyone from doing anything, these days.

As the days pass, I try my best to keep to a routine, trying to bury myself in my work so I can forget about everything that's gone wrong recently. To my surprise, it does help somewhat, although nothing can truly fill the hole in my heart that Tag used to occupy. But I slog through, trying to put on a good face, to pretend like everything's okay when I know it's not. For the most part, I manage to succeed.

The only time my façade cracks is at the first council meeting after Arbois's revelation, three days after Tag left. I haven't been looking forward to it—not that I'm ever really looking forward to a council meeting, but this one even less.

I wait for everyone to settle down before I make my announcement. I have no doubt that informing the council of Arbois's crimes would be 'against his wishes,' as he so delicately put it, so I decide to keep it short. "I'm pleased to announce that I am engaged to Prince Arbois of Jirena Sadai," I say with a sour taste in my mouth, hoping none of them can see through my façade to the distress that underlies it. "We haven't set a date for the wedding yet, but I will inform this Council once we have done so."

The bitterness in my mouth only grows stronger as the councilors break out into polite applause. Most, if not all, of them have relieved expressions, and I almost break as I think about how I should be announcing my engagement to the man I love, not the one who murdered my family. *I'm so sorry, Tag*, I think to myself, trying to hold back tears as their applause washes over me. *I'm so sorry*.

Through some strength of will I didn't know I possessed, I manage to pull myself together, and by the time their applause peters out, I'm back to whatever passes for normal these days.

"This is excellent news, Your Majesty," Voeli says as soon as the applause has stopped. "Congratulations, and I wish you a happy marriage."

The rest of the councilors congratulate me in turn, each sounding happier than the last—although Belling gives me a strange look before adding their congratulations—until I feel like I'm going to burst. At least the council is so collectively relieved that they don't bother to ask why I've changed my mind in the space of a couple days; I don't know how I could possibly give them a satisfactory explanation without implicating Arbois. Instead, I sit there and acknowledge their congratulations with as much grace as I can muster, hoping that nobody notices I'm acting strange. If they do, maybe they'll just think it's nerves; far better for them to think that than to know the truth.

Once that's done, I do my best to settle into my new life as Arbois's fiancé, a life of gray emptiness laced with simmering hatred. One week passes, then two, as the days lengthen and summer comes upon us in full force. At first, I expect he'll want to lord it over me, to rub his victory in my face. But he's apparently content to leave me alone, in no rush to get married now that he has me in the palm of his hand. I suppose it makes sense, in a strange way. He knows it's too late for me to change my mind and send him away, and it's not like he's going to be any more in control of Soeria's army if he convinces everyone that he and I are in love.

However, it quickly becomes clear that even if he's not interested in me personally, he is *very* interested in the military that I nominally control, despite its relative weakness compared to Jirena Sadai's. Two or three times a week, he has me meet him so he can learn more about our army, whether it's a tour of the city walls, going over reports from the quartermaster about our emergency supplies, or so he can interrogate me about troop detachments. I try my best to hold as much information back from him as I can—even if the whole point of me marrying him is so that his country *won't* invade mine, it still feels wrong to give away all of this intelligence—but every time I become evasive, he just smiles at me like I'm a rebellious child, secure in the knowledge that he will find out what he wants to know one way or another. It drives me absolutely insane, but I can't see what I can do about it.

Fortunately, there's at least one person outside my family who's not entirely happy with the new status quo. I meet with Belling about once a week so they can give me an update on the state of the military and bring any important matters to my attention. Given the events of the past few weeks, I thought Arbois might insist on joining these meetings too, but apparently he has better things to do, and is content to let me attend them without him. It's a small silver lining, but a silver lining nonetheless.

"...and lastly, there's the matter of the experimental cannon I've been updating Your Majesty on," Belling says, their tone as dry and brisk as ever. "Major Pressa tells me it is finally ready for testing. She is planning to leave for Fort Alesen tomorrow; there is quite a bit of open space in that area, and the testing can proceed there without too much concern for the safety of any nearby civilians should the cannon fail. I will attend as well and will report back to Your Majesty when I return."

In truth, I had forgotten that this cannon even existed—if I ever actually knew about it in the first place—but it sounds like exactly the sort of thing Arbois will want to see. I'll have to go too, as Major Pressa would never let *any* foreigner attend such a test without a royal escort, even if he is my fiancé. That means I'll be stuck with him in close quarters for at least a week, and I'm sure it'll be a living hell. But if I refuse to go with him, he'll try to force me and if *that* doesn't work, he'll take it out on me—or worse, my family. *I wonder if I could convince them to do the test here instead*? It's not like there aren't any open spaces near Cedelia, so if Pressa is worried about safety, then—

Just then, something shifts in my mind. "What exactly are the safety concerns with this cannon?" I ask slowly. "Is it more dangerous than any other weapon?"

"I believe the danger comes more from the fact that it is untested rather than any sort of qualities of the cannon itself." They shrug. "I won't bore Your Majesty with details, but suffice to say that there are many things that can go wrong with artillery, even if it's been tested exhaustively. However, I can assure you that everyone present at such a test, from Major Pressa down to the lowliest private, is fully trained to minimize the chances of any problems occurring. Even their horses are specially selected and trained for such a test. As long as we keep a good distance from any unsuspecting civilians, I don't foresee any issues."

I try not to grimace. *I had hoped...* It was a long shot anyway. Even if I could somehow make the test fail, how could I ensure that Arbois, and *only* Arbois, was affected? He may be a madman, but he's not stupid. *No, I'll just have to find another way to get rid of him.*

I'm about to ask Belling if there's anything else, but something they just said sticks in my mind like a burr in my boot. *Why would the horses need to be trained*? It's not like they have to *do* anything besides sit there and not buck their riders. *But why would they—*

Then it hits me, like a bolt out of the blue, and almost immediately a plan starts forming in my head. Belling looks at me, clearly waiting for me to respond, but instead I just take a few moments to think, my muscles quivering. *If this works...* I'll have to run it by Ivy and see if she thinks it's plausible, but if I'm right, I could solve my biggest problem without bringing down Arbois's wrath on me and my family. And Emma too—she'd kill me if I left her out. "Is there any way you can move the test closer to Cedelia?" I phrase it as a question, but I'm not willing to take no for an answer. This won't work if I'm forced to go to Fort Alesen. "I understand that you want to make certain no one is harmed if the test goes wrong, but surely there must be somewhere around here that's suitable."

Belling thinks for a moment. "I believe there may be an adequate testing location nearby," they finally say. "I will speak to Major Pressa. I assume Your Majesty and Prince Arbois will attend if the test is relocated?"

I let out a breath, trying not to show the relief I feel. "That's correct. If it's not too much trouble, I would also like you to provide me with a list of everyone else who will be attending, including the soldiers themselves."

It's a slightly odd request, but Belling doesn't even blink. "Of course, Your Majesty. I'll have that information to you within the hour."

"Perfect. Thank you, Belling." *May our next meeting be under better circumstances.* "Now, if that's all?"

They nod, but instead of rising, they hesitate. "Forgive me for asking, Your Majesty," they say slowly, "but are you quite certain it is a good idea to bring Prince Arbois to this test? It's not that I don't trust you, but he *is* a foreign prince, and I don't know that it's a good idea to let him in on a top-secret military project such as this one."

I give them a smile, and even though I can't see my own face, I know there's no mirth in it. "Yes, Belling, I'm quite certain that Arbois should be there," I reply, an edge to my voice that wasn't there before. "In fact, I'm counting on it."

# CHAPTER THIRTY

When I wake the next morning, bleary-eyed and a little nauseous, there's a note waiting for me. I read it as I eat a light breakfast.

> Darien,
> It has come to my attention that the city garrison will be testing a new weapon this afternoon on the outskirts of Cedelia. I wish to be present for this test, and you will escort me. Meet me in the stables after lunch. Do not be late.
>
> Arbois

I breathe a quiet sigh as soon as I'm finished. *Perfect.* It's a little disquieting that Arbois found out about the test on his own, but for once I'm glad he knows about what should be a secret. One thing that Ivy, Emma, and I agreed on during our hasty late-night planning session is that this is our best chance of sending him back to Jirena Sadai for good. Just the thought makes me want to jump for joy.

Yet, my hands are shaking slightly as I continue to eat breakfast, because if things go wrong, the situation could become even worse than it is now. I may have lost Tag, and who knows where Mother is, but at least they—and Emma and Kenessa and Ivy—are safe. If Arbois finds out Emma and I conspired against him, I doubt his response will be measured.

But I'm going to do it anyway, because I can't keep living like I am now, with both my family and my country under threat. If my plan succeeds, then he'll be gone, and I can make sure nothing like this ever happens again.

*If I fail* ... I grimace at the thought of it. *I'll have to make sure that the consequences fall on me, and me alone.*

I get to the stables that afternoon a bit earlier than strictly necessary. Not because Arbois commanded me not to be late, but because I just want to take a moment to be away from it all—the endless meetings, the heavy crown, all the little things that I hate about being king. Here, in the stable, surrounded by the decidedly humble scent of horses and hay, I can almost believe that I'm not trapped by my title.

'Almost' being the key word here.

The first thing I do when I get to the stables is make sure Laya is ready. As I check Laya's bridle, a groom shifts, and a flash of long, dark-brown hair catches my eye, just for a second, as its owner turns a corner and leaves my sight. Even though nobody's looking at me, I continue to act normal, pretending like I didn't just see Emma leaving the stable. *She really waited till the last second.*

It's a good thing I didn't react, because it's only a few moments later that I hear a familiar voice behind me. "I see you got my note," Arbois says cheerfully. "You're on time, too. Excellent. I would have been very displeased if you were late."

I turn to see him standing at the entrance to the stables; his expression seems just as cheerful as his tone, and for a moment all I can think is how good it will feel to wipe that hideous grin off his face. "I'm here," I reply shortly. "Let's get on with it."

"There's no need to be so impatient. It shouldn't take too much longer for the grooms to finish getting my horse ready." He walks toward me, turning his attention to Laya. "Hello, there!" he says to her. "Aren't you a magnificent horse?" When Laya ignores him, he frowns. "Don't tell me your horse is as ill-mannered as you are, Darien."

I push down a feeling of anger. If all goes well, I'll only have to put up with him for a little while longer. "She can't hear you," I tell him, my voice even tauter than it was before. "She's deaf. Has been since she was born."

He stares at me for a moment as though he's not sure whether I'm joking, before breaking out into amused laughter. "Are you serious? Why in the world would you have a deaf horse? You do know you're the king, right? Or are all the other horses in these stables defective too?"

I clench my teeth and silently count to three before I respond. *Don't mess up the plan, Darien.* "Laya is a good horse," I say once I've calmed a bit. "Just because she can't hear doesn't mean she's *defective.*"

He pats me on the shoulder, grinning widely; it takes quite a bit of effort not to snatch his hand away. "Come now, Darien. It was just a joke. No need to get so worked up." He looks around, his eyes narrowed slightly. "Where is my horse? I explicitly instructed the head groom to have her ready on time."

Before I can answer, a young stable hand, who can't be more than fifteen years old, runs up to us. The boy skids to a halt just before he runs into me and bows deeply, his eyes wide, panting slightly.

"Forgive me, Your Majesty, Your Grace," he says, speaking so fast he nearly stumbles over his words. "I was told to prepare Your Grace's horse, but it seems she's lost a shoe. We sent for the farrier, but she won't be here for another hour or two at least."

Arbois frowns again, deeper this time, while I hold my breath. If he insists on taking his own horse, or even postponing the test, then the best-case scenario is that the whole plan is called off. *In the worst case ...* No. I can't afford to think like that. *Everything will be fine.*

Finally, after a few moments of torture, he shakes his head. "I suppose I shouldn't be surprised," he mutters. Then, louder, "Well then, I have no choice but to borrow one of these nags for today, thanks to your incompetence. Go find me a horse that isn't too bad—assuming you can find one, that is—and get it ready *immediately*."

The boy bows again, his body shaking, but makes no move to carry out Arbois's orders.

"What are you waiting for?" Arbois snaps. "Go, before I truly lose my patience!"

At that, the boy squeaks and finally runs off.

As soon as he's out of earshot, I turn to Arbois. "You will not speak to my servants that way," I growl, my voice low. "You will treat them with the respect they deserve."

I wasn't really expecting him to apologize for his behavior, so I'm not surprised when he waves a hand dismissively.

"Servants like that don't deserve any respect," he says, a hint of contempt in his tone. "Not from people like you and me, at least."

I want to argue with him, to demand that he treats my people better than he treats me. But everything is going about as well as it can so far, and I don't want it to get worse. So Arbois and I stand there in awkward silence for a few minutes, until the boy returns with a saddled chestnut mare.

Arbois quickly glances her over. "She'll do, I suppose," he finally says, his tone patronizing. "Come, Darien. Let's go."

Once we're both mounted, Arbois guides his horse out of the stables, and I fall in slightly behind him, with two palace guards following us at a polite distance. Normally, nobody walks in front of the monarch, but he's the one who knows where we're going. It grates on me to be seen following him instead of the other way around, yet I doubt he'd tell me just so I can have the honor of taking the lead. Like many things in the last few weeks, I just grin and bear it as best I can. *Hopefully this will be the last time I need to deal with something like this.*

He leads me toward the eastern gate, setting a brisk but unhurried pace. There's not a single cloud in the sky, and the air is neither too warm nor too cold. It would be a pleasant day for riding, were it not for the company. Unbidden, my thoughts drift back to another day, not too long ago, when I took Tag to the sea of flowers for the very first time. I let myself get lost in the memory, trusting Laya to follow Arbois's horse.

Even though Tag is painful to think about, memories are all I have of him now, and I have to savor them while I still can.

I get so caught up in daydreaming that I barely even notice that we've arrived at our destination until Laya stops walking, the sudden change in motion jolting me back to the present day. I blink a few times and look around. We appear to be on top of a small hill covered in grass that gently slopes down before us to become an empty field. Turning in my saddle, I see that we're a couple of miles outside of the city. Off to my left, about a hundred feet away, are two groups of soldiers, clad in the blue-and-purple uniforms of the Soerian army. Each group is gathered around what appears at first glance to be some sort of cannon, loading the weapons with powder and large, round cannonballs. Part of me wants to scrutinize the soldiers, but I don't want Arbois to see me looking. Besides, it's not like I'd recognize them anyway. I just have to trust that Ivy knows what she's doing; she's already saved my life once, after all.

Behind the soldiers are six large horses and a medium-sized tent, the latter a splotch of red against the green of the hill. Four of the horses are hooked up in pairs to some sort of harness that I assume was used to transport the two cannons, while the other two hold riders, who are watching the soldiers go about their duties. As we get closer, I see that one of the riders is Colonel Belling, and the other one, a middle-aged woman with long white hair, is Major Pressa.

One of the soldiers says something to Belling, who turns and guides their horse in our direction with a quick word to Pressa; the latter continues to keep a watchful eye on the soldiers. Belling nods their head as they get close, their impeccable uniform gleaming in the midday sun. "Good afternoon, Your Majesty, Your Grace," they say. "As you can see, the soldiers are almost ready." They gesture in the direction of the tent. "In the meantime, would you like to meet Major Pressa? Should you wish to rest while we complete preparations, we have refreshments—"

Arbois holds up a hand. "Skip the pleasantries, Belling. I'm here to see the new cannon in action, not waste my time making small talk with subordinates. Tell me, what makes this one better than previous ones?"

Belling's lips thin slightly and their eyebrows draw down slightly, but their voice remains even. "As Your Grace can see, this model is quite a bit smaller than previous models. That means that it can be hauled by two horses instead of four. Speaking of which, we've developed a new form of limber that allows the horses to be harnessed much quicker, even if the cannon is being used at the time. In addition, we have developed a new rifling technique that allows for greater accuracy, and..."

They continue to tell us about the improvements that have been made, while I listen with a growing pit in my stomach. I'd be lying if I said I know much about artillery, but what Belling is describing sounds like a marked improvement over what we have now. If my plan goes wrong—and there is still every chance of that happening—and the cannon works as intended, I'll basically be handing Arbois an advantage over every other nation as soon as we get married. Who knows what something like this could do to an opposing army? He must be salivating at the thought of it! Sure, it's just a few cannons, but if it really is that much better, I doubt it'll take long before we make more. It's not like Arbois will hold back—if he really intends to reform the Empire, he'll need every edge he can possibly get. Maybe, if I'm lucky, the threat of both armies combined will be enough to get other countries to submit without using force.

It's a nice idea, but I doubt that Khoria and Verreene and the rest will give in that easily. Besides, something tells me that even if Arbois doesn't strictly *have* to use force, he will anyway. The very thought is almost enough to make me break out into a cold sweat. *This plan* needs *to work*.

I steal a glance at Arbois; now that Belling is getting into the heart of the matter, he pays rapt attention, presumably thinking of ways to use this new weapon to his advantage.

When Belling finishes, Arbois sits silently, a thoughtful expression on his face. After a few moments of contemplation, he says, "Thank you, Colonel Belling. I'm going to get a closer look now." He rides off without waiting for either of us to respond, Belling and I following shortly behind.

Each cannon is made of bronze and is about five feet long. Arbois approaches the nearest one, which has a soldier standing at attention on either side. Next to one of the soldiers is a metal sconce with a long, thin piece of wood that's smoking at one end, which I try my best not to stare at. As soon as he gets close, Arbois bombards the soldiers with questions, eagerly examining the cannon from horseback as though he's a child and it's a new toy. Which I suppose it is, in a way. The soldiers seem slightly taken aback at the verbal onslaught; both of them look to their commander before saying anything, only responding to Arbois's questions once Belling nods their approval.

Arbois spends a good fifteen minutes examining the cannon from different angles, keeping up a steady stream of inquiries for the bemused soldiers. At one point, he dismounts and raps a hand gently on the bronze breech, seemingly pleased by the ring that sounds when he does, before returning to his horse. In the meantime, I just sit there, trying not to seem suspicious. *It's almost time.*

Eventually, Arbois's thirst for knowledge seems to be slaked—for the moment, at least. He nods to the soldiers, then turns back to me and Belling. "Excellent work," he says, his tone brisk. "Now then, it's time for the demonstration. I would like—"

He cuts off as a sudden commotion erupts behind him.

"Be careful!" someone shouts. "It's loaded, you idiot!"

I turn to see the metal holder falling toward the cannon in slow motion, the soldier who was standing next to it reaching out to catch the lit taper. His horrified expression is so real that I almost wonder if this really is an accident.

The soldier makes a grab for the taper but misses, and it alights onto the cannon, the smoking end coming to rest right above the touch hole, where the fuse is located. As soon as it hits the fuse, there's a flash and a hiss, and then a moment of silence that's so deep that it seems I can hear each blade of grass around me whistling in the wind, everyone frozen in place like they've been encased in clear ice.

Then, almost without warning, there's a clap that's louder than thunder, and my vision fills with white.

# CHAPTER THIRTY-ONE

S ometime later, I'm sitting in a bed in the private infirmary, my ears ringing, when Emma and Kenessa rush in, with near-identical stricken looks on their faces. Emma's mouth moves, but all I can hear is a muffled sound, like my ears are stuffed with cotton.

"You'll have to speak up," I say, hearing myself more through the vibrations of my bones than the sound of my voice. "The healer said it could take a few hours for my hearing to come back."

They both come closer, looking somewhat less nervous.

"Are you alright?" Emma asks. Or, at least, I think that's what she said. It's still hard to tell, even though she's clearly screaming the words, based on the way Kenessa flinches. "Other than the hearing, I mean."

"I'm fine," I assure her. "My ears hurt a bit, but the healer said that should go away once my hearing comes back."

Emma rolls her eyes as Kenessa sighs in apparent relief. "What in the world happened?" the latter asks. "We heard there was an accident and that somebody might have gotten hurt, but nobody seemed to know for certain."

"Arbois and I went to watch the garrison try out a new cannon," I explain; Emma tries her best to look interested, even though she already knows this. "The idea was for us to inspect it up close, and then go to a safe distance while the soldiers fired it. But one of the soldiers made a mistake, and the cannon accidentally went off while we were sitting on our horses right next to it. Laya barely reacted at all, but Arbois's horse was startled by the noise."

"Well, I'm glad you're alright," Kenessa says. "What happened to Arbois? Did he get hurt?" She can't quite hide the hope in her voice.

"His horse bucked him off." I try to keep the relief I'm feeling out of my voice, just in case one of the healers is listening in. "Belling said he looked fine when he landed, but apparently he tried to get up too quickly, and his horse kicked him in the head. It was pretty bad. Belling had the soldiers rush him to the infirmary, but he was bleeding quite a bit, and I don't think he woke up before we got separated." I give Emma a brief meaningful look, careful of the prying eyes and ears around us. "In any event, the healers said they'd update me as soon as they know more. Hopefully that means we'll get some good news soon."

She meets my gaze, her expression carefully neutral. "Hopefully we will," she says. "Hopefully we will."

Not long after that, the healers let me return to my chambers. They say there's no reason for me to stay in the infirmary, but I think they just want us to leave so they don't have to deal with our voluble conversations anymore.

Emma and Kenessa join me in my study. My hearing gets progressively better over the next hour or so, to the point where I can hear them with their voices at a normal volume, although the ringing sound takes longer to recede.

We sit here, waiting with bated breath, for another couple hours, until Arille finally arrives. She holds her head high, but the corners of her mouth are turned down a bit and there are beginnings of bags under her eyes. It may be a trick of the light, but she almost looks dejected; I don't dare to let myself wonder why.

"I apologize for the wait, Your Majesty," she says. Whatever it is she's feeling inside, her tone is as professional as ever. "However, the other healers and I thought it would be best to wait until we had something definitive to tell Your Majesty about His Grace's condition."

My heart is pounding, but I try to keep my tone even. "I understand. Do you have an update for me?"

She nods. "I do, Your Majesty." She pauses and takes a deep breath. "Unfortunately, His Grace's injuries were quite severe. We tried our best, but we were unable to save him."

When she finishes speaking, my heart stops racing. "Thank you, Arille," I reply, trying desperately to sound how I *should* sound in this situation, whatever that is. *Keep it together, Darien.* "I'm sure you did your best."

She bows to me again and turns to go, closing the door behind her. It latches shut with a loud click that resounds in the otherwise silent room. Emma and Kenessa both have near-identical expressions of unease on their faces, and I don't doubt that I look similar.

In truth, the plan was never to kill Arbois. Wound him, perhaps even so badly he'd never be a threat to Soeria again, absolutely. But *kill* him? I knew it was a possibility, but it was never my intention.

But what's done is done. After a few more moments of contemplation, I stand up and walk over to the door, making sure it's closed. The three of us have quite a bit to talk about, and I don't want to be overheard.

The next day, once my hearing is fully healed, I invite the Jirenian ambassador to the palace so I can give her my own condolences in person. Fortunately, even though she's clearly upset about the whole thing, she accepts my explanation that it was nothing more than bad luck.

Together, the ambassador and I make arrangements to ship Arbois's body back to Segaron. She also requests that I hold an official memorial service for him, and I agree with as good of grace as I can muster. *At least after this I'll never have to think about him again.*

The service is held in the same room where Samis's and Father's funerals were held not too long ago. It feels … disrespectful, somehow, but his misdeeds are still a secret, and that means he has to be given the honor that a visiting prince deserves.

Before and during the funeral, I do my best to play the part of a grieving fiancé, but, inside, my emotions are much more complicated. The council seems to think I'm devastated, based on the way they treat me at the meeting where we plan the memorial service, but they're obviously mistaken.

In fact, if I'm being honest, the worst part is that I don't feel bad. I could lie to myself and say it's because he killed my father and brother, but that's not true. Or, at least, not *completely* true. He hurt my family, and I can never forgive him for that, but what truly scared me was what he would have done in the future. He made it quite clear that he was willing to harm my country—not to mention Tag, and everyone else that I love—to achieve his goals. His death could save the lives of tens, if not hundreds, of thousands. If the price of saving those lives is having his blood on my hands...

But it's too late to worry about that now. The price has been paid, and all I can do is try my hardest to make sure I don't have to pay a similar cost ever again.

The days after the memorial service feel ... strange. I don't quite know how to describe it. The entire court is in mourning, and officially so am I. But despite whatever misgivings I may have about Arbois's death my own part in it, I'm happier than I've been in weeks, even if I can't show it. The knowledge that my country, my family, and myself are safe is a powerful balm. In truth, there's just one thing missing, but I don't quite allow myself to think about that just yet, as much as I may want to.

Finally, after one interminable week, the official mourning period ends, and I can wait no longer. The very next morning, I rise early, eat a quick breakfast, and go find Emma in her study. "I need to ask you a favor," I begin, wasting no time on pleasantries. "I'm sorry for dropping all this on you last minute, but I have to leave the palace. I'll be away for a week or two, and I need you to take care of things here while I'm gone. I'm going to—"

"I know where you're going," she interrupts. "Go. I'll make up some excuse for why you're out of the palace. I can handle everything until you get back." A light smile creases her face. "To be honest, I'm surprised you waited this long."

"I am too. But I can't wait any longer." In fact, I'm already walking toward the exit as I speak. "Thanks, Emma! I'm sure you'll do a wonderful job."

She says something in response, but I'm already out of earshot, walking with purpose for what feels like the first time in a while, my heart soaring as I take the first steps on the long journey to Zeteyon, where the man I love waits.

# CHAPTER THIRTY-TWO

T he ride to Zeteyon is uneventful. Two of the palace guards come with me; I don't really expect that I'll need their services, but it's better to be safe than sorry. Neither of them seems to be interested in conversation, which leaves me alone with my thoughts, my anxiety growing slowly but steadily as we draw closer to the Leara estate.

For six days we ride, pausing only to sleep at night or to eat. I set a pace that alternates between a trot and a walk, giving the horses time to recover their energy. Even though I know it's necessary, the periods where the horses are walking feel interminable. I do my best to remind myself that every second that passes is one that brings me closer to Tag.

Toward noon on the sixth day, we cross a river that's wide but so shallow the water only comes up to the horses' knees, and I know we've crossed the border into Zeteyon. Soon after, we peel off the main road onto a smaller one that leads north. My anticipation and anxiety ratchet up then—partially because I'm about to see Tag, and partially because I'm not entirely sure that I'm going in the right direction. In my haste to leave the palace, I forgot to bring a map of this area, so all I have to go by is what Tag and Riella have told me. *He did say the estate is north of the main road. I think.*

Then, midmorning of the seventh day, we crest a hill, and I see a sprawling manor house that's surrounded by vineyards. It looks like what Tag described to me, and it's in the right place, so I assume it's the Leara estate. As soon as I see it, my apprehension doubles, triples, until it takes over my entire mind. While we were riding, I hadn't let myself consider what would happen if Tag doesn't want to see me, or if I can't convince him to come back. Now that I'm here, those possibilities feel very real, and I don't know what I'll do if things go wrong.

When we reach a drive lined with oak trees that leads from the road to the house, I slow Laya to a trot. As I get closer to the house, I see there's a carriage outside with the Leara family crest, a shield bordered in green with a golden-eyed owl in the middle, on it. *This is the right place, then.* My heart lodges in my throat and stays there.

All too quickly, we reach the end of the drive. I dismount and order the guards to stay put, my heartbeat pounding in my ears. *This will go well. It has to.* I walk up to the tall front door and knock on it, the pounding of my fist on the wood sounding like a twin to the *thump-thump-thump* of my heart.

When the door opens, I hold my breath but let it out when I see that the person standing in front of me isn't Tag. Instead, it's an older woman whom I don't recognize, who appears to be half my height. She looks me up and down briefly with her sharp green eyes, taking in my sweaty face and outfit that's expensive, yet dusty from the road.

"Can I help you, my lord?" she asks, her eyebrows slightly raised. "I don't believe we're expecting any visitors."

I know I should be polite, but there's no time for me to explain, not when I'm so close to him. "I need to speak to Tag Leara, right now. Is he here?"

Her eyebrows raise even further. "Is Master Leara expecting you, Lord...?"

"No. Maybe. I don't know. But I need to speak to him anyway." I don't bother to hide the impatience I'm feeling. "Can you please let him know that he has a visitor?"

Before she can respond to me, another voice comes from inside the house, one that simultaneously warms my heart and chills me to my core. "*Darien*? Is that you?" Tag steps forward, as handsome as I've ever seen him, his expression wrought with surprise and disbelief. "I thought I heard you, but I figured I was just imagining it."

I swallow a lump in my throat that wasn't there a few moments before. "Can I come in? I need to talk to you."

He stares at me for a moment longer. "Of course," he says, his tone guarded. "Thank you, Mei. I'll take him from here."

Mei nods to Tag and backs away from the door. I step into the house, not sure how to feel just yet. *At least he didn't turn me away immediately*. Hope and fear struggle within me, neither of them able to gain an advantage and overcome the other just yet.

But underneath them both is love, and when I look at Tag, it grows stronger, swelling in my chest as though it's the very air that I breathe. *I missed him so much*.

Oblivious to the battle going on in my mind, Tag silently gestures me forward and leads me to a room that I assume is his. Once we're in the room and the door is closed, he turns to me. "Darien, what are you doing here? Are you even real? Or am I hallucinating?"

"I'm real. I promise." I hesitate briefly; everything has been leading up to this moment, and how he responds to what I say next has the potential to either make me very happy or destroy me completely. "I came here for you, Tag. I love you, and I'm begging you to come back to the palace with me." I get quiet, so quiet I can barely hear myself speaking. "I need you, my love. I can't do this without you."

A flicker of some emotion I can't quite place passes across his beautiful face. "What happened to Arbois? I thought you said my life would be in danger if I stayed at the palace."

"I did say that, and it was true. But he died, Tag. A couple weeks ago."

Tag's eyebrows shoot up. "I ... see," he says slowly. He shakes his head. "It still doesn't matter. We can't be together, Darien. It will never work."

Ignoring the sudden tightness in my chest, I take one of his hands in mine, hoping he doesn't notice that I'm shaking. "Please don't say that," I murmur. "I know it must have hurt when I sent you away, and I'm sorry for that. But my heart belongs to you, and it always will. You're the only one who ever made me feel like I'm more than just my title. You made me believe that I can be with someone who loves *me*, not my position." I squeeze his hand gently and lock my eyes onto his. "I love you, Tag, and I'm yours for as long as you want me."

Tears well up in his eyes. "I love you too, more than I can say. But I've had some time to think, and..." A few tears fall onto his cheeks, and he pauses to wipe them away before he resumes speaking. "I don't know if that's enough."

Pain blooms in my chest. "What do you mean?" I whisper.

He takes a deep breath, his eyes shining with tears. "Suppose I do come back to court with you. Even if Arbois is gone, that doesn't mean we can be together. I'm still just the son of a viscountess, far too low-ranked to be with you. Sooner or later, you're going to have to marry some powerful lord with money or lands or an army." He hesitates. "I know I offered to be your secret lover when ... the last time we saw each other, but I was wrong to suggest it. I don't think I can watch you be with someone else. Even if it's all for show."

"You're wrong about one thing, my love." I bring his hand up to my lips and kiss it gently. "We *can* be together. You know I don't care about your rank. Your parents could be farmers, or servants, or whatever, and I'd still want to marry you."

His eyebrows draw down slightly. "I believe you, but we both know that's not the problem. Can you look me in the eye and tell me that the council—and the rest of the court, for that matter—will give us their approval? Or will they try to tear us apart at the first opportunity they get?"

"I...." I really wish I could just say that it'd be fine, like my heart is urging me to, but I can't lie to him. "I don't know, Tag. But we won't know unless we try."

"Please, Darien," he says, his voice barely audible. "They'll never approve of me. And it's not just them, it's the rest of the court too. I can't stand the thought of everyone talking behind my back, saying that I'm not good enough for you, or that I tricked you into marrying me somehow." He looks at me, his brown eyes filled to the brim with love and heartbreak. "Maybe if I were stronger, if I had thicker skin, I could do it, but I *can't*."

Tag's face grows blurry; it takes me a moment to realize it's because I'm crying too. "We can make it work," I say, unable to keep the rising desperation I'm feeling out of my voice. "I don't care what anyone else says. It doesn't matter, as long as we're together. If they—"

He gently places one finger across my lips, cutting me off. "You may not care," he says softly, "but I do."

He says it with finality, with weight, each word thudding in my ears like it weighs a thousand pounds. "So, this is it, then?" My voice sounds just as dull as I feel. "You're sure this is what you want?"

He hesitates for a bare second before nodding. "It is," he whispers. "Goodbye, my love."

I stand here for a few moments, stock still, barely able to comprehend what's happening. Then, without taking my eyes from him, I take a step back, then another, toward the door, away from the only man I've ever loved. Slowly, as though I'm moving through molasses, I finally turn away from him, trudging towards the exit.

I'm barely a foot away from the door when, seemingly out of nowhere, Samis's dying words echo in my mind, stopping me dead in my tracks with their burning urgency. *Promise me you won't let anything come between you and Tag.* I didn't know if I could keep that promise back then, but I made it all the same. And here I am, about to walk away from the only man I've ever loved, the only man I ever will love, when the biggest obstacle to us being together is gone. *You two are good for each other, and you'll be happy together.*

Just like that, I stop walking. "No," I hear myself say, as though from a distance. "This isn't right."

I turn back to Tag and go to him, meeting much less resistance than I was just a moment ago. When I reach him, I kneel down before him and take his hand in mine again, my eyes locked on his. "Tag, I understand why you're worried, and I don't blame you. But I won't give up on you just because of what might happen in the future. Sure, some people might be opposed to us marrying at first, but the idea that you aren't suitable just because you don't have the right title is absurd. I don't care what the council—or anyone else—thinks. All I care about is *you*. If anyone resists, I'll do whatever it takes to make them accept you, even if it means opposing the entire council. I'll oppose the whole court if it means I get to be with you."

"How, Darien?" he whispers, tears streaming down his cheeks. "How will you convince them? What if they try to force you to marry someone else? I don't want to come back if I'm just going to be cast aside when the next prince comes along. I won't go through that again!"

I stand up, cupping his face in one hand, the other still grasping his hand. "I don't know. But I do know that if we give up on each other now, we'll both regret it for the rest of our lives. I promise you that I'll give it everything I have. *Everything*." I gaze deeply into his eyes, willing him to hear the truth of my words. "Nobody will ever force me to marry anyone else. There are other ways to protect Soeria besides my marriage, especially now that Arbois is out of the picture. The council can argue with me about alliances or dowries until they're blue in the face. It won't matter. Even if they threaten to take my crown, I will *never* back down." My voice is as strong and confident as I can make it, but there are tears running down my cheeks too. "I love you, Tag, and I always will. As far as I'm concerned, that's the only thing that matters."

When the last word comes out of my mouth, all the hope and fear and anxiety that have competed within me ever since I stepped foot into this room vanish completely, like I took my emotions and formed them into words, leaving only love behind. For a few seconds that feel like hours, he just looks at me, his brown eyes shining with love and fear and anguish. Everything feels completely still, as though the world has stopped dead in its tracks. All I can think about is how badly I want him, how badly

I need him. I silently will him to say that he'll come back, that we can be together, as I struggle in vain against the desperation that's growing within me. "Please, Tag," I say, so quietly it makes a whisper seem loud. "I need you with me."

Finally, after a few more moments of torture, he wraps his arms around me and lays his head on my chest. "I love you too, Darien," he says, his voice a bit muffled. "I love you so much, and that is all that matters." He lifts his head up, his tear-filled eyes finding mine. "You're right. I know I'd never forgive myself if I gave up on you now."

A wave of relief, stronger than any I've ever felt before, crashes into me and washes through me, filling me from the top of my head down to my toes. "Thank you, my love," I say quietly. I move ever so slightly forward, closing the distance between us until our lips meet. I'd almost forgotten how good it felt to kiss him. "Does this mean you'll come back to the palace with me?"

He laughs through his tears, and the sound warms my heart. "It does. You once said you'd always be there for me, and now it's time for me to make the same promise to you." His eyes and his tone are both full of iron resolve. "Darien, I'm yours, for as long as you want me. We're in this together, and I'll always stand by you, no matter what."

I pull him in for a deep, triumphant kiss, hoping he can feel my love for him just as I can feel his for me. When we pull back, he smiles at me, a tender one that's full of joy and contentment. Unable—and unwilling—to stop myself, I kiss him again, deeply this time, letting my hands roam up and down his body. He kisses me back just as deep, and, before I know it, we're in his bed, reveling in our newly reclaimed love for each other, reunited as one.

Sometime later, once we're back in a state where we can speak coherently, we decide to leave for Cedelia the next morning. I'm sure Emma has things under control, but I feel bad for having left her there to deal with the repercussions of Arbois's death by herself. I'm not looking forward to getting back to the drudgery of king all the time, but now that I know I'll have Tag by my side, the idea seems ... tolerable, if not exactly exciting.

When we come down from Tag's room and join his parents and Riella in the library, they all do doubletakes—well, Riella and the viscountess do, at least, and the viscount's eyes widen briefly.

"Darien! What a pleasant surprise!" the viscountess exclaims as she comes over and gives me a hug. "Mei told us that someone was at the door, but she obviously didn't know who you are. To what do we owe the honor?"

"I actually came to talk to Tag," I tell her. "You see..." I briefly glance in his direction, giving him a quick smile that he returns with interest, and take his hand in mine. "Tag and I are courting, and I've asked him to come back to Cedelia with me. Of course, you're all welcome to come too."

If I thought they were surprised before, they're even more so now, although Riella gives me what looks like a knowing smile for a brief second. In any event, their surprise quickly turns to joy, with the viscountess and Riella exclaiming how happy they are for us. The viscount, meanwhile, gives us a brief half-smile before returning to his usual dour expression. From what Tag has told me, that's basically his equivalent of jumping for joy, so I suppose it's good enough for me.

After their excitement has died down, the conversation turns to business, and the three of them ultimately decide to follow us back to the palace in a few days, once they've had a chance to settle their affairs here and make sure the estate won't be neglected during their absence. Thankfully, they accept it when I say I'll explain everything—including why I asked them to leave the palace with no notice—once we've all returned. I don't want to ruin this happy moment by talking about Arbois and his crimes.

Although Riella seems happy too, I have a feeling she might be peeved that Tag and I didn't tell her about our courtship before now. After all, if she had been courting Emma for months and didn't tell me, I would probably be annoyed.

But when I take her aside and gently broach the subject, she just rolls her eyes. "How dense do you think I am, Darien?" she asks. "I knew exactly what you were trying to do as soon as you asked for my advice on that made-up report all those months ago. Plus, don't you think I noticed Tag was sneaking out of our rooms every night and didn't show up until the next morning?"

For a moment, I just stare at her in stunned silence. I should have guessed that she'd figure it out on her own. "If you knew, then why didn't you say anything?" I finally ask her.

"I figured that if you were both trying to keep it secret, there must have been a good reason." She gives me a smile and winks. "Besides, the whole thing was my idea in the first place. I had a feeling the two of you would be perfect for each other before you even met."

I clap my hands together before I can stop myself. *I knew she was trying to set us up!* "Well, you were obviously right. Why didn't you tell me about him before?"

She shrugs. "To be honest, I wasn't sure he was ever going to leave Zeteyon. I didn't want to get your hopes up if you were never going to actually meet each other. By the time I realized that we were all going to live in Cedelia, I figured it would be more fun to let you be surprised. It was a pretty good surprise for you, wasn't it?"

It was, but I'm not quite ready to admit that to her yet. "That means you're not mad at me, then?"

"Oh, I suppose I *could* forgive you." Her smile widens. "But first, you'll need to give me all the details. What was your first kiss like? Who kissed who? When was it? Does anyone else know about you two? Where did you..."

She continues rattling off questions, not giving me a chance to answer one before moving on to the next, while I groan internally. *I suppose I should have seen this coming...*

# CHAPTER THIRTY-THREE

Tag and I leave for Cedelia bright and early the next morning. I can't speak for him, but I'm tired yet exhilarated, ready to face what comes as long as he's by my side.

There's no real reason to hurry other than my vague guilt at making Emma take my place, so we decide to go slowly and take an extra day or two on the road, letting the horses have a break after the pace I set on the way here. The weather is perfect, nearly as sunny as my mood, the summer sun warm but not oppressive.

The ride back is pleasant, and I bask in the glow of being with the man I love again. Sometimes, I catch myself looking at him and just smiling; whenever he notices, he gives me a big grin in return, so clearly he doesn't mind very much. It's so pleasant that by the time we reach Cedelia, I almost don't want to go back to the palace, where I'll have to deal with all the stress and exhaustion that comes with being king.

But then I glance at Tag, and that feeling lessens. *I can handle it as long as he's with me.*

Once we've made our way through the city and reached the palace, I'm glad to see that everything looks normal. Or, at least, nobody's running around like there's a major crisis. Not that I expected Emma to do anything besides an excellent job, but you never know.

"Do you want to get something to eat?" I ask Tag as we dismount. "I don't know about you, but right now I'd love to eat something other than an apple and hard cheese."

"That does sound nice," Tag agrees. "But perhaps we could bathe and change our clothes first? I think I've ten days' worth of dust on me."

I laugh and pull him close to me despite his dusty clothes. "That sounds like an excellent idea." I give him a deep kiss, not caring whether anyone sees. "Let's go to my rooms, then? I'll have the servants send for some hot water."

He nods, and we set off in that direction, both of us grinning widely. Truth be told, I'm looking forward to a nice long bath as well. It may have been a pleasant ride, but sitting in a saddle every day for the last two weeks has taken its toll on my body.

Yet it seems we'll have to wait, because when we enter my rooms, there's someone waiting for us. It takes me a few moments to register that someone is sitting in my antechamber, and once I do, I almost don't believe my eyes. "Mother?" I suppose I should have realized she'd be back by now, but with all that's happened recently, I had almost forgotten she'd been gone. "You're finally back?"

She turns to look at me, a big smile breaking out on her face. "I am, Darien." She stands up and walks over to give me a hug. "I missed you," she says. "Now come sit with us. I understand we have quite a bit to talk about."

*Us?* I was so shocked to see Mother that I didn't even notice that Kenessa and Emma are here too. They both look happy to see me and Tag, but Kenessa looks ... *different*, somehow, in a way I can't quite put my finger on.

"How did you know we got back?" I ask as we take our seats. "Please don't tell me that you've all been sitting in my room waiting for me to return for the last few days."

Kenessa and Emma share an amused look, and Mother chuckles. "Of course we haven't," Mother says. "I'll admit I was a bit confused when I got back and found you weren't here, but Emma told me where you went. I asked the stables to let me know the moment you returned. Fortunately, when I got the message a few minutes ago, the three of us were eating lunch together, so we just came over here to wait for you." She sniffs the air and frowns at me and Tag. "Although, perhaps I should have waited a bit. You smell like a horse. Both of you."

"Trust me, I'm well aware. We were going to bathe, but I suppose that will have to wait."

"Fair enough. In that case, let's get right down to it." She settles back in her seat a bit. "I'm sure you're wondering where I was for the last month or so. I'll get to that shortly, but first, you should know that Emma and Kenessa told me what happened with Arbois." Her nostrils flare a bit, and her cheeks get redder. "Believe me, I wouldn't have left had I known just how much of a monster he was. I knew he was ambitious, but I never thought he would have the sheer audacity, the *ruthlessness*, to do what he did. If he wasn't already out of the picture..."

She pauses and takes a deep breath, visibly calming herself. "But I suppose it worked out for the best in the end. I can't say that justice was done, but at least he won't be able to hurt anyone else in his quest for power. Besides this way we can say we were honest when we told his sister that his death was a tragic accident." She frowns. "Well. Perhaps not the part about it being tragic, but you get the idea."

I glance at Emma, who shakes her head minutely. She hasn't told Mother the truth, then. Maybe we'll tell her what really happened to Arbois someday, but now is not the time. "I was thinking along the same lines," I say, deliberately keeping my voice even. "Now will you please tell us about your top-secret mission?"

"Patience is a virtue, my son," she murmurs. I pretend not to hear her, and she continues at a normal volume. "When we received the message from my brother terminating the alliance with Zeteyon, I told you that it didn't seem like something Zeikas would do. The more I thought about it, the more I became convinced that someone must have interfered in some way—whether it was Rolsteg, Arbois, or someone else. I know we tried to keep our initial message to Zeikas a secret, but in truth, we didn't try very hard. It would have been relatively easy for someone to find out that we sent a message to Zeikas and bribe the messenger to give it to him. Which, I presume, is what Arbois did."

I frown as I consider her words. "I suppose that makes sense. But if Arbois prevented the message from getting to Zeikas, then why did we get a response? Or was Zeikas's response actually a fake?"

She gives me an enigmatic smile. "You're on the right track, but not quite there yet. You see, Arbois *didn't* stop our message from getting to my brother—well, not exactly." I can tell that she's enjoying this. "All he had to do was copy it onto a new piece of paper, with some minor—but highly important—changes, and transfer the seal. Then he could send off his doctored message, with everyone none the wiser. Zeikas would have no reason to think it was anything but genuine."

"And you deduced this all before you left? Where did you go, then?"

Her smile grows wider. "I went to Osella to visit your uncle in person, of course. I thought that if he heard the truth from someone he trusts, he might reconsider his decision."

Things are starting to fall into place. "That sounds like a good idea," I allow. "But why all the secrecy? You could have just told everyone you were going to visit your homeland for a little while, and nobody would have batted an eye."

"Perhaps. But at the time, I didn't know who was behind all of this. If whoever it was found out that I was going to Zeteyon, they might have put two and two together and tried to stop me." Her smile fades when I don't respond immediately. "I'm sorry, Darien. I did what I thought had to do. I didn't mean to cause any of you to worry."

I think about it for a moment, then I accept her apology with a nod. *I guess she's right. In any event, it's too late to change things now.* "What happened when you got to Osella?"

She pinches her lips together and makes a sound that's somewhere between a sniff and a huff. "When I first arrived, he didn't even want to see me," she says, sounding slightly affronted. "Apparently, the letter Arbois wrote requested that Zeteyon pay a hefty tribute to Soeria in exchange for renewing the alliance. Needless to say, Zeikas was quite offended. It took me days to convince him that the letter he received was a forgery, and that I wasn't there to collect money from him. I swear, my brother can be even more stubborn than you are sometimes."

I choose to ignore that last part. "Now that I think about it, I did read a letter the Jirenian ambassador to Zeteyon sent to Arbois, saying something about how Zeikas was suddenly much more amenable to their proposal—whatever it was—than he was before. I suppose that would have been around the time Zeikas got the doctored message."

"That sounds about right. Zeikas mentioned that the Jirenians had been pushing him to enter an alliance with them for the past few months. Although, I'm willing to bet that Arbois never intended to follow through, and that he simply wanted to know when the forged letter reached Zeikas and gauge his reaction to it..." She trails off, lost in thought.

"Did you manage to convince Zeikas the letter was a fake?" I prompt.

She nods. "To my brother's credit, once he finally got it through his thick skull that I was telling the truth, he was quite apologetic, and it didn't take him very long to agree to renew the alliance like we originally wanted."

I feel a huge smile breaking out on my face. "That's wonderful! The alliance is officially back on, then?"

"That's right. And evidently his puerile spat with the Khorians has been resolved, so we don't have to worry that we'll be on our own should trouble arise."

"That's certainly good news." It's a relief to know that Soeria has an ally again, especially now that Jirena Sadai doesn't seem to be an option. "Maybe now the council won't give me as much trouble about courting Tag."

Mother laughs, with just a hint of bitterness in it. "Oh, I sincerely doubt that will be the case. Still, I suppose it's worth a shot. I take it the two of you mean to continue your courtship, then?"

I look at Tag, feeling love swell in my breast as I do. "Yes, we do."

She nods once. "Good. Being back in Zeteyon reminded me just how absurd the notion that someone's value comes solely from their rank is.

From what I've seen, Tag is a good man, and you two clearly make each other happy. I'll gladly give you my support against the council, should it be necessary."

A warm feeling like distilled sunlight spreads through me; from the look on Tag's face, he's feeling something similar. "Thank you, Your Majesty," Tag says, a hitch in his voice. "I really do appreciate it."

Mother waves a hand. "There's no need to thank me. Catherine has stuck by me through thick and thin, and now it appears you're going to do the same for Darien." She frowns. "Speaking of which, I think we're familiar enough that you don't need to call me 'Your Majesty' any longer. Although I'm not sure what you *should* call me. 'Merandia' seems a bit too familiar, and 'Mother' is a bit strange." She thinks about it for a moment, then shrugs. "We'll figure something out, I'm sure."

Tag nods, still smiling widely. "I'm sure we will." Then he turns back to me and gives me a quick kiss. "Well, Darien, it seems like everything has come together nicely, hasn't it?"

I kiss him back. "It certainly has." I look into his eyes for a moment longer, then turn back to the three women sitting across me. "Although, at some point I'm going to have to figure out what to do about an heir. Not that I'm disparaging you, Emma. But something tells me that if I make the council give way on me and Tag being together, they'll just fight that much harder to make sure I adopt someone they consider suitable."

To my surprise, a spark lights in Kenessa's eyes. "I may have a solution for that," she says hesitantly.

From the questioning looks on everyone else's faces, it's clear I'm not the only one who's unsure what she means. "What is it?" I ask.

"Let's say you do adopt an heir," she says. "Whoever it is should be closely related to you, right?"

I nod, still not quite sure where she's going with this.

"I didn't want to tell anyone until I was absolutely certain, but one of the healers examined me a few days ago, and now I'm quite sure." She gently pats her stomach as she speaks.

In a flash I realize what she's saying. "You're pregnant, aren't you?" I hear a quiet gasp from either Mother or Emma. "You want me to adopt the child as my heir?"

Kenessa nods once. "That's what I was thinking, yes. It seems like an elegant solution. I don't think there's any doubt that the council would view your brother's child as a suitable heir. Meanwhile, I'd be able to raise them here at the palace, and you could have a say in their education. From the perspective of succession, it would be as though you had a child of your own." She lets out a quiet breath, looking cautious. "All of this is assuming you're okay with it, of course."

"*Okay* with it?" My wide smile comes back. "Are you kidding? It's a great idea! The council will get off my back, and I won't have to search around for someone they'd find suitable. And Samis..." A not-entire-ly-unexpected rush of grief makes tears come to my eyes. "I know it's what he would want."

Kenessa's eyes are glistening too; in fact, I don't think there's a single dry eye in the room right now. "He would," she says, with obvious relief. "Thank you. I thought you might be willing to go along with it, but I wasn't completely sure."

"I'm glad to hear it," I reply, laughing. "Really, I'm the one who should be thanking you. All of you." I take Tag's hand in mine and squeeze it. "But it seems like we've gotten almost everything settled, so if you don't mind leaving, I'd like to speak to Tag privately."

Tag looks at me, his eyebrows raised, but I remain silent. The three women take their leave; before they've gotten more than a few steps away from us, Mother is already congratulating Kenessa, then asking what sounds like a million questions about her unborn grandchild, with Emma speaking up now and then too. I watch them go with a smile and a sense of pure contentment. I'm sure I'll hear all about my niece or nephew—my *heir*—soon enough, but right now there's something even more important that I have to do.

Once the door is closed behind them, I turn back to Tag, who looks at me with a wide grin.

"What did you want to talk to me about?" he asks. "I thought you said we settled everything."

"I said *almost* everything. There's still one thing left to do, and it might be the most important one of all."

Either he hasn't gotten my hints yet, or he's hiding it. "What is it, Darien?"

"I need to ask you something." I look into his eyes and hold his gaze as I get down on one knee before him, my heart pounding like mad. "Tag, I love you more than anything in the world, and I want to be with you for the rest of my life." I pause for a moment before I ask him the question that I've been wanting to ask him for so long. "Tag Leara, will you marry me?"

To my relief, he reacts immediately, lifting us both up into a standing position and pulling me in for a deep kiss. "I love you too, Darien," he says, a bit breathlessly. "Of course I'll marry you."

When he finishes speaking, there's a huge, happy smile on his face, and I realize that there's a matching one on mine as well. "I'm so very glad to hear that, my love." My smile fades just the tiniest bit. "We won't be able to announce it just yet, you understand. I am supposed to be grieving for my fiancé right now, after all."

He chuckles softly. "So now you're the one who wants to keep our courtship quiet? Well, I suppose turnabout is fair play." He kisses me again, and I feel an overwhelming sense of happiness as I realize that I get to kiss him every day for the rest of my life. "Now we've gotten everything settled, right?"

I gently tap him on the nose; it feels like I'll never be able to stop smiling. "Not quite. We still have to plan the wedding. I'm sure Ivy and Riella will have tons of fashion advice to give us. Once they get over their initial excitement, that is."

He groans. "Don't remind me. Any chance we can run off and get married without all the ceremony?"

"Not a chance, my love. That's what you get for agreeing to marry a king."

He kisses me one last time. "You're worth it." It's clear that he means it. "I love you, Darien."

"I love you too, Tag, and I always will." I've never felt so certain about anything in my entire life. "With all my heart."

# EPILOGUE

## TEN MONTHS LATER

I grin to myself as I walk into the grand ballroom where Tag and I will get married in just a few short hours; it's been nearly ten months since I proposed, and I can scarcely believe the day is already here. The Hall of Lights—named for the multitude of brightly colored glowbulbs hanging from chandeliers and sconces—is by far the most glamorous room in the palace. It's mostly used for formal events, like the annual Founding Day ball, where hundreds of people in resplendent outfits enjoy a banquet dinner and dance the night away. Today, though, the glowbulbs are dimmed; golden sunlight streaming in through the large windows is more than enough to make the room bright. Even so, it looks as resplendent as ever, the perfect setting for what I hope will be a perfect wedding.

I stand in the back of the room, off to one side, watching the servants put the finishing touches on the wedding decorations. Emma directs them, although she seems content to let them do their work without interfering. Almost as soon as she found out that Tag and I had gotten engaged, she asked if she could be in charge of the wedding planning, and I gladly said yes. As far as I can tell, she's doing an excellent job. At any rate, the hall looks even more magnificent than ever, which is quite a feat.

Satisfied that everything's going well, I walk out of the hall and head back to my chambers. There are still a few hours left before the wedding, and even though I'm ready to get on with it, I have a feeling my self-appointed stylist and general fashion manager will want to use every last second she has to make me look perfect.

Sure enough, when I get back to my chambers, Ivy gives me a frustrated look. "Where were you?" she asks. "I have to finish styling your hair. And you still have to decide whether you want to wear any jewelry." She pauses, her eyes slightly narrowed in suspicion. "You didn't go outside, did you? If you messed up your shoes..."

I hold up my hand in mock surrender, as though it will protect me from her verbal onslaught. "Calm down. I just went to see how the hall is coming along." I look past her, out the window. Winter has come and gone, and trees have regrown their leaves, making the land beyond the city walls look like a sea of green. "Although maybe I should have gone outside. It looks like the weather is beautiful."

She looks me over with a critical eye for a moment longer, then nods, evidently reassured I haven't ruined my outfit. "You certainly couldn't have picked a better day," she says. "Now come over here so I can fix your hair. I had an idea, and I know you'll love it. I'm thinking we can..."

I tune her out and let her do her thing. *Some things never change.*

A few hours later, I'm standing by myself outside the hall again. By now, all the guests who are going to show up have already done so, and the great doors that lead to the hall are closed. I haven't seen Tag since last night—apparently in Zeteyon, it's bad luck for the engaged couple to see each other before the wedding. I close my eyes and take a deep breath to calm my nerves ... but to my mild surprise, I find I'm not nervous at all. Instead, when I think about all the trouble it took to get to this point, all I feel is relief and excitement.

At that moment, I hear a voice behind me; I don't need to look to know who it belongs to.

"Are you ready, my love?"

I turn around anyway. Tag is standing there, looking perfect, with a big grin on his handsome face. "I am, my love." I walk up to him and cup his face in one hand, taking one of his hands in the other. "You look amazing, by the way."

"You do, too," he says, still smiling widely. "I suppose we'll have to thank Ivy and Riella when this is over, won't we?"

"We will. But for now, let's just enjoy being with each other."

He kisses me, then lays his head against my chest, careful not to mess up his hair. "That sounds wonderful."

We stay like that for a few moments, just holding each other close, before Tag lifts his head. "You know," he says, "you never did tell me how you convinced the council to let us marry."

I shrug, careful not to mess up my outfit lest I incur Ivy's wrath. "There was nothing to it, really. I just told them that the alliance with Zeteyon was back on, and they agreed that it wasn't necessary for me to marry some foreign prince I've never met anymore. I guess that, plus your family's connection to royalty, was enough for them to deem you acceptable."

He raises one eyebrow. "Come on. There's no way it was that easy."

"I suppose I may have implied that Zeikas would only agree to renew the alliance on the condition that you and I get married."

He laughs and gently punches my arm. "You didn't have to lie to them for me." His laughter fades, and his expression settles into a sweet smile. "I suppose I can't complain though. I'm just happy that everything turned out well."

"I am, too." I kiss him gently, feeling my heart soar as I do. "So very happy."

For a moment, we stare into each other's eyes, the world around us briefly disappearing. Then, one of the servants gives us a signal, and we turn to face the large, ornate doors. As we approach, they begin to open slowly, and the hall quiets as the guests realize the wedding is starting.

When the doors stand fully open, I offer my arm to Tag. "Shall we?"

He takes my arm, his handsome face a picture of eagerness. "We shall."

Together, we begin the long walk down the aisle that divides the row of seats. I look around and see the happy faces of the guests, knowing that none of them could possibly be happier than Tag and I are right now. There are so many faces in the crowd that I recognize—Ivy and her parents, Joram, Voeli, and Arondel and Belling and the rest of the council, ambassadors and envoys from far and wide. Seeing everyone gathered together drives home how special this moment is, how lucky I am to share it with Tag. I even spot Petris holding hands with a tall man with dark hair and blue eyes; Petris sees me looking and waves with his unoccupied hand, he and his date both grinning. *Good for him.*

Tag and I make our way towards the altar, the cheering of the guests crescendoing until it feels like my heart will burst with joy. When we get to the front row of seats, I see Mother, Emma, and Kenessa on one side, and Tag's parents and Riella on the other. Kenessa holds a wide-eyed baby in her arms—my nephew Samir, named in memory of his father. Other than her, all our family members have huge smiles on their faces, and my heart soars even higher as it really hits me. *This is it. I waited so long, and it's finally here.*

When Tag and I reach the far end of the hall, we stop and turn to face each other. Lord Kerion stands before us; presiding over royal weddings is one of his official duties as High Chancellor. This part of the ceremony is short, and to be honest, I don't hear most of what Kerion says. My attention is on Tag, and I gladly let myself get lost in his eyes, as I did when we first met. He looks delighted beyond belief, and even though I can't see it, I have no doubt that there's a similar expression on my face.

Almost before I know it, Kerion finishes his ritual benediction and turns to Tag. "Tag Leara, do you take Darien Garros to be your husband, now and forever?"

Tag doesn't hesitate. "I do," he says, beaming.

Kerion nods and turns to me. "Darien Garros, do you take Tag Leara to be your husband, now and forever?"

I look into Tag's eyes—his deep, brown, beautiful eyes. All I can see is the man I love, the man who stole my heart and gave me his own in return. I love him, and I know I always will, no matter what. It feels like I'm going to overflow with joy and relief and love and wonder, as though I'm a vessel that's filled to the brim. I open my mouth to let the emotions pour out of me, and as they do, they take the form of words, the words that will bind me to him, and him to me, joining us together for the rest of our lives: "I do."

# ACKNOWLEDGMENTS

I'd be lying if I said I ever thought I would write a book, and I'd *definitely* be lying if I said I ever thought I'd publish a book (or two—keep your eyes peeled in April 2026!). The list of people who supported me throughout this multi-year publishing journey is as long as my arm, and I apologize in advance if I've inadvertently left anyone off this list.

First and foremost, I need to thank my family, not just for reading and giving me (occasionally unsolicited) editing feedback, but for everything else they've done. Mom and Dad—who were my first beta readers—Heather and Jay, Pop Bob and Gum Shelle, Aunt Cheryl and Jess and Jerm, thank you all for putting up with me as I metaphorically tore my hair out trying to figure out the perfect words and used you as sounding boards for plot ideas. Special shoutout to my niece and nephew, Sienna and Nate: you both may not be old enough to read this just yet, but I hope someday you do, and maybe you'll be inspired to write (or paint, or cook, or sing, or dance) yourselves. Whatever method of creative expression you choose, I'll always be right there with you, cheering you on no matter what.

Next up are my friends who doubled as beta readers: Matt Blum, Megan Bentley, Dorothy Hill, Moha Thakur, and Ida Walin. Your feedback was incredibly useful, and I really can't thank you enough. Other beta readers who deserve acknowledgement are Nicole Mathias, my critique partner—who read two full, unedited manuscripts without complaining—and Madeline Dyer, my freelance editor. Both of you gave me comments that were insightful, and I don't think this book would be as good as it is without you.

Of course, I can't forget about the entire team at Rising Action, including Alex Brown and Tina Beier. Thank you both so much for taking a chance on me, and helping me bring this story to life! Plus, I can't wait to go through this whole process again next year with *Marooned*.

Last but definitely not least, thank you to my real-life Tag, my amazing boyfriend Eli. I love you, and every day I get to spend with you is a joy. I'm so excited to see where life takes us next.

So that's it—the end of *The Prince's Heart*. Reader, whoever and wherever you are, I hope that you've enjoyed reading about Darien and Tag as much as I've enjoyed writing about them. If you did—and, honestly, even if you didn't—please take a few seconds and rate *The Prince's Heart* on Amazon or Goodreads. Authors like me can't exist without readers like you, and your honest feedback is invaluable to both groups.

Oh, and one final note—there's a chance that you're reading this and you're thinking to yourself, *Hey, I have an idea for a book*. Maybe you have a whole plot in mind, or maybe you just have a germ of a plot. Maybe you've been tossing around an idea for years, or maybe you've been struck by inspiration recently. Hell, maybe you're thinking *That book was terrible, and I could have written it better*. No matter what the circumstance is, my advice is the same: **Write it**. Get it onto paper (or a computer screen). If writing a whole novel seems daunting, write a chapter. Then write another, and another, until you can't write anymore. Worst case scenario, you file it away, never to see the light of day. But on the other hand, maybe someday *you'll* be the one sitting in front of your laptop, typing out acknowledgements for all the people that helped with your soon-to-be published book.

And trust me when I say that's a pretty good feeling.

# ABOUT THE AUTHOR

Ben Chalfin is an intellectual property lawyer by day and a romance writer by night, skillfully bridging the gap between the precision of patent law and the emotional depth of storytelling. Hailing from Maryland with a loyal allegiance to the Ravens, Ben's academic journey took them from Virginia to North Carolina, culminating in a career in Philadelphia—a city that reflects their own blend of innovation and historical richness. Whether drafting patent applications or exploring the complexities of love and loss in their novels, Ben brings a unique perspective to both the legal and literary worlds, celebrating the power of creativity and the human spirit.

Looking for more Romance? Check out Rising Action's other love stories on the next page!

And don't forget to follow us on our socials for cover reveals, giveaways, and announcements:

X: @RAPubCollective
Instagram: @risingactionpublishingco
TikTok: @risingactionpublishingco
Website: http://www.risingactionpublishingco.com

RISING ACTION

Chicago hairstylist Bastian Russo has only three things to his name: a pair of $1,200 shears, a Boystown studio apartment, and a list of men's names written on his closet wall. His constant worry that he's not good enough and his chronic inability to trust are what leaves him heartbroken time and again.

After he adds the latest name, he turns to his best friend, Andres Wood, for solace. But instead of treating Bastian to dinner, drinks, and the usual effortless banter, Andres makes an interesting suggestion: that Bastian should get over the breakup by dating ... Andres.

Sure, Andres is successful and attractive, but he also knows everything there is to know about Bastian—including what an insecure pain in the ass he is. Meanwhile, everyone in Bastian's life, from his mother to his co-workers, thinks he's an idiot for not having dated Andres already. So, what could go wrong?

Everything.

Now Bastian has to sort out his inadequacy and trust issues to prove he's worthy of transitioning from Andres' best friend to his lover. Otherwise, it's a matter of time before one or both of them end up on Bastian's list of Boystown Heartbreakers.

Abigail Meyer and Freya Jonsson can't stand one another.

But could their severe hatred be masking something else entirely?

From the moment they locked eyes in high school, Abby and Freya have been at each other's throats. Fifteen years later, when Abby and Freya cross paths again, their old rivalry doesn't take more than a few minutes to begin anew.

And now Naomi, Abby's best friend, is falling for Freya's producer and close pal, Will. Both women are thrilled to see their friends in a happy relationship – except they are now only a few degrees of separation from the person they claim to despise... and they can't seem to avoid seeing one another.

After their encounters repeatedly devolve into warfare, Abby and Freya's friends decide their age-old rivalry can only mean one thing: true love. Will their friends bring them together? Or will Freya's refusal to admit who she is keep them from discovering their underlying passion?

Keep This Off The Record is a fun and fresh LGBTQ+ story about the freedom to be who you are, even if that means falling for the person you hate.